8/08

WITHDRAWN

PURGATOIRE

**Center Point
Large Print**

**This Large Print Book carries the
Seal of Approval of N.A.V.H.**

PURGATOIRE

Johnny D. Boggs

CENTER POINT PUBLISHING
THORNDIKE, MAINE

This Center Point Large Print edition
is published in the year 2008 by arrangement with
Golden West Literary Agency.

The text of this Large Print edition is unabridged. In other
aspects, this book may vary from the original edition.
Printed in the United States of America.
Set in 16-point Times New Roman type.

ISBN: 978-1-60285-175-7

Library of Congress Cataloging-in-Publication Data

Boggs, Johnny D.
    Purgatoire / Johnny D. Boggs.--Center Point large print ed.
    p. cm.
    ISBN 978-1-60285-175-7 (lib. bdg. : alk. paper)
    1. Large type books. I. Title.

PS3552.O4375P87 2008
813'.54--dc22

2007051254

With much appreciation
to Vicki Piekarski and Jon Tuska,
who know the West, its history, and its literature

Chapter One

Southern Colorado, Autumn, 1893

A dog barked. His horse snorted. The town slept.

Hoofs made a sucking noise as the roan faltered through the muddy street in the cold morning. Laboring with every step, the winded gelding struggled forward, head bent low against the wind. It had been a miracle, Ben Cameron thought, that old Goliad had made it this far, climbing all night up the mountain road after a hard run out of Trinidad along the river cowboys called the Picketwire. He should have stopped hours ago, let the roan graze, taken off the saddle, and rubbed its lathered back, or, hell, simply dismounted and led Goliad for a mile or so along the switchbacks, but Cameron had wanted to put as much distance as possible between him and the dead man back in Trinidad. Despite munching on grass or drinking from the mountain streams only when Cameron had reined up briefly to gather his bearings, or made sure no one followed him, Goliad had never floundered until the last few miles. Now he had played out, but not before reaching town shortly after dawn. The roan had bailed out Cameron one more time, likely saved his life, or at least postponed death a few days.

Still intent on pushing the horse a few more yards, Cameron gave the roan a soft kick while considering the town. He needed to find a livery stable, to reward Goliad and give him a well-earned rest. A blustery wind chilled his face, and he tugged on the collar of his Mackinaw and pulled down the brim of his Stetson, then matched his horse's movement by bending his head low.

The slamming of a door up the street drew quick attention, and his head jerked erect while his gloved right hand rested on the Schofield revolver holstered on his right hip. The town in front of him remained blurred, partly from a lack of sleep, partly from the rye-induced haze, but mostly from his fading eye-sight.

He made out the figure of a tall man in front of a two-story building on the left. THE TEXAS HOUSE. Cameron could read the big, black letters emblazoned across a painting of the Lone Star flag, but the face of the man remained washed out. He wore dark pants, white shirt, and vest. Emptying spittoons, just tossing their contents onto the mud of Front Street. He posed no threat, but Cameron kept his hand on the .45 just to feel safe. The man glanced his way, gathered the brass cuspidors, and returned to the warmth of the saloon. The gent had barely even considered the new-comer, and Cameron couldn't blame him for that. A half-dead horse and its worn-out rider . . . not much to see.

Cameron reined to a stop in front of The Texas House, neither admiring the frame facade nor its plate glass window. Someone had paid a small fortune in freight to build this saloon, but the owner had lacked any business sense. The Texas House? In Ben Cameron's experience, most Coloradoans despised Texans. Why build such an opulent, by Rocky Mountain standards, saloon out here in this rough-hewn burg? Likely the entrepreneur believed the newspaper stories a few years back that had predicted how the Denver & Rio Grande Railroad would run a spur to this town for faster access to the coal being mined here. Miners still worked the coal, but the railroad had not come, and, with the financial panic carving a swath from the East, probably never would. Like many boom towns Ben Cameron had seen across the West, this one would also die. From the looks of the boarded-up buildings and empty lots lining Front Street, the deathwatch had already begun.

To the left of The Texas House, a faded sign announced BILLIARDS, but the windows had been broken and the door ripped off its hinges. Next door, the BANK OF THE CULEBRA RANGE had recently failed, one of many cash-starved institutions out West to go under since the New York Stock Exchange started contracting back in May. To the right of the saloon, the MINER'S COMFORT and JOE'S PLACE, whatever they had been, now housed perhaps a few memories but mostly rats wanting to escape the coming winter. Up the street sat the livery stable and beyond that another store—Cameron couldn't read the name—near the coal-mining operation. He guessed the company store remained in operation to keep the miners on tick, and he spotted livestock in the livery, so it remained in business, although it had seen better days. In fact, now that he thought about it, The Texas House was the only building, with the exception of the Masonic Lodge at the edge of town, on Front Street's south side that did not look abandoned.

Across from the Masonic Lodge were the cemetery, an adobe Catholic Church, and a log cabin. Also on Front Street's north stood a café, hotel, and mercantile, apparently hanging on by threads, and then a scattering of buildings, most of whose occupants had departed for more inviting climes. Smoke rose from the chimney in the marshal's office and jail, so apparently the town supported some type of law. Cameron shook his head. Two years ago, he had turned down an offer to serve as town marshal here. Now that he saw what had almost become his home, he realized he had made the right choice, rare for him, especially these past few years. A few cabins and other businesses dotted the landscape behind Front Street and the Picketwire, but he doubted if many would last the winter.

These days, the town's name certainly fit: Purgatoire.

The Texas House, however, remained strong and inviting. Of course, a warped plank thrown across two whiskey kegs would have looked inviting to Cameron on this morning. Through the open door, he could make out blurs as chairs on tables, the man putting spittoons on the floor, and the shape of a full-length bar.

A dog barked again.

Cameron knew he should ride on to the livery, but his hands trembled for a shot. *Just one drink,* he said to himself as he swung from the saddle and into the street of mud, cigar butts, and tobacco juice. He tied the roan to the hitching rail, and walked inside.

Just one, he said once more, knowing he would say it again when he ordered a second round.

Chapter Two

Clean sheets helped Amie Courtland keep her sanity. She had made a lot of concessions over the years, but long ago Amie viewed that, if she were going to be bedded by filthy, drunken miners and cowboys whose idea of romance was grunting like a hog for a few minutes, or seconds, she was at least going to have something pleasant to sleep on. That meant spending her mornings doing laundry while most prostitutes slept in, but it made her feel better—and cleaner.

She washed the bedding at the river because she couldn't afford taking her things to the Chinese laundry over by the mine, off from Front Street, not with the percentage Diva took from her earnings at The Texas House. After bad nights, Amie would pound out her frustrations on her linen, and during the warm months she would bathe in the cool water and try to cleanse herself, but today felt much too nippy for that.

The town, her home these past eleven months, took its name from the gurgling river that flowed just south of the vacant lots behind Front Street. The Purgatoire. Only the cowhands, who let their Herefords graze in the summer up here and at lower elevations in the winter, called it the Picketwire. Amie liked Purgatoire better; the name usually suited her mood.

The aspens had begun turning gold, which meant Randall Johnson and his cowboys would be here soon to drive Bar J stock to the winter ranges around Trinidad. That meant she and the rest of the girls at The Texas House would be busy. She'd best get her bedding clean now.

She performed her chore in the frigid water, remembering a late spring afternoon years ago when Stan Gibbs found her washing clothes in the river near Blakely, Alabama. Stan had been her beau, had been for thirteen months, and she fully expected to marry him, raise a brood of kids, and live on a farm as they grew old together. That's the way those stories turned out. He had blond hair and eyes as blue as Mobile Bay. His father had been killed while riding with Nathan Bedford Forrest during the War for Southern Independence, and Amie's mother doted on the boy, more than she did her own sons.

Stan had been fishing for catfish the previous week and came away with an awful sunburn. His mother and Amie had chided him for taking off his shirt in such weather, because now Stan's arms and back were peeling something fierce. Yet he had stood beside her, joking, being polite, and then they had started kissing. Amie had tried to push him away, but she really enjoyed him. In fact, at a couple of barn dances she had let him reach inside her blouse. She had let him unbutton her blouse and felt his fingers working her camisole's drawstring. When he had slid his hand lower—he had never done that before—she had moaned, feeling a sensation new to her, had kissed him harder, had realized they were seriously involved, hot, hearts racing, on the sandy shore. It wasn't a sin, he had whispered, if they were going to be married. Truthfully, Amie hadn't cared if they were wrong or right. She had said something, barely understandable, but Stan had known she was willing, and pulled away from her just long enough for them to shed their clothes. He had spread a wet sheet over the riverbank, then was on top of her.

What she remembered all these years later was dead skin. The stuff had flaked off Stan's body all over her and the blanket. She could laugh about it now, and probably would have laughed about it then had Amie's father not discovered them.

"You sum-bitch!" Josiah Courtland had screamed, pulling Stan off and almost drowning him in the river. Amie had wanted to help her beau, but she had been so ashamed she had hurriedly put on her clothes, or tried to anyway. She had been buttoning her blouse, forgetting the camisole, when her father had turned his rage on her. "You damned whore!" he had bellowed, slapping her to the ground. "You whore!" he had repeated. "I work my arse off to provide for you, and you go whorin' like some bitch in heat." He had balled his fist and hit her hard, had hit her again and again until she had lost consciousness, then had dragged her to their home and peeled her hide with his razor strop.

"Whore!" he had yelled while her mother and baby brother Ezra had cried.

Her parents had sent her to a convent in St. Louis later that summer. They probably would have done it sooner, but the beating left Amie in bed for three weeks. She had liked the convent. She had felt safe there—safe from her father—and maybe she would have stayed, but one afternoon as she had strolled along the Mississippi River's banks she heard a familiar voice.

She had turned to find Stan Gibbs.

"I come for you, Amie," he had said.

No longer had he looked like some Alabama hayseed. He was tall—probably because of the high-heeled stovepipe boots—and wore a fine suit of black broadcloth with a red silk cravat and colonial blue shirt. A gray derby covered his light hair. She had held her ground at first but found his eyes irresistible.

"I'm headin' West," he had said, "and you's got to come with me. We can gets married. We'll see Dodge City, Denver, San Francisco."

She had gone with him. They had made love in his

St. Louis hotel room that night, and he had carried her to Dodge City, Kansas, by train, but he hadn't married her. He had registered under the name of Stanley Gibson of Topeka, gambler, telling her later that he chose Topeka because—"I likes the sounds of it."—and he had disappeared into the saloons and gambling dens, maybe the cribs for all she knew. She wouldn't be surprised. Not now. Back then, however, she had been young, and in love. At least, she had thought she was in love, even when she saw him register her as: AMY CORTLIN, MOBILE, ALABAMA, CONCUBINE.

She hadn't really minded "concubine", but it had irked her that he had misspelled her name. Both names! Then he left her in Dodge with no money and a $47 hotel debt. She pleaded with the hotel owner, said she could clean or wash dishes or cook, but the burly man with bad teeth had another idea.

Amie had refused at first, yet finally relented. She no longer had the safety of the convent or protection of her mother, although the latter had never been much of a refuge from her father, especially when he came home in his cups. Besides, two months living in sin with Stan Gibbs had robbed her of her confidence. The Dodge City jail awaited her, and the hotel owner had even mentioned Leavenworth Penitentiary, an exaggeration certainly, but it had scared a seventeen-year-old, unmarried girl on this strange, ugly frontier. One night with a pig to get out of debt. She had closed her eyes and tried to think of pleasant thoughts while the man did his business, then rolled over and went to sleep, snoring. Out of debt, Amie had tried to find a real job in Dodge City, but Stan Gibbs's spirit had dragged her south of the railroad tracks like an anchor.

"I seen you with that gambler. That keeper of yours took me for twenty-five dollars," the man at the Dodge House had told her. "Cardsharp he was. He'd be in jail now if he hadn't lit a shuck out of town. I have no job for the likes of you."

Similar responses greeted her north of Dodge City's famous deadline, and, after three days without food, she realized she had only one option.

In 1882, Dodge City's south side had boomed with Texas cowboys, railroad men, and tinhorns, all of them hell-bent on drinking, gambling, and whoring. No one would hire her to serve drinks, and she couldn't deal poker or even understand faro. She looked rail-thin, a procurer had told her, and didn't have much in the chest department, but she had nice legs, corn-silk hair, and a pretty, unspoiled face that most men, drunk or sober, would find attractive. Her soft Alabama drawl would make those cowhands, most of them Southerners, hot and eager. She could sell her body or starve.

That was the hard truth for an unmarried girl without means in a hell-hole like Dodge. After letting Stan Gibbs and the hotel manager rob her of dignity, what did it matter if she kept on this course? It would be only for a while. "They can buy your body, hon," a fat whore told her one afternoon, "but not your soul, damn them. It's a job. 'The oldest profession', they say. Lots of gals have worked their way West on their backs." So a man named Jenkins got her a crib, for a percentage of Amie's earnings, and she went to work.

She hoped to make enough money to catch a train back to St. Louis, maybe even Alabama, where she'd beg her father's forgiveness, but it didn't happen that way. Jenkins's cut didn't leave her with much, and, when she tried to find respectable work, merchants turned their heads. In fact, a sarcastic writer at the *Ford County Globe* made light of Amie's plight.

It has come to this paper's attention that one Amy Courting sought out the honorable Leviticus Siegel of Siegel's Mercantile on Front Street for employment last week.

My, but business must be poor since all of our free-spending cowboys have gone back to their Texas ranges with the end of the trail season. Our respectable readers don't know Amy Courting, but our denizens across the deadline might recognize Miss Courting as Alabama Amelia, one of procurer Ernest Jenkings's fair but frail Courtezans of the tenderloin.

Tsk, tsk, our sweet Southern Soiled Dove, we hope you can find a job to tide you over until our Texas cowboys return and you can go back to your preferred profession.

Eleven years had passed, and so many towns. Amie Courtland, alias Alabama Amelia, Amanda the Angel, Scar-Face, and other monikers she had long since forgotten, had seen Denver, after all, like Stan Gibbs had promised, but never San Francisco, never west of Colorado's Rockies. Her accent sounded a little sharper, raspier from years breathing in tobacco smoke and drinking gin to kill the pain, but was still distinctly Southern. She remained thin, so skinny in fact that some patrons asked if she were a lunger before they'd pay her for sex, and her hair was still the color of corn silk, but few, drunk or sober, would find her face attractive. A drunken city councilman in Denver had smashed a whiskey bottle against the bedpost one night and rammed the ragged edges into her face in the winter of 1889. So Amie, disfigured, had drifted, now not even trying to find employment in a less shameful field. Her soul felt lost, had been for years, so she whored for six months at a cathouse in Colorado Springs, worked her own crib behind saloons in Pueblo and Raton, and finally wound up at a hog ranch, the lowest of all whorehouses, outside of Trinidad before Diva asked her to come work for her at The Texas House in Purgatoire.

"Don't you see my face?" Amie had asked, tears welling in her bloodshot eyes.

"Missy," the madam had answered, "them scars don't mean a thing to the boys at the Pendant Mining Company. As long as you give 'em what they pay for."

Her scarred face reflected in the river, and she angrily shattered the image with her bedding, ignoring the icy water that numbed her hands and fingers, while biting her bottom lip and trying not to cry.

Louis Venizelos sighed at the sound of the batwing doors slapping in the morning air. He had seen the rider limping up the street and should have locked up after emptying the spittoons, but Diva kept the windows nailed shut, and this place reeked of stale beer, smoke, vomit, and odors of which he didn't want to know the source. Venizelos desired something less malodorous to breathe, and The Texas House needed a good airing out. He had been up all night, pouring forty-rod whiskey for the boys at the Pendant Mining Company, and longed to go to sleep. The Texas House was closed, and he'd have to throw out this vagrant, but that's why Diva paid him twenty a month and a free turn with one of her girls once a week.

The rider shed his Mackinaw and sagged against the bar. He wore a revolver, but most men did, and needed a shave. Venizelos adjusted his wire spectacles and studied the stranger carefully while traversing the length of the bar. Gray-striped pants tucked inside what once might have been a fancy, expensive pair of boots. No spurs. The revolver was a Schofield or some Smith & Wesson; a large knife was sheathed on his left hip. White collarless shirt. He was rolling up his shirtsleeves, the right cuff stained with something dark, perhaps blood. Black

19

vest, frayed from travels, red bandanna, and a hat the color of dirty snow with a Montana crown. Venizelos would not have thought much of this man were it not for the sawed-off Parker shotgun the rider had rested on the bar beside him. That's why Venizelos picked up his billy club leaning against the bar.

He gripped the nightstick tighter as he neared the man. Graying dark hair needing a trim. Thirty, forty, or fifty years old. There was no way to guess a saddle tramp's age. "We're closed," Venizelos said, and tried to swallow when the man looked up with haunting dark eyes.

Venizelos's gaze dropped to the pendant hanging from the man's neck, barely in view behind the calico bandanna. A pewter Scottish thistle hung from a piece of old rawhide.

"Scotch," the man said, "or whatever you have that comes close."

"Yes, sir," answered Venizelos, sliding the stick underneath the bar, out of view. He fumbled for a clean tumbler and grabbed an almost full bottle of Glenlivet—real single-malt Scotch, not just rotgut poured into a Glenlivet bottle—placed the glass in front of the man and filled it, careful not to spill a drop.

"Leave the bottle," the man said, and killed what Venizelos had poured. His hands had been trembling as he lifted the tumbler, and the man sighed as the whiskey burned down. He tucked the shotgun underneath his arm, gripped the glass and bottle, left the bar, and settled into a corner booth, positioning himself so that he could see anyone who walked through the front door. Using the glass behind the bar, he could also detect any movement upstairs near the balustrade.

Venizelos sighed and began cleaning his eyeglasses with a handkerchief. He wondered what Diva would say about him serving whiskey this early. Not that it mattered. He wasn't about to tell Ben Cameron no.

Hanging her laundry on the clothesline behind the frame brothel, Amie heard someone crying. Her sheets danced in the wind as she slowly walked behind the privy. Consuela de la Hoya's back pressed against the woodpile, her legs hunched up tight until she was almost a ball, head resting on her knees.

Diva had given Consuela the name "Vaya Con Dios". Sacrilege? Definitely, but the miners enjoyed the name, not to mention the Mexican whore. So did Randy Johnson, the son of the rancher who provided most of the beef for the miners and town citizens, or had at least when Purgatoire boomed. He had been Consuela's most frequent customer.

Consuela was maybe sixteen years old, and Diva had "rescued" her from the same hog ranch where Amie had been whoring. She stood barely five feet tall, and, in Amie's eyes, was not cut out to be a prostitute. Amie had seen all types, from working for Jenkins in Dodge City to the fancy parlor house on Market Street in Denver, to various cribs, brothels, and one miserable hog ranch. Chinese girls sold into slavery. Women addicted to opium. Sporting girls tougher than their customers. And young girls like Consuela de la Hoya, or even Amie herself years ago, who needed one break to get out of this life.

"Consuela?"

Amie called the name gently, but Consuela still jerked her head up, startled, immediately wiping her eyes, fear etched on her face. Amie felt her heart jump with the panic that Consuela might be pregnant. There were ways to prevent that, Amie had learned over the years, but she had never told Consuela how to protect herself. She had never been able to read Diva, except that she had been fair to Amie and the other girls, but Amie doubted if she would have use for a pregnant prostitute in The Texas House. No, Diva, ever the shrewd businesswoman, would simply throw the girl out on the streets and hire a replacement as soon as possible. Amie had a drawer full of sponges in her room. She should give some to Consuela and show her how to insert and remove them properly.

Another memory flashed through Amie's mind: Back home in Alabama, while recovering from her father's beating, Amie's mother had told her about cottonroot, which could be taken to end a pregnancy. Her mother had been embarrassed even to mention this, and Amie often wondered how her mother knew about this remedy, but Matilda Courtland's concerns were unfounded. Amie wasn't pregnant, and, even if she had been, the whipping her father gave her would likely have killed any child inside her.

Her mind then raced back to the prostitutes she had known who had gotten pregnant and botched their abortions. Two had overdosed on savin, extracted from the juniper trees so common on the frontier. Most tried inserting goose quills or the awful Chamberlain's Utero-Vaginal Syringe, but one had used a dirk. Amie would never forget the sight of her, sitting on the top of the rear staircase at the upscale Cash House in Denver as if sleeping, a river of frozen blood pooled beneath the bottom step, and a frozen crimson waterfall leading up to her corpse.

"Consuela," Amie said desperately, "you're not taking the cold, are you?"

The young Mexican girl blinked, finally grasping what Amie meant, and answered that, no, she had not missed her period. She wasn't pregnant. "It is *Señor* Randy," Consuela said.

"What about him?"

She shook her head. "He has asked me to marry him."

It was Amie's turn to blink in confusion. She had forgotten about the other types of girls who sold their bodies, the ones who thought they'd find a husband in the cribs and cathouses, some gentleman—he didn't even have to be rich—who would take them away from the tenderloin. Amie didn't recall ever being such a romantic, except early with Stan Gibbs, before

23

he had abandoned her. She hadn't been a whore then, or had she?

"Consuela," she said at last, "that's wonderful. You shouldn't be crying out here. You'll catch your death in this cold."

"I am a *puta!*" Consuela snapped, her dark eyes filled with anger and pain. "His father will not let him marry me."

Amie held out her hands, waiting patiently until Consuela grasped them and let herself be pulled to her feet. "Randy Johnson is old enough to vote, old enough to marry, old enough to make his own choices," Amie said softly. "He doesn't strike me as a man who'd ask a girl to marry him if he didn't mean it." She believed little of this, but her words made Consuela wipe the tears from her cheeks, and Amie did believe Randy wanted to marry Consuela, whisk her from Purgatoire to a nicer place, if only a brothel closer to the main ranch east of Trinidad.

"Come on," Amie said. "You should get to your room."

"Should I tell Miss Diva?" Consuela asked.

She thought about this before replying. "No, not yet. If Randy gives you a ring, then you should tell her."

"But he has given me a ring, Amie. I am just too ashamed, too afraid to wear it. It is very beautiful."

Amie struggled for words. She felt a pang of jealousy, of regret, but she painted on her best smile as she did for the impetuous boys of the Bar J Ranch or the Pendant Mining Company when they paid for what the girls called "horizontal refreshments". She thought back to the early days in the Dodge City crib, when she had prayed Stan Gibbs would ride back to town and take her away, apologize for being a cad, take her on to San Francisco. How naive, how stupid she had been. Amie had been working in Raton in 1890 when she read in the *Colfax County Courier* that a gambler named Stanson Gibbs of Topeka, Kansas, had been shot dead while cheating at his faro layout in Las Vegas, New Mexico Territory. She could never know for sure, but she felt that out-of-luck tinhorn had once been the Alabama hayseed she thought she was in love with. When she folded the paper, Amie didn't feel sad, nor did she feel glad. That Amie Courtland was dead, and had been for years.

"I want to see that ring, Consuela," Amie lied, and led the teenager into the back door of The Texas House. They went through the kitchen and into the saloon, where she saw Louis Venizelos cleaning shot glasses, watching a man sitting alone in a corner booth. Diva would have a conniption once she woke up. The Texas House wasn't some saloon where saddle tramps could drink before breakfast. The batwing doors pounded, and another man walked inside. Amie knew Joshua Reed by sight, although he had never been a customer, as far as she knew, of any one of Diva's girls.

"Hurry upstairs to your room," Amie told Consuela,

and watched as the girl, now frightened, made a bee-line for the staircase. Amie stood still, holding her breath as Marshal Reed pushed back his coat, and rested his right hand on the butt of a revolver.

"Mister," the young lawman told the stranger sitting in the booth. "You're one sorry son-of-a-bitch."

Chapter Three

The lathered, cold, winded roan horse had stopped him. Having stoked the fire in his office and swept out the empty jail cells, Town Marshal Joshua Reed was on his way to the Dead Canary Café for breakfast when he saw the exhausted gelding tethered to the hitching rail in front of The Texas House. Reed felt his ears redden as boiling blood rushed to his head. He couldn't understand why anyone would have gelded such a magnificent animal, a Tennessee Walking Horse maybe sixteen hands with a broad chest, compact body, and muscular frame. What galled him even more was why anyone would abuse a horse like this. The Walker looked half dead, and likely wouldn't live much longer without water and grain.

Reed patted the animal's neck, forgetting his hunger, and stared at the open doors of The Texas House—as far as he was concerned, the biggest blight in Purgatoire. Ordinances prohibited prostitution within the town limits, but Mayor Potter Stone told Reed he would look the other way or look for another job, especially since the town had started to go bust. Diva's establishment kept the miners happy, and the miners kept the town alive. Potter Stone and the few merchants who hadn't packed up and left had too much invested in Purgatoire to believe it would fail. The panic wouldn't last forever. The railroad would come. Until then, until civilization came here, the God-fearing residents of Purgatoire would tolerate Diva's wretched business on Front Street.

But damn if some saddle tramp could leave his horse to die on the street while he helped himself to the flavors inside. Reed pushed his way through the loud, flapping doors and spotted the bartender and fiddle player, a Greek whose name he couldn't pronounce, and two prostitutes over by the bar, then saw the man in the corner booth, calmly sipping whiskey before seven-thirty in the morning.

One of Diva's little chirpies, a Mexican probably in her teens, lifted the hem of her skirt and hurried past him and up the stairs. The bartender set a tumbler and polishing rag on the bar, and stared at Reed, while the other woman, a blonde with a badly scarred right cheek and forehead, gripped her fingers and pressed her lips together. Ignoring them, Reed stepped closer to the bum in the booth, pushed back his coat to reveal the star on his vest, and rested his right hand on the butt of the single-action Colt holstered high on his hip.

"Mister, you're one sorry son-of-a-bitch."

His voice carried an edge to it. Reed had learned

that if you sounded tough, you could buffalo most drunken miners and cowboys, take the starch out of them, and cart them to jail to sleep it off. Reed had never planned on becoming a lawman. He had hoped to raise horses, but had found himself working in the Pendant for a grubstake when the town's previous marshal, Horace C. Bentham, slipped into the Picketwire while drunk last winter and died of exposure. With the backing of the Pendant bosses and town leaders, Joshua Reed had been sworn in as interim town marshal. The money was better—you didn't go in debt to the Pendant store—his lungs felt lighter, and, for the most part, keeping the peace in a town like Purgatoire seemed far less risky than mining for coal.

At least it had until Reed spoke those words to a total stranger, and saw the shotgun resting on the table beside the bottle of Scotch. When the man turned to face him, Reed's throat went dry. The eyes looking up at him were dead.

"Marshal," the bartender whispered, "that's Ben Cameron, The Scottish Gun."

Reed blinked. He knew he shouldn't, but he couldn't help himself. Ben Cameron had barely moved, simply turned a bit in his seat, although now his right arm had dropped beneath the table. *Don't back down,* Reed told himself. *I don't care who he is.*

He did care, however. Reed knew that Ben Cameron had been offered the job as town marshal before it wound up going to Horace C. Bentham. He had seen the dime novels in mercantiles from St. Joseph to Denver, and he had heard the stories. Ben Cameron, The Scottish Gun. A Ranger down in Texas with Captain Leander McNelly in the 1870s. Pinkerton detective. Marshal of Caldwell, Kansas. Ben Cameron was the Ranger who had shot bandit Efrain Concepción dead along the Rio Grande, the shootist lauded by Buffalo Bill Cody who had left gunman Wes Evans dying on the streets of Cheyenne, Wyoming. Ben Cameron, The Scottish Gun. Stock detective. Hired assassin. Cold-blooded killer.

He could make out the thistle hanging from a rawhide cord. The Greek bartender hadn't lied. This man truly was Ben Cameron.

"Is that your horse outside, Mister Cameron?" Reed wanted to sound unintimidated, but he knew he had failed. He couldn't match Cameron's stare. It felt like he was gazing into a corpse—his own—so he looked at where the gunman's right hand had disappeared, half expecting to see it appear suddenly holding a revolver.

Cameron didn't answer, didn't even budge.

"A horse like that ought to be treated better, Mister Cameron," Reed tried again. "We've got a pretty good livery just up the street."

Cameron's right hand shot up from underneath the table, and Reed stepped back involuntarily, stupidly releasing his grip on his Colt, although, even if he had tried to pull the pistol, he would have been too late. He ground his teeth and closed his eyes briefly, expecting a bullet to tear into his heart at any second, but forced his eyes open to see something glittering in the air, arcing over the chair-covered tables and landing on the hardwood floor.

A silver dollar rolled, twisted, and landed in front of Reed's boots.

"That's mighty good advice," he heard Ben Cameron say. "Why don't you take ol' Goliad to that livery you been praisin', rub him down, and give him plenty of water and a bucket of oats?"

Reed looked up at the gunman, whose right hand now rested on the stock of the shotgun on the table. He swallowed, knelt, and picked up the coin, never taking his eyes off Cameron. Reed had forgotten about his anger, had lost his appetite. He slid the dollar into his coat pocket and turned on his boot heel, heading for the batwing doors, hurrying, feeling the heat rise to his head again, imagining the bartender's, whore's, and gunman's mocking laughter, although silence filled the inside of the cathouse, and feeling like the biggest coward in all of Colorado.

It had worked this time, Ben Cameron thought after the young lawman left. *Bluffed him.* He shot down another drink to stop his hands from trembling, felt the whiskey warm his insides, calm his nerves, stop the shakes, then he poured another. He heard the marshal leading old Goliad down the street, and Cameron felt ashamed. Then again, many gunmen would have killed the impetuous greenhorn, lawman or not, for such a verbal insult, but the marshal had been right. *Sorry son-of-a-bitch* was an appropriate description. Cameron should have apologized, should have taken care of his horse before he fought off the shakes, but, well, Ben Cameron couldn't back down to some snot-nosed boy with a star pinned to the lapel of his vest. Ben Cameron didn't care for his horses. That's what stable hands were for, or greenhorns wearing a badge. That's what the dime novels said, and he had to live up to his reputation. He downed the Scotch, and felt better until he thought about why he had ridden to Purgatoire.

He had tried to bluff that boy, a ne'er-do-well likely younger than the marshal he had just buffaloed. Only that kid had refused to fold.

His luck had been going pretty good that night at Las Animas Saloon and Gambling Parlor in Trinidad. He had been winning at poker, and everyone in the watering hole had wanted to buy him a drink. That's what it was like when you were Ben Cameron. His vision had become fogged, and he had known he should take his winnings and head to his hotel room, if he could find it, and sleep it off. Someone, however, had brought him another whiskey, and the cards had been dealt. Cameron had picked up the paste cards, stared, snorted, and held them up to a hurdy-gurdy girl standing behind him.

"Do you see what I see here, ma'am?" he had asked.

"I don't know," the girl had answered in a nasal drawl, and the crowd surrounding the table had laughed.

"Well, what do you see? I want to know if this hand's as good as I think it is."

More laughter. The girl, thinking she was the butt of a joke, had said: "Mister Cameron, I can't tell you that. Then these other players'll know what you have."

"Whisper it," Cameron had said, and the girl, blushing from the hoots and cackles, had knelt beside him, and told him what he held. Ben Cameron had pinched her butt as she had walked away, and the saloon had roared with louder hoots and howls. They had thought he was funning her—so did the girl—but he hadn't been able to tell what he held.

A pair of tens, not a great hand, but he had bet twenty dollars and bluffed the tinhorn in the striped shirt and the merchant in the bowler hat into folding. The cowboy with the handlebar mustache and the rawhide-looking kid in the black Boss of the Plains had matched him. The tinhorn dealer had passed the cowboy three cards and the kid one.

"How many?" the dealer had asked.

"Two," Cameron had said. He had thought about standing pat, but figured the others would call that bluff. He had kept the king kicker, and tossed the jack and eight onto the deadwood. The tinhorn had dealt the draws, and this time Cameron hadn't needed some saloon dancer to tell him what he held.

His luck hadn't stopped. A ten and a king. Cameron's bluff had now turned into a full house.

"Fifty dollars." He had tossed three greenbacks into the pot.

The cowboy had twisted his mustache. "He's tryin' to buy it," the kid had told him, but the cowboy had shaken his head, saying—"Then he bought it."— before tossing his hand on top of the deadwood.

"Well, Mister Scottish Gun, you ain't buyin' it from me," the kid had said, matched Cameron's bet, and raised his last $100.

Cameron could have raised, bought the pot through table stakes, but that's not how he had played poker. He had called the boy, who showed a straight to the queen. The poor kid had turned ashen when Cameron revealed tens over kings.

After raking in the winnings, Cameron had tossed the loser a $5 note. "I never leave a man busted," he had said. "Buy yourself a drink and breakfast."

"You cheated," the boy had said icily. "Dealt off the bottom, you son-of-a-whore."

Cameron had leaned back, his right hand disappearing below the table. The merchant in the bowler had said in a placating tone: "Frank, Ben wasn't even dealing."

"Go find your brother, Thompson," the tinhorn had added.

"I ain't leavin' till I get my money back from this cheat." Cameron hadn't moved. He had said evenly: "You're leavin' . . . alive or dead."

Usually, that had worked. Cameron had lost count of the times he had scared some drunken, sore loser into accepting his generosity, but the besotted little oaf had sprung out of his seat, clawing for a Remington stuck in his waistband. The hurdy-gurdy girl had screamed. He had stood himself, reaching behind his back, shunning the Schofield for the knife, easier to reach in his position. He had whipped the Bowie from its sheath, and sliced wildly. The blade had connected, blind luck considering how drunk he was, tearing through the boy's throat. The young face had turned white, and the Remington fell to the floor as blood sprayed the green felt tablecloth and Cameron's shirtsleeve. Thompson had gripped the back of a chair, tried to speak, and fallen to the floor.

Cameron had felt sick, from the whiskey or the gore, he wasn't sure, but he stood calmly, wiping the blood off the knife blade and his hand with a bar towel someone had handed him before shoving his winnings into his hat. The saloon had turned quiet. Even the hurdy-gurdy girl had stopped shrieking.

"You knew him?" Cameron had asked the merchant.

"Frank Thompson," the man had answered. "Keno's brother."

He had heard the name Keno Thompson before but couldn't place it. Cameron had tossed a gold piece on Frank Thompson's blood-soaked corpse.

"To bury him," Cameron had explained.

"His brother will want to bury you," the tinhorn had said.

"He can find me."

Before leaving Las Animas Saloon and Gambling Parlor, Cameron had bought his shotgun back from the bartender. He had sold it—collecting twice its worth, for it was Ben Cameron's shotgun—to buy into the poker game. As he had walked into the crisp night, Ben Cameron heard the excited whispers. *Ben Cameron and Keno Thompson would be facing off on the streets of Trinidad at dawn. . . . Ben Cameron backed down from no man. . . . Cool as ice water, that killer. . . . Tomorrow would be something to see.*

A saloon filled with dunces. They had believed all those penny dreadfuls that had been printed about The Scottish Gun. Well, he wasn't about to stay in Trinidad. Maybe he had been afraid, but mostly he had felt sick. Sick that the killing had sobered him up, sick of what he had become. Cameron hadn't even gone back to his hotel room—nothing there but a few clothes and his grip. He had pulled on his Mackinaw and headed for the livery, stopping at some bucket of blood to buy a bottle of Taos lightning to drink along the way, and left Trinidad at a high lope.

Down the Picketwire he had rode, not knowing where he was bound until by chance, fate, providence, or Satan, he had somehow spotted the sign illuminated in the moonlight, pointing down a road that led into the mountains. He had nudged old Goliad closer, squinted until he could read the sign.

PURGATOIRE, it had read.

Chapter Four

The last person in the world Louis Venizelos wanted to see at that moment came barreling down the stairs, which creaked under her weight. Between puffs on a long nine cigar, Kate Weiss, known to everyone in Las Animas, Huereano, and Costilla counties as Diva, unleashed a cannonade of profanity. She wore a Japanese kimono over her unmentionables, none of which could hide her ample breasts, double chin, or beer belly. Diva might have been, Venizelos thought, the most hideous creature he had ever known, although he had seen the tintypes and *cartes de visite* in her office upstairs and realized The Texas House's madam had been a comely woman twenty or thirty years ago. Now she was fat—"big-boned", she called it—with dull green eyes and matted hair, not quite red or blonde, but something horribly in between.

After letting loose with final myriad curses, Diva pitched her cigar into the closest spittoon and pointed a large finger at Ben Cameron. Her glare remained locked on the silent gunman, but she screamed her question at Venizelos: "What are you doin' lettin' some rummy in at this time of the morn? Vaya Con Dios woke me up, shriekin' that our dumb oaf of a lawdog was fixin' to shoot it out down here. Now what's goin' on?"

"That's Ben Cameron, Diva," was all Venizelos could think to tell his boss.

She stopped venting long enough to catch her breath after her brisk descent, then studied the gunman in the booth.

Cameron ignored the madam, just sat staring at the wall but likely not seeing anything, lost in his thoughts—whatever thoughts went through the mind of a killer like The Scottish Gun.

"Shit," she finally said.

"I'm not fooling, Diva."

Her eyes returned to Cameron. "You mean all them nickel and dime dreadfuls I've seen around here and there are about . . . *him?*" She let out a belch and laugh, closed the kimono, and walked to the bar. "Pour me a drink," she ordered Venizelos, who had anticipated the request, and had his hand on the jug of port wine underneath the bar. He filled a goblet and slid it toward Diva, who shook her head, and asked: "What about you, Alabama Angel? You think this walkin' whiskey vat is the legendary Ben Cameron?"

Venizelos, who had forgotten all about Amie, glanced at her, saw she had moved down the bar a bit, and now stared soulfully at Cameron. "It's him," she murmured without taking her eyes off the gunman.

Diva drained her goblet in two swallows and, fortified, turned back to face the killer. "I don't care who he is." She plodded toward the booth, knocking over one stacked chair deliberately to grab the man's attention. Cameron considered her now, dropping his right hand underneath the table. Sweating despite the coolness of the morning, Venizelos reached for the Webley revolver near the money box. Would a man like Ben Cameron kill a lady? Not that Diva was a lady, but still. . . .

Venizelos didn't like this one bit. He could see himself getting gunned down by Ben Cameron simply because he was paid to protect Diva and the girls, and, well, he couldn't show yellow—especially since Diva might be testing him. Venizelos had never killed a soul, never even fired a gun in anger. Certainly he had broken a few jaws and throttled many a drunk and belligerent jackass, but the line between busting heads and shooting to kill stretched pretty wide; he never wanted to cross it.

"So you're the legendary Ben Cameron." Diva let out a corrosive laugh. "The Texas House, Mister Scottish Gun, don't open till four in the p.m."

Cameron flipped her a coin, slower than he had done with Marshal Reed, and Diva caught the money in a fatty hand. She examined it closely before testing it with her teeth. "Twenty dollar gold piece," she said to no one in particular, then deposited the money between her breasts.

"What'll that buy me?" Cameron asked dryly.

"Well, I guess I can make exceptions for a man o' stature such as yourself," she answered with a wicked grin. "But understand this, that money just keeps this place open for you this morn. It don't buy you no whiskey, and it don't buy you no horizontal refreshments." She winked in Amie's direction. "You can buy a turn with our Alabama Angel, though, if you like. You don't mind, do you gal?"

Amie did not reply, just kept staring at Cameron as if he were a ghost or a god, Venizelos couldn't tell which.

Tossing back her head, Diva laughed again and told the gunman: "Or you can have me, sugarfoot. I'm more woman than any gal in Colorado."

Another coin flipped toward the madam, who caught it with a smile. "What you buyin' now, friend?" She loosened her gaudy kimono.

"Privacy."

That shut her up, which at first surprised Venizelos. Her face hardened, and she closed the silk garment around her waist tightly. Venizelos expected Diva to change her mind, order him to toss Cameron into the streets, but $40 in a place like this could buy many things, including Diva's tolerance, her silence. "Suit yourself," she said coldly, and headed back upstairs, flipping the second gold piece nonchalantly, but Venizelos had worked for her long enough to know she was furious with Cameron and would take it out on somebody—not The Scottish Gun, of course, or any customer, but one of the girls, or maybe Venizelos himself.

He sighed, stifled a yawn, and angrily dunked Diva's empty goblet in the wash basin full of soapy water. Venizelos didn't clean his boss's glass thoroughly—he never did that any more—but wiped it dry with a dirty rag, and set it beside the clay jug.

Would he have to nursemaid Ben Cameron until the other bartender, Joe Miller, showed up later that afternoon? He wanted to go to sleep.

"Would you like some coffee, sir?"

Venizelos blinked, barely recognizing Amie Courtland's voice. He slowly understood the question had been addressed to the gunman and watched with surprise as Cameron wet his lips, squinted in the direction of the prostitute. Leaning back in the booth, Cameron pushed away the empty glass with his fingers toward the bottle of Scotch.

"Coffee." The word came out as if it were Greek to The Scottish Gun. Venizelos even thought he caught the faintest trace of a smile. "Coffee. Yes, ma'am, that sounds pretty good."

Of Diva's six chirpies, Amie Courtland—given the moniker "Alabama Angel" by Diva, who wanted all of her whores to sport what she considered exotic names—was one of only two that Venizelos respected, if only slightly in Courtland's case. He had never even slept with her but attributed that to her face and the fact that he found Dirty Denise more to his liking, and he had often fantasized about taking Denise out of this hell-hole, trying a new life together, maybe down in Arizona. Still, Amie had a brain, a sense of decency, and he often wondered what had brought her to this sordid little world? Maybe her face. Her right cheek looked like a map of Colorado's Rockies. Somehow, she often reminded Venizelos of himself, the son of a carpenter in New

40

York City. Venizelos had come west to build things, only to become a pretty good bare-knuckle pugilist because of his tall, muscular frame and quick hands. A bum knee, however, ended his dreams of squaring off with the "Boston Strong Boy", John L. Sullivan, and sent him to saloons and cathouses to pour drinks and break up fights. Still, it beat trying to make a living with hammer and screwrdriver in the Fourth Ward.

"I'll put a pot on," Amie said. She stopped before entering the kitchen. "Go on to bed, Louis," she added. "I'll take care of things down here."

"You sure, Amie?"

"Sure."

"You're an angel, child. I'll lock up the front before I hit the hay. See you tonight."

After pouring two cups of coffee, Amie slid into the booth across from Ben Cameron, and set the coffee pot on a dish towel she had laid on the table. "Sorry," she said as she lifted her own cup. "No sugar and no milk."

"Black's fine." He blew on the cup before taking a sip. His twang spoke of the Deep South. She had always figured Ben Cameron to speak with a Scottish accent, like the dialect described in those dime novels written about The Scottish Gun.

"Would you like me to fix you something to eat?" She had blurted out the question, which came to her like a thunderbolt. It sounded more like an apology, and it was, considering the stock in the pantry or in the smokehouse out back. "We don't have much, but I think there's some elk stew I could warm up."

"No, thanks." He lifted a finger off the pewter cup and pointed slightly toward his stomach. "Don't know if I could keep real food down."

So they drank their coffee in silence. She refilled their cups, and they sipped without saying a word as the morning whiled away. Amie had a million questions to ask him, but she lacked the nerve. The coffee in the pot had grown cold, and Cameron simply stared at his empty cup, fingering the rim absently. Amie knew she should go upstairs and catch some sleep, just in case Randall Johnson's cowboys reached town today and felt like whoring all night, but she didn't want to leave without talking to this man, the only person she knew who could tell her about the death of her brother James so long ago.

"You served with Captain McNelly's Rangers down in Texas?" she asked timidly.

"For a spell." He concentrated on the empty cup. "Till consumption got him." His laugh came out more as a sigh. "Done just about everything there is since then. Even tried the Pinkerton Detective Agency for 'bout two years."

"I know."

He looked up with dark, sad eyes, accentuated by the bloodshot whites, and he stopped playing with the coffee cup.

Amie sucked in air, slowly exhaled, and explained.

"I've read just about everything ever written about you. When Diva, the big lady in here earlier who owns this place, said she'd seen those half-dime and dime novels here and there, she probably meant here. I got about a dozen or so up in my room. And anyway. . . ."

"You shouldn't believe them stories. . . ."

"Amie. Diva calls me Alabama Angel, and I am from Alabama, but my name is Amie. Amie Courtland."

"Alabama. I grew up in Mississippi."

She smiled. "I thought so. You haven't lost your accent. Always figured you'd talk like some Brit."

"That was Colonel Hall's idea." Colonel Thaddeus Hall had written most of the nickel and dime novels about Ben Cameron. She had eight of his titles on her chest of drawers upstairs. "Like I said, Amie. Them stories ain't nothin' more than a fanciful writer's lies. Most of those boys never even talked to me, or knew me, before poundin' out them dreadfuls."

"I've also read the book you wrote, *The True Life of the Scottish Gun by Himself, or, Chilling Accounts of My Career as a Lawman and Detective.* It's upstairs. . . ."

"Ma'am," he said with a laugh, "I didn't write that, either. Colonel Thaddeus Hall did one weekend in Chicago."

"But it's true. . . ."

"Some of it. I was there with him, talkin' to him, but he said he had to dramatize some of it, make my life more palatable for the reader. His words, not mine. So a bunch of it's pure hogwash."

She dropped her gaze and mumbled something. "The part about the Concepción raid, when you killed that Mexican bandit. . . ." She made herself look up. "Was that true?"

"Some of it, I reckon. Some. . . ." He shuddered, closed his eyes.

"There was another Ranger," Amie said softly, not wanting to pry but needing to know. "A friend of yours. James Courtland. You wrote that he was killed in the raid, hit by a stray bullet, but you didn't say much else. Well, I guess a few paragraphs, but. . . . And in all the other stuff I've read, James is never mentioned. I was wondering. . . ." She brushed away a tear.

"He was . . . ?"

"My big brother. He left home when I was eight or so, went to Texas."

She watched as Cameron's hand left the empty coffee cup and reached for the bottle of Scotch. Hands shaking, he pushed out the cork and somehow managed to fill his glass without spilling a drop, then threw back his head as he killed the drink.

"I was wondering," Amie began, "if you could tell me a little about him? He was a boy when Pa . . . when he ran off to Texas. I'd like to know all about him, at least about how . . . ?" Her voice trailed off.

"Lady," said Cameron, the friendliness gone, the Mississippi drawl harsh, "it's like I said. Most of them books ain't nothin' but lies, and I don't recollect no James Courtland. Now, if you don't mind, I'd like to sit here and drink. I paid good, hard money to be left alone, and don't need some carved-up whore pryin' into my past."

Upstairs, Amie unlocked her trunk and rummaged through the old clothes and junk until she found the old cigar box at the bottom. Moments passed and tears fell before she could bring herself to unlatch the fastener and open the lid. Ben Cameron's words ran through her mind again, and the memories came forth—the dam had burst. Amie finally found the nerve to open the box, and lift the first yellowed envelope as if it were worth a fortune. She pulled out the crinkling paper and, lying back on her small bed, dabbing her eyes with a handkerchief, read the letter one more time.

18 Apl 18 & 75
Burton Washinton county Texas

Sissy
 I tak pencil in hand in hops that U Mother & Ezra Jacob Victoria & the dogs are in good health the Turkey bisnes didnot pan out so i hav enlistD as a ranger undR Capt L. Mcnelly a puny litle guy with a wikked cough who dont look like much but is a reel Helion Am payd 50¢ a day & found We are headed S. to stop rustlin & murder

*but do not fear 4 my safty, little sister 4 U kno i
can tak care of myself*

*Besides my bunkie is a good man with a gun
who arived in texas about the same time i did His
name is Benjmin Alxandr Camron & he hails from
Viksberg, Misisipi mor about him latR*

There hadn't been any more, though. James had
gone on to ask about the crops, the fishing, then jotted
down a few descriptions of what life was like in
Texas before signing his name and asking in a post-
script to give Victoria and Ma a peck and pat his
brothers' heads. He never mentioned his father.
Josiah Courtland had run James off the farm, much as
he would chase away Amie, more or less, seven years
later.

She folded the letter, and returned it to its envelope,
grimacing as another small piece in the corner flaked
off and drifted toward the floor. Amie didn't bother
opening the second envelope again, didn't want to see
it wither away, or read it. Besides, she knew its contents by heart, probably even better than she remembered the first letter. Addressed to Josiah Courtland,
the second letter contained only a terse account of the
death of Private James S. Courtland a little less than
a year after he had joined the Rangers. Captain
McNelly had not mentioned Ben Cameron, only said
James Courtland had been killed in the line of duty,
that he had died bravely and gamely and had not suf-
fered. McNelly also wrote that the late, brave

Ranger's personal items would be forwarded at a later date. Amie had stolen the letter after her father announced James's death and went outside to get drunk. The package containing James's watch, Bible, spurs, and a deerskin pouch had arrived two weeks later. She would have stolen those, as well, but her father took them to Mobile, where he sold them to buy two quarts of corn liquor.

Amie had often wondered about James, how he had really died. Maybe that's why she had not resisted too much when Stan Gibbs seduced her with the promise of taking her West. She had been in St. Louis, picking up a copy of the latest Wide Awake Half Dime Library book about Ben Cameron, serving as marshal in Caldwell at that time. Stan Gibbs said he was going to Dodge City, and she naïvely thought that maybe the peace officer of Caldwell would have reason to ride to Dodge City, and she would introduce herself and learn the particulars of her big brother's death.

Of course, that had never happened, but now here came Ben Cameron, the man who could answer just a few questions, only Amie realized that the man she had so long admired from afar was no gentleman. Cameron was nothing but a drunk, a rude, mean-spirited heel who could go straight to the devil.

Chapter Five

Joshua Reed sorted through the Wanted posters until his growling stomach forced him to stop. He looked up at the wall clock only to find it had stopped—he had forgotten to wind it again—so he pulled out his pocket watch. 12:15. He rubbed his tired eyes and pushed away from the desk, disappointed that his search of about a hundred dodgers had revealed nothing. He had hoped to find something posted on Ben Cameron, round up a posse, and haul the man-killer off to jail, but the gunman wasn't wanted in Colorado, or anywhere else for that matter, by the law.

After pulling on his hat and jacket, Reed stepped outside thinking about the Dead Canary Café. He had at last regained his appetite after eating crow in The Texas House that morning; at least no respectable citizen had witnessed his belittling.

Purgatoire had come to some semblance of life since he had disappeared inside his office. A whistle blew at the mine, and Reed could hear the annoying bellowing of the preacher in front of the main gate to the mining property. The preacher had arrived about a week ago, spitting out fire and brimstone in front of the Pendant, The Texas House, the jail, the Chinese laundry, everywhere except the Catholic Church at the far edge of town. Must be Protestant, Reed figured. The preacher's irksome bass voice carried throughout the streets no matter where he set up his pulpit, and Reed had considered arresting the shabby-clothed, dirty vagrant or at least running him out of town. However, there was no law against preaching, and most miners seemed to enjoy those sermons, even if the Word did not stop them from sinning. It was something new, a fresh form of entertainment, cheaper than whiskey, cards, and The Texas House's soiled doves. Reed wondered how much money the preacher made, if any of the miners or townsfolk dropped a coin or two in the grizzled old coot's battered slouch hat that served as his collection plate.

Reed headed away from the jail and the Pendant, guided by the aroma of fried ham and fresh biscuits at the Dead Canary, and did not glance across the muddy street at The Texas House although he couldn't help but wonder how Ben Cameron's horse was doing at the livery? He found Potter Stone and Glenn Boeke standing on the rotting boardwalk in front of the restaurant, Mayor Stone working a toothpick on his molars, and Boeke, a former newspaperman, staring down Front Street toward the bridge over the river. Boeke had arrived fifteen months earlier with plans of opening a newspaper in town, but his press had been destroyed when a freight wagon went over the treacherous mountain road during the winter. He took his loss with the calmness of a gambler, saying *The Purgatoire Enterprise* wasn't meant to be for the time being but that he might buy a new press and equipment after the railroad spur arrived.

That's why he said he stayed in town, but Reed didn't believe him. Boeke remained in Purgatoire because he was broke. He worked twice a week at the town mercantile as a clerk, and performed other odd jobs around town when not trying to charm someone into buying him something to eat. It seemed the mayor had been his mark this afternoon.

"'Afternoon, gentlemen," Reed said pleasantly.

"Marshal," responded the mayor, pitching his toothpick into the street. Boeke remained transfixed on the bend in the road past town. "Glenn here's convinced that he hears horses, thinks it's the Johnson crowd coming in to gather their beef. I say it's the stage from Trinidad."

"Mules pull that stage," Boeke said. "I heard horses."

The mayor rolled his eyes, and Boeke laughed.

"Reckon it's time for both," Reed conceded. The stagecoach seldom brought anyone to town these days, so that didn't concern him. Likely the only reason the Trinidad-based company still sent a Concord up the mountain road once a week was because of the mail contract, and the fact that, while few people paid to go to Purgatoire, more people kept leaving. Randall Johnson's cowboys, however, were another matter, something Reed would fret over. The Bar J boys caused little trouble, but Reed could not ignore the presence of a gunman. "Mayor, you should know that Ben Cameron's in town, over at The Texas House," he said, his stomach souring again.

The newspaperman blinked and stared at Reed. "Who's Ben Cameron?"

Mayor Stone snorted. "You really are a greenhorn, Glenn. Where is it you come from . . . Indiana? You never read about The Scottish Gun?"

Boeke shook his head, and Stone laughed. "Ben Cameron's a shootist. Wore a badge in Texas and Kansas, worked for the Pinkertons. Fought in the Lincoln County War down in New Mexico, served as a stock detective in Wyoming. Killed probably twenty or thirty men. We offered him the job of marshal a few years back, but he turned us down." The mayor addressed his next comment at Reed. "You don't think he's decided he wants your job, after all, do you?"

"Not if he's at The Texas House," Boeke answered with a hoot. "I'd say he has more pressing needs."

As Stone cackled and slapped his thigh, Reed felt his ears burning again. He excused himself and had just pushed open the screen door when the first of Randall Johnson's cowboys came loping around the bend, the horses' hoofs churning up mud.

"You have good ears, Glenn," Stone told the journalist. "I'll buy you supper tonight." His face tightened, and he turned to Reed. "I'll tell Randall about Cameron. Doubt if there will be any trouble, but you never know. Eat your dinner, Joshua . . . biscuits aren't burnt too bad today . . . and don't worry about The Scottish Gun. I don't think one of the Bar J cowboys will go gunning for him, or that he's here after one of them. But make sure no strangers get off the stagecoach when . . . or if . . . it finally arrives this afternoon."

A cold wind swept off the mesa and blew dust into Keno Thompson's eyes as he stood in front of the fresh grave in Trinidad's pauper's cemetery. Thompson had gotten good and drunk the night before, passed out near his bedroll in the wagon yard, and slept through his brother's funeral. That wasn't right. Somebody should have woken him, told him Frank had been murdered, almost decapitated the stories went, and was being planted that morning, but no one in Trinidad had cared much for the Thompson brothers.

Fact was, Keno Thompson thought as he pulled off his grimy bowler and crushed a clod of dirt with the toe of his boot, nobody anywhere cared much for any of the Thompsons of Yell County, Arkansas. When Pa had been struck by lightning on their hardscrabble farm, only kinfolk—and not all of them—and one of Judge Parker's deputy U.S. marshals had turned out for the funeral, and the lawdog came only because he wanted to make dead certain that Mal Thompson was, indeed, a corpse. He had made Keno, then just a yonker, and older brother Terry open the lid of the coffin, but that didn't do no good. Pa had been toting an axe on his shoulder when the bolt struck him dead, welding the iron blade to his head. That had been the first dead person Keno ever saw, and, although far from his last, it remained the grisliest. It had been too much for the young deputy, too, who vomited all over Pa's charred face.

Brother Terry had cackled over that, then slammed the lid, almost pinching off the deputy's fingers. Once the lawdog had mounted up and rode off, Maw had read some Scripture—pretended to, anyway, for Maw had never learned her letters, nor had any of the Thompsons—and they had lowered Pa into the earth behind the barn.

Judge Parker and his lawdogs had been after Pa more than two years for running whiskey in the Indian Nations, but they never got him; God did. The law did get brother Terry, although not Parker's marshals. Nope, Terry had gotten himself arrested after trying to rob a bank in Baxter Springs, Kansas, and was swiftly tried and hanged. Keno's older sister had run off with a drummer and died of typhoid up in Montana, where her husband was shot to death by vigilantes, and little brother Jimmie had been killed by Comanches after consorting with some sorry little squaw around Fort Sill. That showed how little the law thought of the Thompsons, he figured, trusting prairie niggers more than white folks. Those murdering Comanches weren't even arrested because the Indian agent and bluecoats all said the killing had been justified. Maw had raised holy hell over that, and she'd raise even more once she heard that her baby boy was gone to glory.

Keno Thompson could see that wrinkled old hag

clearly. She'd practically twist his ear off, spit snuff in his eye, and whip his backside with Pa's old razor strop. "You was supposed to look after Frankie," she'd tell him, "you good for nothin' dog." Then she'd cry out in misery: "Oh, God, why did you have to take my man Mal? Why did you have to take Terry and Jimmie and Doris and her man Cletus? And now you done taken Frankie. Why did you have to leave me with Alastair?"

Alastair. He had always hated that name.

Well, he would have to get someone to write his mother a note sometime, mail it to her in care of Uncle Preston Zeske over in Van Buren. Uncle Preston had been the one to ride out and read the letter announcing Terry's hanging, Doris's death, the shooting of Cletus, and Jimmie's scalping. Keno would have to say that Frank got his throat cut after catching a man cheating at cards, that she could have those grave-diggers dig up Frankie and send him home if that's what she wanted, although she hadn't felt the need with her other young ones. He'd also have to swear to her that he'd go find Frank's killer, track him down if it took him the rest of his life, and shoot down the coward. He'd have to do that because of her. She'd demand it, and he wouldn't have her tormenting him in his dreams the rest of his life. No, if he killed the man who killed Frankie, Maw might even show him some kindness.

He pulled his hat back on and spit on his brother's grave. Keno Thompson had never wanted that boy to tag along with him—that had been Maw's idea, too. Frank had been Maw's pet, while Keno had been nothing better than one of those lazy old hounds full of fat ticks and suffering from the mange. "Brother, I reckon you're burnin' in hell by now," he said. "Say hello to the brothers and Pa, you sorry son-of-a-bitch."

Thompson heard the horses whinny before he turned to walk down the hill. A big man with a brushy red mustache and Whitney shotgun opened the gate for him while five others remained mounted, hands on pistol butts or cradling shotguns or Winchesters. One man on horseback held the reins to Red Mustache's bay, and another horse, a buckskin mare, stood grazing beside the fence surrounding the cemetery. Thompson spat again. The buckskin was his—his at least since he had stolen it in Laramie, Wyoming. The welcoming committee had thrown his saddle and traps on the mare, and had come here to see him off.

"You missed the funeral," Thompson told the red-mustached man, who pushed back his coat to reveal a marshal's badge pinned to the lapel of his vest.

"We were here," Red Mustache said, "buryin' your brother. You paid your respects?"

"Reckon so."

"Then there's your horse, Keno."

Thompson pushed the tail of his coat behind his holster just to spite the lawdogs. "Where's Frank's?" he asked. "And his saddle and tack?"

"Paid for his burial," answered Red Mustache, thumbing back the hammers on his ten-gauge. "Now, you want to ride out of Trinidad, or you want to stay here with your brother? Makes no never mind to me."

"Who killed him?"

The lawdog took pleasure in his answer. "Ben Cameron."

One of the deputies on horseback added: "Your brother drew on Cameron, Thompson. We got thirty witnesses who say it was self-defense."

"I hear Frankie caught him cheatin'," Thompson challenged.

"Horse apples," replied the man on horseback. "Frank was drunk, Keno, and a poor card player to boot."

The shotgun barrel inched closer to Thompson's stomach. "Cameron left town, too," Red Mustache told him, "so there ain't no point in you stickin' around here, Thompson. You've worn out your welcome."

Thompson took his hand off his Colt and gently pushed the shotgun barrel to one side. "Always knew Ben Cameron was yellow."

"He left town to avoid bloodshed," argued the man on horseback. "The man who killed Wes Evans in Cheyenne ain't no coward."

"Yeah." Thompson headed for his buckskin. Ben Cameron. Now that was a fine pickle, but he wasn't afraid. The deputy on the horse had been reading too many newspapers and yellow-covered tripe.

Thompson had heard that Cameron wasn't much of anything no more, a saddle tramp and occasional gambler who'd do just about anything for a drink. The once-great marshal of Caldwell and legendary Texas Ranger had last been seen pouring drinks for customers at some hog ranch in southeastern Wyoming. At least, that's what Thompson had heard up in Denver. Besides, if he killed The Scottish Gun, Maw would have to be proud of her only surviving child. He'd be in all the newspapers. Folks would be buying him drinks, not running him out of town with scatter-guns.

"Where did Cameron go?" he asked after checking the cinch—it would be just like those lawdogs to leave it loose so he'd get pitched while climbing one of the passes—and swinging into the saddle.

"We don't know," Red Mustache answered.

"I'll find him." He thought briefly that perhaps they were lying to him, that Cameron remained in town, but, no, those scalawags didn't have that much brains. Thompson spurred the buckskin, and headed south. He couldn't see Cameron going north, not with winter coming, and it didn't matter anyway because the Denver police were probably still looking for the Thompson brothers after they had robbed that cobbler's shop three weeks back, and he had no intention of getting any closer to Denver than Trinidad. Nor did he want to ride across the plains to the east, not as cold as it kept getting, where nothing grew to stop the wind, so that left south or west. Thompson put his horse into a trot and rode for Raton Pass. He knew a whorehouse just across the border where the whiskey and women came cheap. If he didn't find Cameron in Raton, he'd ride back to Colorado and check out the mountain towns.

He had to. Maw would rip his head off if he gave up too easily.

Chapter Six

By the time Joshua Reed finished dinner, the stagecoach had arrived, depositing mail and a whiskey drummer who crossed the quagmire and complained to Reed about the lack of a plank across the street to prevent one from soiling his shoes. Ignoring him, Reed headed for the stagecoach. He warned the old jehu and messenger—they generally spent the night, not wanting to risk that mountain road in the dark, making the run to Trinidad at first light—of Ben Cameron's presence before heading for the livery. The stable hand, Moses Keller, wasn't around, typical, but Reed didn't care. Cameron's Tennessee Walker looked much better, and he didn't care about that, either. He saddled his bay gelding, rode west out of town, taking the left fork past the Pendant Mining Company, and headed for the clearing across the Picketwire where the Bar J boys had set up camp.

"Swing down, Marshal," Jack Tompkins, Randall Johnson's foreman, sang out in a Texas twang, "an' help yourself to some of Quincy's grub."

"No thanks," Reed said as he dismounted. "Just ate in town."

"Coffee then?" Tompkins said.

After wrapping the reins around an aspen sapling, Reed smiled with a nod toward the cowhands holding tin plates and cups, waiting in line by the chuck wagon for their afternoon meal. "Working hands, first," he said, which earned the respect and appreciation of the waddies. "Is Mister Johnson around?" he asked the foreman.

"Headed back to town after we set up. Chasin' that tryin' son of his. Must 'a' just missed him." *While I was in the livery,* Reed thought. Tompkins set his own plate down, picked up a clean cup, and cut in line to fill it with steaming coffee, ignoring Reed's protest, then handed it to him, saying: "The mayor's already been here, if you're here to warn the boys 'bout Ben Cameron."

Reed thanked him for the coffee. "I just wanted to make sure. Don't want. . . ."

"You'll get no trouble from the boys here, as long as he don't hog The Texas House," Tompkins assured him with a wink. " 'Sides, after Stone dropped in, Boss Johnson had me round up all the boys' hardware. Anything that shoots is now stored in the chuck wagon."

He felt relieved as he examined the cowboys and realized that they, indeed, were not heeled. Even the coffee tasted better, and he offered Tompkins a weak smile. Worry quickly returned, however, and he asked the foreman where Johnson's son had gone, although he had a good idea. Everyone in Purgatoire, and probably most in Trinidad, knew that Randy Johnson was sweet on one of the prostitutes working at The Texas House.

Tompkins tossed the dregs from his cup to the ground. "Randy Johnson would have to squat to piss, Marshal," he said. "Now don't you go an' tell Boss Johnson I said that, but that boy ain't gonna face down a man-killer, even over that child of a whore he fancies. 'Sides, his daddy's likely found him now an' is layin' down the law."

Most of the cowhands had taken their coffee, beans, and biscuits, and were lounging underneath the aspens while the cook sat on a boulder, peeling potatoes. Tompkins refilled his cup with black coffee, and shook his head in reflection. "I saw Ben Cameron once. Caldwell, Kansas, back in 'Eighty-One, maybe 'Eighty-Two."

"Did he kill one of your men?"

"Pshaw." The foreman shook his head with a hearty chuckle. "Texas waddies ain't got the sense God gave a mule, but they know better than facin' down a shootist, even when they're in their cups." He jutted his jaw toward his current collection of cowhands, and reassured Reed. "Colorado waddies ain't no smarter. No, Cameron didn't kill nobody when we was in town. Didn't have to. Already had a reputation back then. I was trail bossin' a herd from Uvalde County. He had a drink in the Last Chance Saloon with me, told me the rules, an' I agreed. He was a younger man then. Weren't we all. Strappin', good-lookin' fella, fit as a fiddle."

"He's changed." Reed tossed his empty cup into the wreck pan.

"Bet his eyes ain't changed none," Tompkins said. "He had the look of Cain in those eyes."

Reed didn't respond to that. The bay gelding snorted, and Reed gathered the reins, thanked Tompkins and the cook for the coffee, and swung into the saddle. He rode back to town in silence.

Ben Cameron had not moved, except once or twice to step out back and relieve his bladder. He stared at the bottle of Scotch and now empty glass in front of him, vaguely aware of the conversation around him. The fat madam sat at a table, haggling with a drummer over the price of shipping whiskey by wagon from Trinidad. The drummer was overmatched.

So Cameron had found yet another cathouse. He had guessed The Texas House to be a fancy saloon when he had reined up along Front Street, not some house of ill repute, but that's the way his luck had turned. The last job he had held, other than itinerant gambler, had been serving forty-rod whiskey at the Thirteen Mile Hog Ranch in Laramie County, Wyoming. That had lasted six weeks, until the proprietor of the establishment tired of Cameron's drinking the supply of rotgut and asked him to leave, *pronto.*

The Texas House prostitutes had made their way downstairs for breakfast—breakfast to them, anyway—but the young woman Cameron had insulted that morning remained upstairs, as did the Mexican teenager. The four girls who had disappeared into the kitchen were a rough lot, although not the hideous, tortured creatures he had known back at the Thirteen Mile. One of the girls, a tall blonde with a nose broken more than once, had given him a wink, asking if she could join him, before the bartender, refreshed from his nap, told her to mosey along elsewhere. The bartender had called her Cindy, but Cameron didn't know if that was her real name or some handle like "Vaya Con Dios" or "Alabama Angel". A delicate Oriental with long, black hair, a freckled redhead with a sack of Bull Durham, and a brown-eyed, chubby-cheeked brunette comprised the rest of Diva's stable. A second bartender had also arrived and stood wiping down the long bar with a rag. The first bartender Cameron had met had disappeared into the storeroom to refill bottles after rolling out one keg of beer.

Cameron had considered this group and quickly dismissed everyone, but, when the door swung open, he reached for the shotgun. A barrel-chested, broad-shouldered man in duck trousers and a linen duster stepped into the dim lighting of The Texas House and headed straight for Diva, spurs jingling as he walked. He wore a fancy bone-colored hat and carried a quirt in his right hand, but, as far as Cameron could make out, he wore no gun. Cameron didn't feel completely satisfied, and, although he pulled his hand away from the sawed-off Parker, he reached underneath the table and pulled the Schofield out of the holster, resting it on his lap. With his left hand, he poured another drink.

"Why, if it isn't the King of the Picketwire, Mister Randall Johnson," Diva spoke while flicking ash from her cigar to the floor. "We heard your boys ride in. You lookin' to head 'em off at the pass, or get an early . . . jump on things?"

"I'm looking for my son." The man's voice was toneless.

Diva cackled, craned her neck, and yelled: "Vaya Con Dios!" When no reply came after a minute, she shouted the name again. Still nothing. "Consuela!" the madam tried again. "Consuela de la Hoya, get your tiny rump downstairs. You got a gentleman caller!" Silence answered her shouts, and, after another drag on the cigar, she changed tactics.

"Alabama Angel! Wake up, gal!"

A hinge *squeaked,* and Cameron made out the figure of Amie Courtland standing upstairs, wiping sleep or something from her eyes. "Angel, drag that Mexican's arse out of bed and kick her downstairs before I come up there and whip her stinkin', bean-eatin' hide."

Amie Courtland disappeared briefly before reemerging from another door. "She's not here,

Diva!" she called out, which prompted a chorus of curses from both the madam and the rancher, although they swore at different people. The big man stormed out the front while Diva headed to the bar and filled a goblet with wine. The small, bald-headed drummer followed her at a safe distance.

"Aren't we done yet, Charlie?" Diva asked the drummer after taking a long swig.

The drummer laid a paper on the bar, worked on it with his pencil, and slid it toward her goblet. "How's that?" he asked.

"That'll do," Diva said. "I suppose you want the usual."

Blushing, he shuffled his feet.

"Joe," Diva told the second bartender, "give this man a token. Just one." She drained her wine, signed the contract, and clapped her hands, screaming for her girls to get upstairs, get dressed, and get ready, that the Bar J boys were in town and business would be booming.

The girls filed out of the kitchen and upstairs, and Diva disappeared into the storeroom with the other barkeep. After the drummer slid his token into his vest pocket, he picked up his glass of whiskey and timidly approached the booth.

"Buy you a drink, sir?" he asked.

Cameron shrugged. He had finished the Scotch, but the craving remained. Someone always wanted to buy him a drink, and he seldom rejected any hospitality. He slid the shotgun out of the way, and the drummer sat down, offering his hand across the table.

"I'm Charlie Carr, sir, originally from Topeka."

Cameron took the man's hand. "How does a man from Topeka become a whiskey drummer?"

The drummer cackled, but didn't answer. Instead, he shouted for Joe the barkeep to bring another bottle. It wasn't Scotch, Cameron noticed as the bartender set something on the table. The drummer filled Cameron's glass, then his own, and said: "I arrived in Cheyenne on the UP the day after you shot Wes Evans down." He let out a sigh. "Sorry I missed that, Mister Cameron." He raised his whiskey with a grin. "To your health, sir."

Cameron lifted his glass wearily. *"Salud."*

Halfway down the stairs, Amie Courtland stopped and grimaced when Consuela de la Hoya walked through the rear entrance to The Texas House just as Diva exited the storeroom with her hands full of whiskey bottles.

"You stop right there, gal," Diva said, and the Mexican's smile vanished, her face paling. Diva walked with intense purpose, set the bottles on the bar, and stormed to the quivering child, lashing out with a wicked slap that brought tears to Amie's eyes as she watched in fear.

"You been givin' Randy Johnson a freebie. I don't tolerate that, you good-for-nothin' greaser. He pays like all the rest." She slapped her again, backing Consuela to the wall. "He can afford it. I can't!"

When Diva raised her hand again, Consuela blurted

out: "But, *Señora,* Randy has asked me to be his wife." She held out her hand, revealing a ring.

"What the . . . ?"

"*Por favor, Señora,* do not strike me again."

Diva stared at the ring as if she were struck dumb. Slowly she lowered her hand, and did not speak as Consuela wiped tears from her inflamed cheeks and bit her lower lip.

"When's the date?" The question came from Louis Venizelos, who stood in the doorway to the storeroom with a case of whiskey. That was just like the Greek bartender, Amie thought, as her legs began to work again, and she walked downstairs. Venizelos often played The Texas House's peacekeeper.

Consuela flashed him a timid smile. "As soon as Randy tells his father," she replied. The bartender ignored Diva's glare, returned Consuela's grin, and walked to the bar. "We are going to go to Denver, Randy tells me, for our honeymoon," Consuela continued, excited, forgetting the beating from Diva. "Then go all the way to Montana, perhaps, and start a ranch, small at first. . . ." She stopped, embarrassed at her excitement, and faced Diva again. "I thank you for all that you have done for me. I hope. . . ."

Diva grabbed Consuela's arm, dragging her toward Cameron's table where she yelled at the drummer to produce the token. The runt of a man almost spilled his drink as he fished the coin from his vest pocket, mumbling something to Diva that Amie could not understand.

Still enraged, the madam snatched the token from the drummer's fingers, and savagely swung Consuela, sobbing uncontrollably, into the drummer's arms, the force almost knocking both of them into the booth where Cameron sat sipping whiskey, ignoring the commotion.

"Take her!" Diva yelled.

"But I was drinking with Ben Cameron. . . ."

"I said take her upstairs now. And you!" She pointed a fat finger at the girl. "If and when Randy Johnson marries you, fine, but until then, you work for me. Stop cryin', you pathetic greaser. Stop it, I say!" She raised an open palm as if to strike again, but the little drummer stepped between them, mumbled that everything was OK, and dabbed Consuela's eyes with his hanky. The girl pressed her lips tightly, thanked the drummer in Spanish, and swallowed.

"Go on, now!" Diva screamed as the drummer led Consuela away. "Get out of my sight, the both of you. And hurry back down, Vaya Con Dios, because you gonna get a lot of work tonight. I guaran-damn-tee you that."

Out of breath, Diva slowly headed back to the bar, where Venizelos had poured her more of that dreadful port wine. Amie stood at the bottom of the stairs as the drummer and Consuela passed her. Embarrassed, Consuela stared at the wall, and the drummer ignored Amie. Amie wanted to say something but couldn't find the words, and then the two had passed her.

Slowly she moved to the bar, careful not to attract any attention, lest Diva turn that rage on her.

After draining the goblet, Diva barked something and stormed out the back door for the privy.

"Well, I knew that was bound to happen," Venizelos said as he poured Amie a cup of coffee. "She'd have her pound of flesh."

Amie took the coffee, understanding. A storm had been brewing inside Diva since Cameron insulted her that morning. Amie glanced at the gunman, unfazed by the outburst, just refilling his glass from another bottle. Briefly she stared at him with contempt, but sighed as Joe Miller opened the door and two of the Bar J cowboys rushed inside, asking for whiskies, demanding music. Venizelos deftly filled two shot glasses, collected the money, and fetched his fiddle and bow from beneath the bar. As soon as he started "The Virginia Reel", one of the cowboys grabbed Amie's arm and began trying to dance, even though the "Reel" needed at least eight dancers, and the cowboy and Amie were the only ones swinging to the sawing fiddle.

Amie put on her best smile, clapping her hands to encourage her partner while deep down dreading the night to come.

Chapter Seven

"An abomination!" the preacher shouted outside The Texas House, his voice barely audible over the boisterous laughter and fiddling wailing from the intemperate bucket of blood. "This house is an abomination in the eyes of the Lord! Be gone. Remember, the wages of sin!" The preacher's sermon fell on deaf ears as cowboys pushed him aside to make their way through the batwing doors. "Death!" the preacher yelled to their disappearing backs. " 'For the wages of sin is death.' " He spun around and stepped toward the next group of waddies, spouting Scripture one more time with the same results: " 'Lift up thine eyes unto the high places, and see where thou hast not been lien with. In the ways hast thou sat for them, as the Arabian in the wilderness . . . and thou has polluted the land with thy whoredoms and with thy wickedness.' "

Joshua Reed had to credit the persistency of the cuss, about the shabbiest-looking man this side of Ben Cameron. The second wave of Bar J boys also ignored the preacher before entering The Texas House. With the exception of Reed, nobody else could be found on the streets of Purgatoire, and, although the preacher considered Reed briefly, he didn't cross the thick mud to try to save his soul. Instead, he leaned against a wooden column, tucked the Bible underneath his arm, bowed his head, and prayed.

Reed left him like that, and headed for his office for a cup of coffee. The Texas House wouldn't likely pose any problem tonight, at least nothing out of the ordinary. None of the cowboys had been armed—Randall Johnson and Jack Tompkins had kept their word—unless one of the boys was carrying a Derringer or some other hideaway gun, but Reed doubted that. The Bar J waddies were honest cowboys, not gunmen, living on forty a month and found. They'd get drunk, blow off steam, and risk catching an ungentlemanly disease by heading upstairs with one of Kate Weiss's prostitutes, although Mayor Stone swore up and down that the madam ran a clean business, even brought in a doctor from Trinidad to check out her girlies twice a year. That was another one of Stone's arguments to keep the house operating. Reed wondered how often Potter Stone frequented The Texas House. He had never seen him go inside. Likely used the back door late at night. What did it matter?

Reed opened the door to his office, surprised to find a visitor had helped himself to coffee. Pulling off his jacket and gun belt, Reed stepped to the gentleman, sitting at the desk, and held out his hand. "'Evening, Mister Johnson. I hope you haven't been waiting too long."

The rancher had a firm grip. "Not long, Reed." Smiling, he raised the cup. "Your coffee's better than anything Quincy pours. If you ever get sick of marshaling, see me about a job as our cook. Pays better and you don't get shot at."

Reed laughed, settling into his chair. "I haven't been shot at here, Mister Johnson. And I can't handle a chuck wagon, plus my cooking's pretty bad, so I'll have to pass on your offer." He turned serious. "Thanks for disarming your boys, sir.

"Not a problem. No sense in tossing coal oil on dying embers."

They fell silent. Reed remembered he had come back to the office for coffee, so he rose, walked to the stove, and filled another cup before returning to his chair. "What can I do for you?" he asked.

"I've commandeered one of your cells, Reed," Johnson said casually, continuing to sip from the tin cup, only not even looking at Reed now.

Reed stood. The jail only had three cells, and the lock was broken on the one he used as his bedroom. He crossed the room, opened the heavy door separating his office from the jail, and peeked inside. A young man in cowboy trappings lay unconscious, half sprawled on the cot and floor.

"That's. . . ."

"My boy," Johnson finished. "Call it drunk and disorderly conduct. I'll pay the fine, plus extra for your trouble. I want you to keep him locked up till we ride out in four, five days, after we've rounded up our cattle."

Reed took a deep breath, trying to figure this one out, and walked into the jail for a better look at the rancher's son. Chair legs scraped against the floor; Johnson had followed him.

"That's a nasty bump on his head," said Reed, finding Johnson in the doorway.

"He'll live."

Stalemate. Both men waiting. Reed decided to play his hand first, but chose his words carefully. "Mister Johnson, with all due respect, sir, the town jail is not the place for family discipline. Drunk and disorderly conduct? I've never seen your boy take even a sip of liquor."

Johnson's face lost whatever friendliness it had shown. "Keep him locked up, Reed. I don't want him anywhere near that whore."

So that was it. Reed figured this had something to do with that prostitute Randy Johnson had been seeing. Well, Johnson should have left the boy back in Trinidad. "Why not just keep him tied up at your camp?"

"I want him in jail. My boys will be busy, and Quincy can't watch over him all the time. He'd get loose, come in here, maybe light out with that. . . ." He spat into the empty slop bucket at the nearest cell. "He stays here." Johnson's eyes became distant, vacant, his next words a mere whisper. "I don't want Randy around. There's something . . . I wish . . . I wish The Texas House burned to the ground."

"A few here in town would agree with you," Reed said, and Johnson blinked, focusing, as if he had been miles away from Purgatoire. Perhaps he had been.

"Do we have an understanding, Reed?"

You didn't argue with a man like Randall Johnson, not and win. Reed had tried, and had lost. If he told the rancher no, Johnson would simply head over to Potter Stone's and get the mayor's approval. Reed could appeal to the town council, but of the six board members duly elected two years ago, only two remained in town. Officials hadn't seen fit to replace the four men who left in search of more promising futures, and the two survivors would never take a stand against either Potter Stone or, especially, Randall Johnson.

"Agreed." Reed watched silently as the rancher set his cup on the stove, pulled on his coat and hat, and went outside. Reed stood there for a few minutes, dismissing the notion of cleaning the bloody knot where, most likely, Randall Johnson had savagely applied a pistol barrel. He headed back to the office, closing and bolting the door behind him, and dropped into his desk chair. He took a sip of his coffee, now cold, and stared at the greenbacks the rancher had left on the desk. A bribe.

It sickened him, but he pocketed the money anyway, leaving a few bills to pay for Randy Johnson's fine and court costs for public drunkenness and disorderly conduct.

He had pissed in his pants.

Ben Cameron intentionally spilled his whiskey glass, letting the contents pour onto his trousers to cover up his loss of bladder control. Laughing, he cursed his fake carelessness, shaking his head while reaching for the bottle for a refill. He had forgotten the times he had pulled off this act, but it worked again. A big-hatted cowhand sitting across from him asked merrily: "Waterin' your horse, Ben?"

That resulted in a hearty chuckle from the drunken whiskey peddler, who had returned after his brief tryst with the Mexican. Cameron smiled at the cowboy with the thick Texas drawl. Ben, the waddie had called him. Things had gotten mighty friendly here, but the night, and Cameron's memory, kept falling out of focus, shattering like a broken mirror. He couldn't recollect the cowboy's name.

Looking through the tobacco smoke, he realized things had not slowed down at The Texas House. Cowboys paraded Diva's girls upstairs to their rooms, then came back down for whiskey or beer as other cowhands took their turns on the dance floor downstairs and the beds upstairs. Cameron didn't see how prostitutes did it, one after another, all night. He took another sip, placed the glass on the table, trying to guess how Colonel Thaddeus Hall would paint over the hard fact that the hero of his journalistic career kept winding up at brothels. The Scottish Gun had fallen from the streets of Caldwell and Cheyenne, even Chicago, from the dime novels, national newspapers, and a standing invitation to join Buffalo Bill Cody's Wild West arena show, to a hog ranch in Wyoming and now another cathouse in Colorado. Well, at least The Texas House was a step above the Thirteen Mile Hog Ranch, and the whiskey here wouldn't blind a man.

He told himself he wouldn't drink any more tonight—well, after he finished the glass he had just poured. Cameron needed sleep, but he had to gain some control. He knew he could do this. John Barleycorn and the hard life he had been living the past few years had definitely taken a toll, but he hadn't lost all willpower. He wiggled his toes inside his boots, felt the circulation returning, slowly regained feeling in his legs.

The cowboy said something, and Cameron looked up. He couldn't remember when the cowhand had joined the drummer and him in the booth. Cameron couldn't remember much these days.

"How's that?" he asked, as though the bartender's fiddling and cowboys' laughter had drowned out the man's question.

"Nothin'," the cowboy drawled, lifted his glass, and drained its contents before looking upstairs. Someone came through the loud-flapping doors, catching the waddie's eye, and he choked on his whiskey and swore. Recovered, the man said: "I ain't never seen the boss in no whorehouse, not even since his wife went to glory."

Squinting, Cameron spotted the tall figure of a man pause to study the surroundings before walking to Diva. The two spoke briefly before retiring into the madam's office in the far corner of the building.

"Ain't got much taste in women," the drummer said lightly. "You couldn't pay me for a turn with that crone."

Cameron remembered the cowboy's name now:

Tompkins. Back in Texas with McNelly's Rangers, Cameron had known a man named Tompkins. Not this fellow, though. Ranger Eli Tompkins had died in the fall of 1875 of dysentery. This cowboy's name was Jack, not likely any kin to the dead Ranger, and worked as ramrod of the Bar J outfit. Cameron recognized the rancher, Tompkins's boss, as the man who had entered The Texas House earlier in the day, the one Diva had called "King of the Picketwire" . . . Randall Johnson.

The rancher exited Diva's office and strode outside, angrily pushing through the doors, disappearing into the darkness. Diva came out shortly thereafter, puffing on a cigar, but Cameron couldn't make out her face. She flipped cigar ash on the floor, surveyed the scene downstairs and, perhaps satisfied, returned to her office.

Cameron trained his eyes on another scene. A cowboy was leading, more like dragging, the Courtland girl upstairs, already working on the buttons to his trousers with his free hand, encouraged by hoots and howls from his comrades below. Cameron killed the whiskey in his glass and watched until her door slammed shut. Downstairs, another cowboy led the red-headed prostitute called Dirty Denise through the front doors for fresh air. Less than five minutes later, the bespectacled bartender stopped fiddling, and strode outside as well, but the dancing prostitutes and waddies didn't seem to notice, or care, that the music had stopped.

Even though his vision kept failing, he hadn't lost his touch, taking in scenes, studying everything around him, a habit from what Colonel Hall called "Cameron's star-packing days". Cameron thought of the Courtland girl, and looked back up at the closed door. A foggy haze enveloped his brain, and he lost his train of thought, sighed, and let his gaze return to his booth—where he could see clearly—smiling at the drummer and cowboy, who all night had been buying him drinks, telling him stories, enjoying themselves. A glance down revealed that someone had refilled his whiskey glass.

Forgetting his vow, he lifted it, and drank.

Louis Venizelos had learned to hear things above the din of fiddling, drinking, and carousing, so he knew something was wrong outside even if no one else at The Texas House did. He set the fiddle on the bar top, pushed through the batwing doors, looked to his left, and charged, picking up that lunatic of a preacher by his throat and slamming his stinking body against the wall.

"You miserable sky pilot!" he thundered, slapping the preacher with his free hand before lowering him to his feet. "You touch Denise again, I'll kill you." He threw the man over the empty hitching rail and into the mud. Panting, he whirled toward Denise, who held a hand against her cheek, red from where the parson had slapped her. The cowboy she had walked outside with was gone. Likely he had left long before

the preacher accosted her. Likely Denise, after countless trips upstairs with the Bar J boys, had postponed
returning inside a while. Likely the preacher had
approached her to inform her that she was damned,
and, when Denise filled his ears with unchristian language, he had slapped her. It didn't matter.

Turning back to the preacher, who had pulled himself out of the mud, Venizelos pointed at the sorry
vagabond. "If you. . . ."

Denise, however, stopped him. "It's all right," she
said softly. "He ain't hurt me none."

When he looked back at her, she smiled sadly, and
whispered: "He was just preachin' to me, Louis."
Dirty Denise sported curly hair the color of carrots,
wet from sweat after a night of dancing and fornicating, had thin lips, teeth browned from smoking too
much. Freckles covered her fair skin, giving her a
softer appearance than any of Diva's other girls,
except maybe the Mexican. Dirty Denise—she had
admitted to Venizelos that Denise was her real name,
Denise Benbrook, from Eureka Springs, Arkansas—
could have been twenty-five or forty-five. He had
given up trying to guess the ages of prostitutes, but he
thought her to be on the younger end. "Didn't mean
nothin'," she told him. Maybe she hadn't cursed the
preacher.

"He slapped you!" he vented.

"That don't mean nothin', neither. C'mon, hon, let's
go back inside."

Denise could lead him anywhere, and he forgot his

anger. She took him by his arm and steered him toward the entrance, hearing the preacher shriek at them from the swampy street: " 'Woe unto them! for they have fled from me . . . destruction unto them! because they have transgressed against me . . . though I have redeemed them, yet they have spoken lies against me!' "

He felt fairly certain he could walk, although if anyone wanted to kill him to avenge some pal's death or just to build a reputation, they would have found Ben Cameron defenseless even with that Parker shotgun and Schofield revolver close by. A wave of fear overcame him—the lad he had killed back in Trinidad had a brother, and a face suddenly materialized with the name, Keno Thompson, a two-bit assassin from Arkansas or Missouri who had killed a couple of so-called rustlers during a range war up in Wyoming a year or so back. Killer. Back-shooter. Piece of Southern trash who would have been known for nothing but petty thievery and robbery if he had not drifted into Carbon County.

The panic vanished almost as quickly as it had come. Keno Thompson's reputation wasn't the kind that instilled fear in a gunman. He likely wouldn't care that his brother was dead at Cameron's hand.

Still, Cameron needed sleep, a place to hide, and there were worse places than a whorehouse. Hell, he had been hiding at the Thirteen Mile Hog Ranch before drifting south.

Hiding from what? No one was chasing him. He wasn't wanted for any crime. What . . . ? The answer came to him, though, and he frowned. *Hiding from myself.* He had been running, hiding for years now. Some hero, this Scottish Gun.

The drummer had called it a night, but The Texas House still showed no signs of slowing down. A group of miners had joined the festivities; two of them were about to engage in fisticuffs over who had dibs on the Oriental, China Rene. The second bartender, a bruising man twice the size of the leviathan miners, stood waiting to brain those two if things got out of hand. The rest of the prostitutes, *sans* Diva, were upstairs. And the Courtland girl. She stood at the bar, nursing a gin and bitters, talking to the music-playing bartender with the eyeglasses, who had stopped fiddling.

"Well," Jack Tompkins drawled, "reckon, since I don't want to tangle with them Pendant boys an' everyone else is occupied, I'll spend my dollar on that butchered-up dove before callin' it a night. Pleasure talkin' to you, Ben. Glad you recollected me from that time in Caldwell."

Caldwell? Oh, yeah, Cameron remembered, blinking, trying to comprehend everything the Bar J foreman had told him. He had bossed a Texas herd to Kansas back when Cameron wore the star of city marshal. *City* marshal? Caldwell had delusions of grandeur. It was a rough-hewn burg on the Chisholm Trail just across the border from Indian Territory that went through lawmen like the trots. Cameron saw Tompkins slide out of his seat and stare at Alabama Angel, working up the nerve while finishing his whiskey. Cameron tried to swallow, but his throat turned suddenly dry. He didn't know what he was doing, or thinking, but found his voice after the foreman called out: "Hey, Angel!"

"Tompkins."

The waddie shot him a curious look. As the Courtland girl downed her drink, put on a smile, and walked over, Cameron managed to drag himself from the booth. The girl stopped, frowning, her hard eyes boring through Cameron.

Said Cameron: "How 'bout if I take this one for now?"

Tompkins shrugged, not one to tell The Scottish Gun no. Cameron wasn't so sure about Amie Courtland.

"How much for all night?" he heard himself ask.

"Night's almost finished," she answered sharply.

"How much?"

"Twenty-five."

Steep. That was a Denver price. Still, nodding his approval, he grabbed the shotgun, cumbersome in his inebriated state. Her stare never wavered, but Diva had come to fill her goblet, glancing over to make sure her girls weren't dilly-dallying, so Amie Courtland shrugged and said without enthusiasm: "Let's go."

Cameron took a deep breath, held it a moment, slowly exhaled. He hoped he could make it up that staircase without falling on his face.

81

Chapter Eight

A parched voice called out early in the morning: "How 'bout a drink?"

"Jesus, mister!" Amie Courtland exploded from a rocking chair in the corner of her room. She had slept there all night after Cameron passed out in her bed before he even tried to unbutton his trousers. He had paid for the night, though, and Amie didn't feel like having Louis Venizelos or Joe Miller throw him out so she could let the Pendant and Bar J boys lay on top of her for a dollar a poke, of which Diva collected half. That was last night, however, and this was this morning.

"You puked all over yourself. Now, I gotta wash my sheets again. You smell like a privy, too. Please get out of my bed and out of my sight."

Her neck hurt from sleeping in the rocker. When Cameron didn't budge, she threatened him again. He said nothing, maybe still drunk, probably living off his reputation as The Scottish Gun, but Amie had unbuckled his rig last night, and both gun belt and revolver lay underneath the bed, plus she had unloaded the shotgun before leaning it in a corner.

He started sobbing, which first embarrassed her, then angered her. With another curse, she gripped the doorknob.

"James Courtland," he said softly. "We called him Jamie."

Slowly she turned, watching with some amazement as Cameron managed to swing his boots—she hadn't tried removing those after he passed out—off the bed, and pull himself into a sitting position. Amie thought he'd puke again, but he shook this off and ran fingers through his greasy hair. When he looked up, those haunting eyes made Amie sad.

"You remember him?" Not sure she trusted him.

"In my lucid moments," he answered. He saw she wasn't amused, and apologized. "I remember." His laugh came out as a hoarse cough. "Sometimes I wish I didn't."

Her hand had dropped off the doorknob to her side. "Tell me," she whispered. "Anything."

"A drink," he pleaded, and she dropped to her knees, reached underneath the bed, and found her gin comforter beside his arsenal. She started to hand him the bottle, thought better of it, and poured two fingers into a china coffee mug, giving this to him.

With shaking hands, he took it, killed the liquor quickly, and sighed. "That's better." Strange, but he didn't ask for more. He seemed more focused now, aware of his surroundings and his own wretchedness. "Guess I could use a bath," he said.

"Come on," she told him, still not certain if she believed he even remembered her brother. "The water's cold, but I need to do my laundry anyway. Promise me. . . ."

He answered her with: "Jamie Courtland, private, Texas Rangers. My first friend. His eyes weren't blue like yours, more hazel, I reckon. Worst speller, worst handwriting I ever saw."

Hearing that, Amie helped him out of bed, and he leaned against the wall for support while she stripped off the bedding, ignoring the stench of sweat and vomited whiskey. He didn't ask for more gin—another surprise—nor did he demand the return of his revolver or shotgun. Reaching up, he tentatively fingered the pewter thistle hanging around his neck, dropping his hand when he caught his reflection in the mirror. He staggered to the table below the looking-glass and stared at himself, running a hand over the vile, crusted beard stubble on his gaunt face.

Amie balled up the bed linens, slid past him, opened a drawer, and pulled out a bar of soap. If he noticed her presence, he did not show it. She also picked up a copy of Cameron's autobiography, but he concentrated on his squalid appearance. After dropping the book and soap into her bundle, she asked him: "Ready?" Only after she repeated the question, a bit louder the second time, did he nod.

She opened the door, and he followed her.

"Let me out of here!"

Curses echoed Randy Johnson's demand, followed by the irritating noise of a tin cup rattling the bars of the jail cell.

Joshua Reed let out his own oaths, and crawled out of the bed next door to his prisoner's cell. "I can hear you! Stop that infernal racket." Reed combed his hair with his fingers and looked through the iron bars separating the cells. Randy Johnson seemed a bit stunned to find the town marshal bunking in the cell next to him, but, once he recovered, he tossed the tin cup to the floor and walked closer, gripping the bars and staring.

"What am I doing here?"

"Drunk," Reed lied, sighed, and shook his head, changing his tone: "What do you think you're doing here?"

"My father," he snapped, releasing his tight grip on the bars and testing the knot on his skull. "That sorry bastard." The anger returned, directed again at Purgatoire's marshal. "You can't hold me here. You know I wasn't drunk. I swore to my dying mother I wouldn't touch the stuff, and I haven't. And I know all about *habeas corpus*."

"Nearest lawyer's in Trinidad, though." Reed couldn't keep up his facade. Randy Johnson was right, and his father, not to mention one Marshal Joshua Reed, stood on the wrong side of this argument. "Look, don't yell at me, because I'm on your side." Reed's voice fell to a whisper. "But your father has a mighty long arm in this state. You know that. That's why you're in our miserable calaboose. I'll fetch us some coffee, some breakfast, then work on softening your father." His eyes locked on the ugly wound. "I'll also bring you hot water and rags to clean that head of yours. That must hurt."

After leaving Randy Johnson stewing in the cell,

Reed walked over to the flimsy hotel where the jehu and messenger prepped the stagecoach for the return trip to Trinidad. He peered through the door's window and saw no one inside.

"Just me and Curt," the jehu said as he climbed into the driver's boot. "Ain't decreasin' Purgatoire's population none on this run."

A pity, Reed thought. He had hoped Cameron would take his leave, and, when a man shouted from the hotel lobby, Reed felt a reprieve. He sighed audibly when the whiskey drummer stumbled outside and spilled his luggage onto the warped boardwalk.

"You almost missed us," the jehu said while the messenger swore underneath his breath and dragged the drummer's luggage toward the rear compartment.

"Sorry. Busy night." The middle-aged man's red-rimmed eyes, bedraggled appearance, and stiff, awkward movements told Reed all he needed to know. "These damned Sodoms will kill me yet," the drummer moaned. "Gotta be in Raton next." He sighed, ducked his chin toward his throat, eyes bugging, and turned two shades paler, fighting nausea. Somehow, he kept his mouth closed.

"Try not to puke or shit all over my Concord, jasper." The jehu punctuated the sentence with a stream of tobacco juice. A thin trace of a smile began to form on Reed's face, and he stepped back to watch. The passenger struggled to get inside, the messenger secured the luggage, climbed up beside the driver, rested a shotgun stock on his thigh, and, a minute later, the jehu whipped the team of mules to take the stagecoach out of town.

One day, Reed thought, *I'll be on that stage, leaving this place forever.*

A half hour later, Reed had finished his breakfast at the Dead Canary, and received a plate of cold ham and eggs to take back to his prisoner. As he carefully maneuvered the shabby boardwalk, trying not to spill Randy Johnson's grub, a slamming door woke up one of the town's noisy dogs, and Reed shot a glance at The Texas House. The little Mexican prostitute had just come outside, in a hurry, not concerned about anyone on the street. At first, Reed thought she might be trying to catch the stage, but he dismissed that idea for that was long gone by now. She was after something, or someone, else and slipped something into her coat pocket. Bundled up against the morning chill, she ran one block before cutting down an alley, moving southeast, out of town.

"Wrong way," Reed said to himself. "Your paramour's in jail. He won't be waiting for you today."

The Picketwire's frigid water left Cameron breathless, and the world began spinning. He thought he might throw up again, or pass out, drown, but the dizziness passed, his vision cleared, and he saw Amie Courtland pounding her sheets and his clothes relentlessly.

Cameron picked up the bar of soap and began scrubbing. He sat in the shallows in only his long-handle underwear, and those looked so threadbare he might as well have been naked. Stones lined the river bottom—not the most convenient place for a bath—and he asked the prostitute if Purgatoire didn't have a bathhouse.

"Closed up, oh, thirteen, fourteen months ago. I guess you could get a hot bath at the hotel, though, and sometimes I use that." She pointed to a tub near the brothel's rear entrance.

He vaguely recalled noticing the hotel as he rode into town. Probably had ticky mattresses and no chinks between the logs to keep out the wind. That wasn't the reason he had not stopped at the hotel, however. He knew himself better than that.

"The Texas House looks more like a saloon than a. . . ." Trying to make conversation, he had failed. He scrubbed away harder, daring not to look in the prostitute's eyes.

She answered him, though, without showing any offense. "Used to be one. Diva was running a brothel over by the Chinese laundry, but, when the town started going bust, the owner of The Texas House sold it to her. There was a stink about that in town, it being right on the main street, but that died. A month or so after she bought the place, she got rid of some of her girls, hired me and Consuela. Louis, too. He's the bartender with the eyeglasses."

Amie tossed him a towel after he climbed out of the river, almost slipping on the slick stones. The river water had helped, but he still needed a shave and a real bath, with hot water, sometime soon. Watching Amie examine his frayed clothes, he felt embarrassed. Once, he had been outfitted in the best wardrobe on the frontier, and, while working in Chicago for the Pinkertons, he daily looked like a walking advertisement for Bloomingdale's. His gaze fell to the book beneath a pine. *The True Life of the Scottish Gun by Himself, or, Chilling Accounts of My Career as a Lawman and Detective.* More memories came to him from yesterday. Amie said she had read most of the accounts about Ben Cameron, including his autobiography, ghost-written by Colonel Thaddeus Hall.

She turned as he sat down, leaned against the tree, toweled himself off, and stared at the worn leather-covered book published by G. W. Carleton of New York in 1885.

"We should get inside." Amie began hauling in her laundry. "You'll catch your death out here."

He forced himself to pick up the book, grimacing when the cover fell off.

"It's all right," Amie assured him. "It's been like that a spell."

The book almost opened itself to a well-read section. His vision didn't suffer when reading; his problem came seeing clearly at ever-shrinking distances. His teeth chattered as he scanned the page.

Efrain Concepción was getting away. I raked my trusty steed's side with big-rowel spurs and charged through the bedlam. Hot lead sang all around me, but in spite of all the deafening musketry I managed to hear another horse race right behind my powerful roan, Goliad. Chancing a glance, I saw my bunkie, Private James Courtland, reins held in his teeth and a brace of Colt's Navy revolvers affixed to his hands as if welded there.

"That a boy," I said, and knew Efrain Concepción would not escape Captain McNelly's pursuit on this occasion.

We cleared the brush and charged on. The Mexican badman rode a good Texas Quarter Horse, no doubt stolen from one of his many nefarious raids, a horse with a lot of bottom, and one that would give Goliad a run for his money.

Ten or fifteen minutes later, our mounts carried us to the banks of the Rio Grande, shallow but wide, and surprisingly treacherous. Turkey vultures lined the banks, as if expecting a fresh meal soon on this hot, summer day. Great foresight those birds had. Private Courtland's mount began faltering, dropping farther and farther behind me, so I figured I would go this fight alone, not knowing all this while whether our comrades, indeed even our captain, lay dead or dying on the Texas landscape a few miles to our north.

It mattered none. All that mattered was that I end the bandit's reign of terror, and, at a full gallop, I jerked my Sharps carbine from its scabbard.

That is when, perhaps a quarter mile ahead of me, Efrain Concepción surprised me tremendously. He wheeled his horse around, hoofs splashing in the shallows of the norte americano side of the Rio. Like my partner, he, too, shoved the reins into his mouth, and charged like a medieval knight in a jousting contest. Firing his Colt revolvers, he came at me like the headless horseman from Washington Irving's story.

No one ever questioned the bandit leader's bravery. Perhaps he knew he could not outrun me for so intent was I on pursuing him to the ends of earth and had been steadily closing the distance between us.

Yet I admit to you, dear reader, that fear churned in this Son of Scotland's stomach at the beginning of our duel on horseback. "Outrance", Sir Walter Scott put it. A fight to the death. A bullet tugged at my collar, another left a sizable hole in my hat, and a third grazed my cheek while a fourth tore out a chunk in my left thigh that I did not feel until hours later. The other shots went wide, and I brought the Sharps to my shoulder, cocked, fired, and, as Goliad cleared the acrid smoke, saw Efrain Concepción somersault over the back of his steed, which raced past me, disappeared into the brush a few rods later, and returned to its home, riderless.

Efrain Concepción's lifeblood flowed from underneath his spread-eagled body and into the Rio Grande, fittingly, I suppose, considering all of the violence that river had seen. I turned my horse and rode away, with a heavy heart discovering the body of Private Courtland, my friend, lying on his side, six-guns still clutched in his hands in death. One of the

Mexican bandit's bullets that had missed me had struck him—a one-in-a-thousand chance—and I am not ashamed to tell you that I cried for this senseless death and cursed the fiend who had wrought it.

Yet Private Courtland knew the risks, and he had died bravely. Upon our return to Brownsville, Captain McNelly read over his grave, as well as the graves of four other Rangers who had given their lives for justice. I did not mourn my bunkie too long for he had died a good death, and that is all that matters.

Numb, he closed the book.

"Come on!" a voice called to him, and he looked up to see, through vision blurred from tears, Amie offering her hand to him again. He took it, letting her help him to his feet.

"Let's go inside to the kitchen," she said. "Warm you up, put some solid food in you, and let our clothes dry. Come on." She smiled. "You owe me a story."

He felt ashamed again. "It ain't nothin' like in that book, ma'am," he said. "Wasn't even summer that it happened, but late winter."

"I understand." Her words shocked him out of his despondency. "But I want to know anyway."

Chapter Nine

South Texas, February, 1876

"¡Chingada madre, amigo, eres el mejor pistolero de todo el mundo!" said the Mexican with a strange grin, his dark eyes filled with pain from the bullet in his shoulder, and a bit of respect for the young man who had put it there. If he realized the fate Captain Leander H. McNelly had in store for him, he did not seem to care.

"What's that he said?" asked Ben Cameron, still holding a smoking Navy Colt converted to take brass cartridges.

"He admires your shooting," answered Tom McGovern, "though his language is not totally complimentary."

Another voice commanded Cameron to holster his revolver, which he did immediately as Captain McNelly rode into the camp. McGovern, the Rangers' interpreter, knelt beside a smoldering campfire, and cut away at the Mexican's bloody muslin shirt. Another bandit lay dead a few yards away, left hand gripping a Remington revolver by the butt, right arm snagged in a mesquite branch. The third man, a boy in his early teens, had also been shot, but his wound was not superficial like the burly Mexican's, nor through the heart like the dead man's. He had been gut-shot, making his wound the least merciful.

The scene suddenly cleared to Cameron. His ears stopped ringing, and the bitter smell of gunsmoke dissipated. He had been riding with the Rangers for less than a year, had been involved in several engagements against outlaws, but, until this morning, he had never killed a man.

"Report, Ranger Cameron," said McNelly, still on horseback, in a quiet but authoritative voice.

Cameron cleared his throat, shuffled his feet, and stuttered. Only twenty-one-years old, on the frontier just a few years, he felt tongue-tied talking to a man like the captain. Certainly McNelly wasn't much to look at: medium height, not much thicker around than a telegraph pole, small nose, unkempt dark hair, and prematurely graying mustache and goatee. When McNelly removed a handkerchief from his mouth, Cameron detected the specks of blood on the yellow silk. The captain was having another bad day with his lungs. If the outlaws the Rangers had been chasing down in South Texas didn't soon kill McNelly, consumption would.

Despite his appearance, McNelly was a born leader, and, while his voice might have lacked power, his steel gray eyes shone clearly, forcefully, and Cameron had learned to look his commanding officer in the eye when talking to him. He forced himself to look up now, and tried to speak clearly.

"Me and Jamie seen the smoke from their campfire. I sent him back to fetch y'all, then tried to sneak closer for a better look-see, usin' mesquite for cover.

There was only two of 'em, and I had planned on waitin' till y'all got here, but just a few minutes after Jamie rode off, this feller here—" he pointed to the bandit McGovern was doctoring—"rode into camp, hootin' and a-hollerin', and the other boys started for their mounts. I guess they knew you was comin'. I was only about twenty yards from 'em, so I ran in, yellin' at 'em to throw their hands up. When they didn't, I started shootin'. Don't really know what all happened, sir, how I even hit a one of 'em."

McNelly's eyebrows arched in some sort of appraisal, and he stifled a cough. "You charged in here, Cameron, three-against-one?"

He dropped his eyes to his scuffed, dusty boots, no longer able to hold the captain's gaze. "Well, Capt'n, it's like you told us. Odds don't matter when you're in the right."

The captain didn't respond, just nudged his horse closer to the wounded bandit, who was busy telling McGovern something in Spanish. When the interpreter stood, the Mexican pressed a rag to the bullet hole and grinned at McNelly, who ignored the prisoner.

While this was going on, Jamie Courtland sidled up next to Cameron and whispered: "Why didn't you wait for me, Ben? I wanted to shoot some Mex'cans."

Cameron shrugged in reply, listening to his captain.

"What did he tell you?" McNelly asked McGovern.

"Pretty much what Cameron said, Captain, only his version has Ben running in here while they was having a peaceful talk, not hurting nobody, and shooting his friends. The boy got hit first, he says, while he was about to go tend his sheep. Sheep, my arse. Greaser don't say nothing about that Spencer carbine in the boy's hand, and I don't see no sheep. The greaser here got shot off his horse, and I'll bet you a month's wages, when Sergeant Armstrong runs down that animal, it'll have a Texas brand on it. The third man emptied his gun at Cameron, but Ben put one slug clear through his heart. The greaser says the boy's name is Jose Vittore, and the dead one is Donato Muñoz."

The saddle creaked as McNelly twisted his wiry frame to look at Cameron.

"You hit, Ranger?"

The question took Cameron by surprise. He suddenly checked his stomach, chest, arms, and legs, wondering if a bullet had struck him and he didn't know it. He had heard stories from the late War Between the States of men being killed minutes before they realized they were dead. Yet he saw no blood, and he shook his head, found his voice at last, answering: "No, sir. I don't think so, Capt'n."

McNelly turned back to the Mexican before Cameron finished. "And his name?" he asked McGovern.

"He won't say."

"Corporal Rudd."

A Ranger on a big bay gelding at McNelly's side pulled a book from his saddlebag, thumbed through the pages, and reported: "There's no Donato Muñoz in the book, sir, but Jose Vittore is wanted for rustlin', horse theft, and attempted murder in Brownsville."

"Does the description fit?"

"Yes, sir, to a T . . . five-foot-two, maybe a hundred pounds, black hair, black eyes, and missin' the upper joint of the left thumb. He's our boy."

"*Boy* is correct, Corporal." McNelly sighed. "They're getting younger all the time. You think these men are part of Efrain Concepción's renegades?"

"No doubt, Captain," McGovern answered.

McNelly guided his horse to the wounded boy, barely conscious, but begging for water. He stared down at the boy briefly, noticed the Spencer carbine one of the Rangers had kicked a few feet away from the lad. A minute passed before McNelly urged his horse and returned to McGovern, Cameron, the other bandit, and the waiting Rangers.

"Sandoval," McNelly said. "See to it."

Smiling, Jesús Sandoval dismounted and led his paint horse to an oak tree along the creek bed near the Mexicans' camp. Cameron tried to swallow, but his mouth had turned to dust, and his stomach started dancing. The sight of Sandoval made Jamie Courtland's face turn paler than Cameron's. They knew what Sandoval would do, for they had seen it too many times in their months with McNelly's battalion. Although on the state payroll as a scout, Jesus Sandoval did far more than just track for the captain. A lean, graying *Tejano* with wild eyes and rotting teeth,

Sandoval wore greasy buckskins, Apache-style moccasins, and a silver crucifix that seemed out of place. After tossing a rope over a stout limb and securing the other end to the oak's trunk, he walked toward the Rangers.

"The boy first," McNelly said softly.

Sandoval stopped, puzzled, but soon grinned. The scout had to be mad, Cameron thought. No sane man cherished his work so much, especially this kind of work. After nodding his understanding, Sandoval covered the ground quickly, stooped to pick up the dying boy, and tossed him over his shoulder, not caring that the boy's blood stained his buckskins or that the agonizing screams chilled everyone else in the camp, except the captain. The paint horse stood waiting patiently, the lariat's noose dangling over the shadow, and, when Sandoval reached the spot, he sighed, saying in a hard accent: *"No bueno.* He cannot stand up in the saddle."

That was Sandoval's favorite way of hanging a prisoner. He'd make the condemned man stand atop the saddle for a better drop, and despite many a man's cries and shaky legs, Cameron had never seen the scout botch a hanging. The necks always snapped.

"Por favor," Sandoval said meekly, addressing McNelly.

"Help him," ordered the captain, those hard eyes falling on Cameron, who felt his legs turn to rubber. Beside him, Courtland drew a sharp breath.

"You heard the capt'n," Corporal Rudd told Cameron, and explained. "You shot him. Go help Jesús."

Over the years, Cameron had blocked the hanging of Jose Vittore from his memory. He couldn't piece together how he and McNelly's butcher had strung up that boy, who almost passed out before the noose went over his head. The rest of that day, however, remained etched in his brain no matter how much whiskey he drank.

The wounded Mexican's face turned ashen as the body of Jose Vittore swayed in the breeze. Once Sandoval tossed another rope over the limb, Cameron positioned the paint horse so that the saddle sat underneath the noose. The scout remained beside the hanging corpse and the paint horse while Cameron walked slowly back to camp, all the time thinking he might lose his breakfast. He stuck his hands inside his trousers after seeing how the boy's blood had stained them while he had played executioner.

"Get up," McGovern told the Mexican, and kicked his boots.

"Madre mia," the bandit said in a hoarse whisper, looking up at McNelly. *"Por favor. Yo soy Miguel Rodriguez."*

"Take him," McNelly ordered. "We are burning daylight."

"But," the bandit said as McGovern and Cameron lifted the man to his feet, "I am not in your damned book!"

He had spoken English and, with surprising strength, broke loose from McGovern's and Cameron's hold, and took two steps toward McNelly before finding himself staring down the barrels of dozens of rifles and pistols.

"I am not in your book, McNelly," he said again, softer this time. "Check it."

"I don't need to," McNelly said. "I have no doubt there is not a Miguel Rodriguez listed for crimes in Texas." His face hardened as he added: "Nor do I have any doubt that you are a lying, murdering snake not worth wasting any more precious breath on with conversation." With a nod from McNelly, Cameron and McGovern retook the Mexican's arms.

"Please!" he screamed while being dragged to the oak.

Only when the man stood trembling, standing on the saddle of Sandoval's paint horse, did McNelly kick his horse forward. He reined up and swept off his black hat. "I will give you two things, *Señor* Rodriguez. If you like, you may tell your confession to *Señor* Sandoval, which he will carry to a priest."

"I have nothing to say to this *diablo,*" the bandit said, and spat in the scout's face.

Sandoval merely smiled and wiped off the saliva with his bandanna.

"Then you have one chance, sir, and that is to tell me where I can find Efrain Concepción."

Cameron studied the shadow on his boots. He had seen McNelly and Sandoval hang their prisoners before. "Summary justice," McNelly called it, and the Mexican bandit must have known that, even if he talked, confessed everything to the Rangers, even if he promised that he would personally guide the *gringos* to Efrain Concepción, McNelly would execute him. The second chance McNelly offered was nothing more than a cleansing of the soul. The bandit didn't take the captain's offer.

"I will see you in hell, McNelly." The bandit choked out the words, laced with fear, although he had undoubtedly tried to sound defiant. The laughter in his eyes had long died away. No longer did he smile, not with death so close. He had just finished the sentence when the body of Jose Vittore turned in the wind, his sightless eyes facing Miguel Rodriguez or whatever his real name might be, and a low moan came out of the dead boy's lips like some final whisper. The Mexican almost slipped off the saddle in fear. Even McNelly's eyes widened, and Cameron took an involuntary step back. To Miguel Rodriguez, the dead man's whisper must have been a warning from perdition, a last chance to do right on this earth, and he took it, turning to McNelly, practically screaming: "Efrain is supposed to cross the river at Guerrero on the second night after the full moon! He plans on raiding the big ranch north of Carrizo Springs. We scouted the Dolan Ranch and were on our way down to his encampment where the San Juan and Pesquería meet. That is all I know, McNelly. I swear to it. I . . . ."

Jesús Sandoval did not let the man finish. The Mexican had said all McNelly needed to know. It was like the captain had said. Rodriguez was *not worth wasting any more precious breath on with conversation.*

The neck snapped loudly, and Miguel Rodriguez, like all the others Jesús Sandoval had hanged, died instantly.

Chapter Ten

"I thought you was gonna wet your britches when that dead Mex'can started moanin', Ben," Jamie Courtland drawled as they rode along the trail southeast of Eagle Pass. "Thought I might join you, too. First time I ever seen me a haunt."

"Wasn't no haunt, Jamie," Cameron said, although he didn't feel much like conversation. "Tom McGovern said it was just air escapin' after the boy was dead. Freak thing, that's all."

"*Freak* is right. Scared that other Mex'can somethin' fierce."

They fell silent as McNelly led the Rangers into a canter, then a full gallop, a warm wind blasting their faces as they weaved through the thick brush country. Most, if not all, of McNelly's men originally hailed from Southern states and could handle the heat. Elsewhere, February meant snow, ice, and bitterly cold north winds, but along the Texas-Mexico border winter remained a stranger; indeed, even spring and fall seldom arrived. "It's hotter'n hell," a Ranger from Missouri had once remarked, to which Tom McGovern had replied: "Because we're closer to it." Having grown up near Mobile Bay, Jamie Courtland felt comfortable in this climate. So did Ben Cameron, although it could get cold back home in Vicksburg.

Of more concern than men to Captain McNelly were the horses, so he would keep up a gallop for a mile or two, then slow to a trot, before finally making his Rangers dismount, and lead their horses for ten minutes every hour. When they neared the ford across from the Mexican town of Guerrero, the captain sent Sandoval and McGovern across the border. Exhausted, the rest of the group took shelter in what passed for shade, chewing on jerky, sipping tepid water from canteens, honing knife blades, or cleaning and loading pistols and Sharps carbines.

"Never have understood why the capt'n don't allow us to use them fancy repeatin' rifles," Jamie Courtland said while sliding the Ranger-issued Sharps from its saddle boot. That boy always had something to say.

"Hit a fella with a Sharps and he stays down," Cameron answered, repeating McNelly's words.

"Yeah, but. . . ." Courtland shook his head, checked the breech, and pushed the .50-caliber single-shot rifle into the scabbard.

"Besides," Cameron continued, smiling for the first time since the previous night, "the state of Texas couldn't afford to pay for all that ammunition you'd waste if they issued you a Winchester, not as poorly as you shoot."

"I ain't that bad." Courtland sounded like a pouting schoolboy, which widened Cameron's grin. Today he especially appreciated his friend's ceaseless banter. He started to forget about the men he had killed. "I bet I could 'a' killed me all three of them Mex'cans if you'd let me stay and you'd gone ridin' for the capt'n 'stead of me."

Cameron's smile vanished. "I wish I had gone for the capt'n," he whispered.

"Huh?"

"Nothin'."

Courtland changed the subject. "Ben, I ain't never heard of no San Juan River, or that Pesky-whatever."

"Must be in Mexico."

"Be a lot of Mex'can bandits I could kill down there."

Two days later, as the sun slowly began to rise from behind the tops of the mesquites and brush, Sandoval and McGovern returned to camp on lathered horses. McNelly rose stiffly from a rock, closing his Bible and suppressing a cough, and approached the two men, his officers and sergeants slowly following.

"C'mon," Jamie Courtland said. "Let's tend them horses."

Cameron rolled his eyes. Courtland wasn't being polite; he wanted to hear what the captain and scouts had to say. Cameron didn't cotton to the idea of helping a callous hangman like Jesús Sandoval, but he, too, found himself a bit curious, so he followed his bunkmate.

"They're camped right where the greaser said they'd be," McGovern was saying when Cameron took the reins to his black mare. "We got a few days before the full moon, if that greaser wasn't lying about when they plan on hitting the Dolan spread."

"How many men?" McNelly asked.

"At least fifty," came McGovern's reply. "About even."

Cameron led the mare a few yards away before he began working the cinch on the saddle, taking his time, patting the horse's neck and side as he worked and listened. With a grunt, he pulled off the saddle, set it in the shade, and put the soaking saddle blanket on top to dry. Next, he began rubbing down the horse, looking over the mare's back to find Courtland doing the same.

"Do you think they will ride together?" McNelly asked Sandoval. "Cross the border at the same place and time?"

"*No, mi capitán.* They will split up, three or four groups, meet at the springs, attack the Dolan Ranch from all sides."

"Could we ambush them at Carrizo Springs?" Sergeant Armstrong asked.

"Perhaps." Sandoval grinned. "Perhaps not. Efrain Concepción is no fool. When the men I hanged and Cameron killed do not arrive, he may become suspicious, call off his raid, and wait. He is wily, that *hombre*."

McNelly bowed his head as if in prayer for several moments. When he looked up, Cameron felt a chill race up his spine.

"Is Concepción in that camp?"

"Si." Sandoval's grin widened.

"Captain," Sergeant Armstrong cautioned, "if you're thinkin' what I think you're thinkin'.

"My thinking is this," McNelly said, straightening his back like a lightning rod, his soft voice carrying strength and conviction. "We have an opportunity to rid this country of Efrain Concepción. If we wait for him to cross the river, we could lose him. Dolan, his family, his cowboys could be killed."

With a stern shake of his head, Armstrong continued his argument. "But if we cross the river, Mexico could consider that an act of war. And it's a hard ride to the confluence of the San Juan and Pesquería."

"I don't care one whit what the Mexican government thinks," McNelly said. "They have been harboring this bandit for too many years. But you're right. When we cross that border, we do so as Texans, not Rangers. Did you see any sign of Mexican troops?"

"No," McGovern replied, "but they're out yonder. I promise you that, sir. And we won't be able to hide our trail from them, not as many as we are."

McNelly pursed his lips. "Gather the men. I'll ask

for volunteers. Anyone who chooses to stay on the Texas side of the Rio Grande will still have a job when we return."

"If we return," Sergeant Armstrong said.

You didn't tell Captain McNelly no, so everyone volunteered to cross the border. They forded the river at midnight and rode the rest of the night, using Sandoval's eyes to guide them through foreign country. At dawn, they rested their mounts in the brush while Sandoval and McGovern rode out to scout the bandit camp. Cameron understood why the Rangers avoided the main roads. This *was* an invasion, and McNelly wanted to leave no evidence the Mexican government could use to assail Austin, Washington, or declare war on the United States. When the two guides had not returned by sundown, McNelly seemed unconcerned; he ordered the Rangers to mount, and they pushed on, making camp shortly before dawn along the muddy Rio San Juan. An hour past sunup, McGovern and Sandoval returned on well-used mounts. Once again, Jamie Courtland volunteered Cameron to tend to the scouts' horses.

"What is the nearest town?" McNelly asked as Cameron unsaddled McGovern's mare.

"Onofre," replied Sandoval, "though as a town it is *no bueno*."

"Mexican soldiers?"

"Not in Onofre. We can kill Efrain and his men easily."

"Very well . . . Sandoval, do they know you in Onofre?"

"No, mi capitán."

"Good. I want you to ride to Onofre, tell the *alcalde* to keep his people in the village. Stay there to make sure he obeys, but don't tell him we are Rangers. You'll have to pick your way back to Brownsville alone."

McNelly stifled a cough. "Your horse is done in, Sandoval. Take. . . ." A quick glance found Cameron and Courtland. "Take Private Courtland's. He will stay here with a few others, our rear guard."

Cameron's friend cursed underneath his breath.

"Mine's worn out as well, Captain," McGovern said. "Do I take Cameron's mount?"

McNelly started to nod but stopped, likely remembering Ben Cameron's charge into the Mexican camp back in Texas. Cameron wished he would forget it, but the captain shook his head. "Cameron rides with me. You will stay here, Mister McGovern. And Sergeant Armstrong. If all goes well, we shall meet up here, but, if we are struck down, I want you two to make sure those fortunate among us return home safely."

"When do we attack?" an officer asked.

"Immediately. . . ." This time, the captain could not stop his coughing spell. He glanced at the handkerchief, frowned at the blood, and added: "Volunteers only. If no one wants to go into that camp, I'll ride in alone."

108

• • •

"Ain't fair at all, Ben," Courtland pouted as Cameron saddled Goliad. "How 'bout if I take your horse, Ben, so I can kill me some Mex'cans?"

Cameron had no qualms about staying behind and letting his young bunkmate take his place, but the captain would frown on that. Orders were orders, and McNelly wanted Cameron in this battle.

"I expect, Jamie, that we'll all have our chances. When we hit their camp, the bandits will likely run right toward you."

Courtland kicked up dust. "Capt'n must think me yeller, Ben. That's how come I ain't goin' with y'all. Just because I ain't never kilt me no badman. . . ."

"That ain't true, Jamie. The capt'n put Sergeant Armstrong in charge of y'all, and he ain't no coward. Nor is Tom McGovern. You'll get your chance at shootin', pard."

The nightmare of his own bloody baptism back in Texas caused him to frown. "I'd put it off as long as possible," he added, more to himself than to his friend. Courtland didn't hear.

In the gloaming, they spurred their horses and charged into the quiet bandit camp. Cameron swung his rifle to the right, then left, waiting, sweating, confused. *Where were all those Mexican bandits?* Heart pounding, he reined in Goliad, hearing Corporal Rudd's curse. Campfires flickered; someone had even left a coffee pot on one, and the aroma drifted through the desert air and scrub, but no one stood in the camp except fifty Rangers.

"Gentlemen," McNelly said, "we have been hornswoggled."

"That damned Sandoval!" someone snapped, but McNelly shook his head.

"I would trust Jesús Sandoval with my life, sir. No, it is Concepción who has tricked us. My guess he is riding toward the Rio Grande at this moment."

No sooner was this said than a Ranger named Brubaker galloped into the camp, jerking his horse to a stop so suddenly the gelding stumbled, almost spilling the rider. "Capt'n!" he shouted. "There's a passel of Mex soldiers lopin' toward us. Must be two hunnert. We ain't got a chance if we don't light a shuck for Texas *pronto!*"

It seemed as if McNelly almost laughed. "Another present from Concepción, I warrant. Gentlemen, we have to make the border!" He raked his spurs across his mount's ribs, and led the Rangers north on a hard ride all that night and the following day.

A few Texas newspaper editors later theorized that Efrain Concepción never planned on raiding the Dolan Ranch, that he had sent the three Mexican bandits north knowing they would be captured, knowing at least one of them would confess, and thus anticipating Captain McNelly's raid south of the border. Ben Cameron never bought any of that. To his way of thinking, a scout had spotted the Rangers and warned Concepción, who rode out for

Texas, tipping off the troops to the whereabouts of the *gringo* invaders. Somewhere along the ride north, Concepción must have decided on something even better: He set up an ambush just south of the Rio Grande, and McNelly led the Rangers right into it.

Horses and men screamed, caught in the enfilade. For a second, Cameron thought he was back home in Vicksburg, just a boy, holding his crying mother as Union artillery raked the city with cannon shot, the starving Confederates returning fire. The memory vanished, and he quickly understood his plight. He fired his Sharps, almost losing his seat in the saddle when he attempted to shove it back into the scabbard while Goliad hurdled a dead body. Righting himself, he jerked one rein hard to the right to bring Goliad to a stop. A bullet tore through his hat, and he reached for the Navy Colt, bringing the reins to his mouth while touching the stallion's ribs with his spurs.

Goliad exploded. Cameron fired once at shadows, trying to pick a real target. Horses galloped past him, and his ears rang from the concussion of gunshots, echoes, screams.

"*¡Gringo!*"

Cameron wheeled toward the shout, ducking in the saddle as a bullet whistled past him. He leaned forward, fired a shot underneath Goliad's neck. To his surprise, the Mexican trying to kill him cried out in surprise and pain. Cameron raked the spurs again, not looking back to see if the man he had shot had been killed.

"Make for the river!" McNelly called out above the din of battle.

Cameron craned his neck, trying to find the captain, but couldn't see much through the smoke and dust. He made out another figure, fired, reined up again when the Colt's hammer *clicked* on an empty chamber. Rangers roared past him. He started to spur Goliad, stopped at the sound of a cry: "Capt'n's down! Capt'n's down!" Then, McNelly's voice: "Damn you men, ride! Make for the river, damn you. That's an order you Texas sons-of-bitches!"

Never had he heard the captain swear.

He pulled on the reins and loped toward McNelly's voice, away from the river.

A bullet ripped off his hat. Another tore a furrow across his right thigh. Spotting McNelly, he vaulted from his saddle and handed the officer the reins to Goliad. "Take him, Capt'n," Cameron pleaded, ducking as a bullet *buzzed* past his ear.

"You have your orders, Cameron," McNelly said sternly, raising his revolver at Cameron's face. "If you do not. . . ." A coughing fit almost doubled him over—briefly Cameron thought the captain had been hit. Hacking up blood and phlegm, McNelly dropped his Colt into the sand. Cameron holstered his own revolver and caught McNelly before he fell. He heard another horse, saw Sergeant Armstrong dismounting, firing his revolver. Goliad danced nervously as bullets whined, but Cameron managed to push the captain, now unconscious, over the saddle, and picked up the captain's Colt.

"Come on!" Sergeant Armstrong said, and, pointing toward a mesquite thicket and gripping the reins, ran forward. Cameron followed. About ten yards from the trees, Sergeant Armstrong looked back. When he did, another figure emerged from the trees.

"Look out!" Cameron bellowed.

He didn't remember aiming the captain's revolver, didn't even know he had fired until the pistol barked twice, and the figure disappeared. Neither Armstrong nor Cameron slowed until they had made it behind the tree shelter.

"Hell's bells, Cameron," Armstrong said as he stared at the body of the Mexican Cameron had shot twice in the chest. "That's Efrain Concepción himself."

Cameron didn't care, didn't even look at the dead bandit. He was standing over another body. He quickly dropped to his knees.

"Oh, sweet Jesus Almighty," Jamie Courtland groaned when Cameron rolled him over, cradling his head in his arms. "Oh, dear God, Ben, don't tell my mama it was like this. Don't tell her it was like this. Don't tell her. . . ."

Blood trickled from both corners of his mouth. He swallowed, cursed, cried out in agony. Bullets clipped the mesquite branches, and Armstrong's horse screamed, dropped. Crouching behind the dead animal, Armstrong returned fire, emptying his pistol, then slid behind the dead horse's belly.

"Mount up, Cameron," Armstrong ordered. "You got to get the capt'n out of here. I'll hold 'em off."

"I can't leave Jamie, Sergeant . . . ," Cameron began.

"He's done for, damn it. Gut-shot. Now get Capt'n McNelly home, Ranger!"

"You best run, Ben," said Courtland with surprising strength.

Cameron could only shake his head.

"My horse played out," Courtland went on. "Sandoval's horse, I mean. Never got to kill me no Mex'can." His eyes regained focus, and he gripped Cameron's arm. "Get out of here, Ben. Ain't no sense in us both gettin'. . . ." Pain returned, and he screamed.

Numbly Cameron heard himself telling Sergeant Armstrong: "You take the capt'n, Sergeant. Courtland's my pard." Slowly he lowered Courtland's head to the damp earth. There wasn't time for argument. Armstrong tossed his reloaded revolver to Cameron, jumped to his feet, grabbed the reins, and pulled Goliad and Captain McNelly toward the Rio Grande.

A body popped through the thicket, and Cameron fired. The man screamed, turned, and ran, shouting something about Concepción, likely telling his friends that the leader was dead or wounded. That seemed to stop the gunfire, at least momentarily. Cameron pulled the trigger twice, but no one answered. Maybe they thought Concepción might still be alive and had stopped shooting for fear of hitting their leader.

"Ben . . . ," Courtland whispered.

"Hold tight, Jamie," Cameron said. "I'm gettin' you out of here."

"No, you ain't. . . . I . . . Ben . . . finish me."

He froze at his partner's request. Toward the river, new gunfire erupted, and he realized Sergeant Armstrong and Captain McNelly were caught again, on the Mexican side of the border, unarmed.

"You gotta help the capt'n," Courtland whispered. "Ben, don't leave me to them butchers."

More gunfire in all directions. Cameron ducked. The Mexicans had started shooting into the thicket again, probably now believing Concepción was dead. Above that, another scream, Armstrong's: "Cameron! Come quick!"

Cameron's shadow covered Courtland's face. He looked at his friend only once, saw his eyes closed, mouth whispering a prayer: "Now . . . I . . . lay me . . . down . . . to . . . sleep . . . I . . . pray . . . the Lord . . . my . . . soul . . . to keep. . . ."

The pistol bucked in Cameron's hand, and he ran toward Armstrong and McNelly.

"Nothing in life comes easy," McNelly told Cameron as they stood over the grave behind the Methodist church in Brownsville, Texas. "Nothing will be easy for you, either, Benjamin."

It was the first time McNelly had ever called him by

his first name. Cameron had shot his way through the bandits that had McNelly and Armstrong pinned down, had personally pulled Goliad through the river to Texas, and, once the Rangers reached Brownsville, had become a celebrity.

Safely back in Texas, McNelly never denied leading the attack in his reports to Austin. The Mexican government quickly raised a stink about the invasion, but President Grant and Governor Coke elected not to act, eventually dragging on correspondence through channels until the Mexicans gave up. Efrain Concepción would torment Texas no more, and the price paid—five dead and sixteen wounded Rangers—seemed a bargain to the people of south Texas, if not Cameron.

When he looked back on that day, he found it amazing that Captain McNelly had the strength to stand, let alone give a eulogy and speak to a troubled young Ranger. Likely McNelly didn't want anyone to see how weak he really was, how much the consumption had raked his lungs. That's why Colonel Thaddeus Hall omitted McNelly's weakness in all of those books.

As Cameron fingered the Texas Ranger badge made from a Mexican *peso,* McNelly kept talking in his quiet voice: "Ranger Courtland wore that badge proudly, as should you. You want to resign, I will not badger you to stay with me. If what happened sickens you, I understand. Truthfully it sickens me, but I would do it again. If you wear that badge, or any badge, do what you think is right. Not always legal, but right. That's the only way to tame this land."

Once McNelly left, a stranger walked to the grave, handing Cameron a flask of rye. He had a thick mustache, wire spectacles, and a checkered vest covering a bulging belly. "Sometimes," the man said softly, "words are not enough to kill the pain. My name's Thaddeus K. Hall."

Chapter Eleven

Southern Colorado, Autumn, 1893

" 'Course, your brother ain't buried in Brownsville," said Cameron, staring at the cup of cold coffee before him. "We left him in Mexico. Left two others, too. Them other two, guys named Brubaker and Whitt, didn't die till we was in Brownsville. Anyway, Colonel Hall made up a bunch of lies after talkin' to some of the boys. Interviewed me at the cemetery, but I didn't say much, even after I drank his hooch. Don't think the colonel ever figgered that half-dime novel he wrote about me and the Rangers would be nowhere near as big as it become. But it was something, and then I was bein' wrote up in *Frank Leslie's Illustrated, Harper's Weekly.* From then on, the colonel was writin' 'bout me all the time, followin' me like a flea chasin' a hound, plyin' me with whiskey, even took me to Washington to meet President Hayes back in 'Seventy-Nine.

"Before I knew it, I was a national celebrity. Got offered the marshal's job in Saint Jo, Texas, did that a spell, then moved north to Caldwell. Reckon the capt'n's words stuck with me, 'cause I hardened myself. Capt'n was right. You had to be hard, downright mean, had to do what needed to be done to survive in hell-holes like Caldwell and the Wyoming ranges.

"Guess there was a tad of truth in some of Colonel Hall's stuff, but not much. He stretched it most of the time. Hell, all the time. After Kansas, next it was the Pinkertons, then I got hired on as a stock detective in Wyoming. A few other jobs between 'em. Reputation got me through most of my jobs. I was The Scottish Gun." He chuckled, fingering the pewter thistle. "Never knew why Colonel Hall made that name up. Told him my great-grandparents was Scotch-Irish, but I'm pure Mississippi. Guess he thought it was catchy, bein' Scottish. Reckon it was, as many as them dreadfuls sold. He bought this here thistle in Chicago, give it to me to wear. Don't rightly know why I keep the damn' thing."

He could follow his career from place to place. St. Jo Town Marshal, 1878 to 1880. Riding for John Chisum and later Pat Garrett during the Lincoln County War in New Mexico Territory, 1880 to 1881. Caldwell City Marshal, 1881 to 1884. Running a faro layout in Dodge City in late 1884 and early 1885. Pinkerton agent, 1885 to 1886. Touring the East in Colonel Hall's harebrained stage play during the winter of 1886. Then over to Wyoming, rounding up or running off rustlers, or maybe just small-time ranchers carving up the spreads of the big outfits, killing Wes Evans in 1889. Gambling between jobs. Lately, though, his career roamed from saloon to saloon, brothel to brothel, anywhere he could work for, buy, or steal a drink.

Shaking his head, Cameron pushed the cup away and leaned back in his chair. "Last story I read said how I had killed thirty men in fair fights. Truth is, I've killed six. Maybe three or four more. It was hard to tell what I did down in Mexico. Colonel Hall once wrote that I didn't count Mexicans and Indians, but I never shot at no Indian, and the only reason I can't count the Mexicans, 'cept for Concepción, is you just can't tell in a fight like that. I hit a few, know that much, but got no way of tellin' if they died or not. So six is the number I know for sure." He froze momentarily, recalling the dead punk in Trinidad.

"Seven."

Another thought crossed his mind, and he made himself look up at Amie Courtland. "Eight . . . if you count your brother."

She said nothing. She didn't have to, for Cameron could read the shock, the anguish, the dulled comprehension in her face. He had killed her brother. Yeah, Sergeant Armstrong would have pulled the trigger if Cameron had not volunteered, and, yeah, Jamie Courtland would have died anyway, gut-shot like he was, died slowly, in agony, or would have been butchered by bandits. He had killed his friend out of mercy. At least that's what he told himself. It seldom helped.

He wanted a drink. Needed one and slid his hands underneath the table, sitting on them to stop the shakes. He thought maybe he should not have confessed everything, should have lied to ease her pain, told her Jamie Courtland died in battle without ever feeling the bullet that killed him, like the colonel wrote in that stupid autobiography. More lies. The colonel often told him that little lies, and sometimes bigger ones, never hurt anybody. Too late now.

The rye Colonel Hall had given him at Courtland's grave had helped, and he had remained with McNelly, tendering his resignation in 1878, a year after the captain had succumbed to lung disease. Then it was off to St. Jo on the Chisholm Trail where mostly he had busted a few heads with a pistol barrel, a Schofield by then, rounding up drunks and keeping the peace. His drinking had been social, and it wasn't until Caldwell, when he next met up with Colonel Hall, that he found himself popping corks more frequently, consuming John Barleycorn to dull the pain, block out the memories. Caldwell had been tough on many lawmen's nerves. It sat just across the border from Indian Territory, thus attracting more than thirty-a-month cowhands looking to blow off some steam. He probably would have died there, shot down by some jasper on the owlhoot, if he hadn't been invited to run that faro deal in Dodge. A short time later, Hall had helped him land a job with the Pinkertons—most likely, Cameron figured now, to give Hall something to write about. Faro had its limits, and even the colonel couldn't make up a novel about bucking the tiger that would sell.

He had learned a lot about the detective side of law enforcement while in Chicago, and, although the job had lacked the daily stress of keeping the peace in Caldwell, he had found himself drinking more and more, especially when Hall showed up, needing to write another novel. Three botched assignments due to drunkenness had led to his dismissal—a resignation, if you believed the colonel, to return to the frontier (after that dreadful, short-lived theater career) among the elements more suited to The Scottish Gun. Stock detective—a more polite name for hired gun, or assassin—in Wyoming. It had been in Cheyenne that he had met Wes Evans, a gunman brought in by the smaller ranchers to rid the big outfits of their assassin.

Evans had ambushed Cameron in a dark alley, but his Remington had misfired, and Cameron's Schofield had sent three bullets into the killer's stomach. As bad as Cameron's vision had become, it was a miracle any of the bullets hit their mark, but they had. The gunman had staggered into the street, falling in the dust underneath a street light. Cameron could recall walking up to Evans, seeing the blood seeping from his mouth, hearing the dying killer's whispers: "Now I lay me . . . down to . . . sleep . . . I . . . pray . . . the Lord. . . ."

Courage of the Scottish Gun; or, Death Comes to Wes Evans. That had sold almost as well as *Blood on the Border; or, The Texas Rangers' Scottish Gun*, Colonel Hall's first Ben Cameron novel.

He had trained the barrel at Evans's head, couldn't miss at that range, even with his fading vision, but stopped, no longer seeing a forty-year-old balding killer with a black mustache but a young boy from Alabama just across the Rio Grande in Mexico. He hadn't been able to pull the trigger, and walked, practically ran, to the nearest saloon, finding himself well in his cups by the time Wes Evans had died. *Courage of the Scottish Gun.* Courage, hell. Maybe he had been brave down in Texas and Mexico with Captain McNelly, or perhaps he had been just too afraid to know better. McNelly had inspired courage, but the only bravery Cameron could find any more came in a corked bottle. He had to change; he was just so scared.

The door flew open, letting in a blast of cold air, and Diva stepped inside, stopping abruptly at the sight of Amie and Cameron in The Texas House's kitchen. Her eyes locked on Cameron, and he realized he sat in his long johns, towel over his shoulders, clothes hanging near the stove to dry. Diva recovered, closed the door, and said: "Well, ain't this a pleasant surprise. What got y'all up so early? I reckon my Alabama Angel decided to wash more than her laundry this blustery morn."

Cameron shrugged, even more uncomfortable. Amie said nothing. The madam's gaze drifted from Amie to Cameron as she muttered something Cameron couldn't understand. "Well, y'all enjoy yourselves." Giving up on attempting conversation, Diva removed her coat and entered the saloon.

A long silence followed. Cameron couldn't think of anything to say, having spoken more to Amie than he could remember telling anyone. She finally found the strength to stand, whispering—"I need to think about this."—and leaving him alone. He sat there for several minutes, fighting the urge for another shot, feeling his resolve weakening. At last, he stood to check his clothes, found them dry enough, and dressed. When he walked into the main room, Amie stood against the bar, sipping a glass of gin or some other clear liquor. He walked past her, climbed the stairs, and entered her room, where he found his hardware, buckled on his gun belt, reloaded the shotgun, and returned downstairs. By then Amie was gone, leaving an empty tumbler on the bar.

The saloon was empty. He placed the shotgun on the table at his booth, walked behind the bar, found a glass and a bottle of whiskey, not even looking at the label, fished out a few greenbacks from his vest, and found his place. The clock chimed half past ten.

"Alabama Angel! You up there, hon?"

She sat up on her bed, groaned, and rubbed her head. Three glasses of gin in the morning had not been smart. She answered Diva's call, but the madam likely didn't hear, and she stumbled to the dresser, splashed her face, then reached for a towel. A pocket watch slid off the towel and rattled on the wooden top. Solid silver, it looked like. Not hers. Likely Ben Cameron's. She popped the cover, checked the time. Three-thirty-nine.

"Courtland! Damn you, gal, answer me!"

"I'm coming, Diva!" Amie shouted back, started to snap the watch but caught the inscription inside. She brought it closer and read:

> TO BEN CAMERON
> IN DEEP APPRECIATION
> FOR YOUR SERVICES
> AS OUR CITY MARSHAL
> THE PEOPLE OF CALDWELL, KANSAS
> 1884

She left her room and stuck her head over the railing, silver watch still in her hand, and found Diva standing next to the big rancher, Randall Johnson, by the bar. How many times had Johnson been here the past two days? She had never seen him inside before, always figured him to be the type that would cross a muddy street to avoid walking down the boardwalk in front of the brothel.

"Wake up that damned Vaya Con Dios, Angel!" Diva shouted, shaking her head and reaching for a goblet of port wine.

Just nodding hurt. She walked next door and tapped on Consuela's door, softly, so not to inflame her miserable headache. No answer, so she turned the knob, and stepped inside. A crucifix hung on the wall over the bed. Strange, but she hadn't noticed that before, or the rosary beads on her dresser. She turned down the lantern—some of the girls had lamps in their rooms, but Amie and Consuela had lanterns—and noticed the coal oil was low, as was her own. She'd have to ask Louis Venizelos or Joe Miller to fill them sometime soon. The bed had not been made, not that Diva cared about such matters. Not finding Consuela, Amie bit her lip, massaged her temples slightly, recalling the rage Diva had flown into the last time Consuela had disappeared to see Randall Johnson's son. This time Diva might whip her. She also recalled, vaguely, footsteps that morning, the squeaking of Consuela's door. Amie had been asleep in the rocking chair, and the slight noise had waked her. Consuela must have left early that morning. She dreaded telling Diva, but had no reason to lie. It was obvious the young girl had gone, but her clothes remained here. She'd be back. At least Amie thought she would.

She closed the door behind her and started to tell Diva, but the madam must have read the expression on Amie's face because she cut loose with a litany of curses. "That bean-eatin' whore's done run off on me!" Diva snapped, drained her goblet, and poked Randall Johnson in the chest. "Likely run off with your son, damn it all to hell!"

"Not Randy," Johnson replied. "He's locked up in jail."

"Well, she's gone, damn it." Diva pivoted and pushed the empty goblet toward Venizelos. Randall Johnson also turned back, said something to Diva, and left.

"That means we'll be one whore short tonight if those Bar J boys are still feelin' frisky," Diva mumbled after the bartender slid the goblet back to her. "I'll tan that girl's hide if ever I catch her, shorely I will."

Amie felt confused, not quite comprehending Diva's reasoning. And why was Randy Johnson in jail? Her head pounded. Maybe she'd understand once the hangover subsided. Looking back at the pocket watch in her hand, she moaned, remembering the time. Almost four o'clock. The Texas House would soon be open for business, and most likely the Bar J boys, at least those who hadn't spent all their money last night, would be back to burn the rest of their pay. The Pendant miners, thinking the more the merrier, might join them. It would be another miserable night, especially if Consuela didn't come back.

She looked downstairs again, catching a glimpse of Cameron in his booth. Her gaze fell to his watch. This was the Ben Cameron she had worshipped, had wanted to know, the man so brave, so feckless the citizens of an entire town had presented him a silver watch upon his resignation. Likely years ago she had even held a schoolgirl's crush on The Scottish Gun.

Amie didn't hold him responsible for Jamie's death. She thought she might, but, no, Cameron had done what had to be done. Had he stayed behind, he would have been killed, probably along with McNelly and that Ranger sergeant. Jamie had died because his horse had given out. Maybe he would have lived had he not been riding the hangman's mount, or maybe he would have died anyway. You couldn't second guess these matters, not almost twenty years after the fact. She thought she might hate Cameron after he told her what had really happened, and perhaps she had, briefly. Perhaps she would again after the hangover wore off, but she didn't think so. This morning, he hadn't been a sharp-tongued, callous scoundrel. He had been human, sober, and she had seen something in him, distant, maybe even unreachable, but something soft, decent, something that warranted a beautiful watch and kind sentiment.

Downstairs, though, the Ben Cameron of today lifted a glass and drank.

Chapter Twelve

The door jerked open, letting in a blast of autumn wind along with vibrant fiddle music, shouting, and singing from The Texas House. Joshua Reed had just collected a spoon, empty cup, and supper plate from Randy Johnson's cell and turned to identify the late-night visitor. He had left open the door separating the cells from the office and immediately recognized the big man who slammed the door shut and strode across the office to the jail.

"I want to talk to my son," Randall Johnson said.

At the sound of his father's voice, Randy Johnson leaped from the bunk, gripping the iron bars and showering the visitor with curses. "What for, Dad? Want to beat me with that pistol of yours again?"

Reed felt like a voyeur, a silly one at that, holding a greasy plate, spoon, and tin cup in his fingers.

"You pathetic piece of dung!" the rancher roared in reply. "You run around fornicating with trash. . . . God be praised that your mother isn't around to hear it."

"She ain't trash! She's a good girl, a God-fearing woman, and I love her. . . ."

"Well, she's gone! Lit out of town this morn. That's how much she loved you back, boy!"

"You're a liar!" Randy spat at his father, and the rancher, his face blistering, charged like a rabid wolf. Reed stepped between them, taking the full force of Johnson's body, felt himself being slammed backward into the iron bars. Pain raced up his spine, and his head cracked against the cell door, dulling his senses, but only briefly. Lucky for him, and he knew it for he could have cracked open his skull. Randy Johnson's fists flailed away between the bars, connecting with Reed's throbbing head and shoulders more than his father. The plate, cup, and spoon rattled against the bars, dropped to the floor. Randall Johnson struck out at his son—a stupid move, his knuckles skinning an iron bar. Despite the pain in his head and back, Reed managed to get his arms underneath the rancher's shoulders, and pushed him back. Johnson hit the far wall, blinked, took a step forward, eyes blazing.

Reed never carried a gun while feeding the prisoners, even a generally timid, harmless one like Randy Johnson, so he crouched, gripped the plate, and flung it at the rancher. That seemed silly, too, but the big man threw up his hands defensively as if Reed had lashed out with a whip. The spinning plate glanced off Johnson's thick forearms and *clanged* off a cell door.

"Stop it!" snapped Reed, picking up the cup and feeling like a fool for using tinware in self-defense. "The both of you, calm down!"

The towering rancher blinked, recovering, but his son kept the curses flying. Reed spun around and, with surprising strength, pushed Randy, sending him crashing against his narrow cot in the corner. Whirling back, he summed up courage to threaten the powerful rancher.

"That's enough, Mister Johnson," he said. "Now step outside into my office or I'll have you in jail . . . I don't care how many beeves you brand or how many senators you know."

"He's the one who should be behind bars," Randy mumbled. "Ought to swear out a complaint for assault."

"Shut up, Randy," Reed said, and, to his surprise, the young man obeyed.

"I was going to see if you wanted out, if a night in this pigsty was enough." Randall Johnson spoke in a rather calm voice considering the round of fisticuffs. His skinned knuckles seeped blood. "But I guess you need another few days to cool off."

"She ain't gone, Dad!" Randy shouted. "We're gettin' married, and to hell with you."

"She's gone, Son. Not coming back, I warrant."

Randy was still cursing his father when Reed closed the door, which only muffled the young man's verbal assault. Reed caught his breath, motioning at the chair in front of his desk, but Randall Johnson shook his head.

"We'll have the bulk of the herd rounded up within the week," the rancher said. "I'll pick up Randy on our way home, if that's all right with you." Johnson suddenly looked tired.

He must be, Reed thought, to be asking him permission for anything. Dumbly Reed answered with a nod. "That girl?" Reed began. "Did she really leave town?"

Johnson's head bobbed. "Lit out this morning is what that fat madam says." He wiped his bleeding knuckles on his coat sleeve. "Sorry for the outburst, Reed." He glanced at the thick door, shaking his head at his son's dull shouts. "That boy . . . I'll never make a man out of him."

Before leaving, he tossed a gold piece on Reed's table—another bribe—and left without another word. The prisoner kept cursing, and Reed collapsed in his chair with a sigh, pulling open a drawer and sliding the coin inside, not even checking the denomination. Randy's voice must have given out, or else he heard the front door slam when the rancher left, because the office fell quiet. His stomach rumbled, and Reed thought about fetching a cup of coffee, but a vision played through his mind, once, again, even a third time. He could see the Mexican prostitute running out of The Texas House.

What was her name? The Pendant boys called her Vaya Con Dios, but that was the hideous madam's creation. He pursed his lips, thinking. *Consuela.* He wasn't sure how he remembered that; Randy Johnson must have told him. He didn't know her last name. Probably no one did except Randy Johnson, and perhaps Diva. He pictured seeing her that morning. The young girl had taken off, running, heading out of town, but wearing only a coat, a bonnet covering her head. She couldn't have caught the stagecoach, and she wouldn't have tried walking down the mountain road to Trinidad, not without provisions. Maybe she was meeting somebody. Or Randall Johnson had left her a horse, paid her money to leave Purgatoire and leave his son alone. That made sense. He closed his eyes, trying to see what she had slipped in her coat pocket. Money? No. A note?

He snapped himself out of that bit of detective business with a sharp shake of his head. Tentatively he reached back and tested the small bump on his head where he had been catapulted into the bars. It didn't hurt much any more. He pushed Vaya Con Dios into the far recess of his brain. What did it matter? She was gone. Another soul had fled Purgatoire, yet he remained with the damned.

Cold as the night had become, the air felt refreshing, cleansing, as Amie Courtland made her way to the privy. She couldn't tarry out here; Diva would throw a royal conniption as busy as the night had become, what with Consuela gone, and all. Amie could not figure out where Consuela had run off to, or why, and she worried for the young girl. Maybe she had just grown sick of the profession, had tried to make it back home. If that were the case, Amie wished her Godspeed.

She did her business, took a deep breath outside the two-seater, and picked her way in the darkness back to The Texas House, guided by the fiddling of Louis Venizelos and the dim lights.

"Sister?"

Amie froze, not recognizing the voice, heard a twig snap behind her, and ran several steps, stopping in better light when the deep voice cried out: "Wait, sister, for the love of Jesus, please, I beg of thee!"

She turned toward the voice only, not sure, not quite trusting, retreated farther back toward the brothel until backing into the pine tree that served as one end to her clothesline. Light shone on a brutal but smiling face. Amie bit her lip once she recognized the preacher. She shouldn't have stopped;

Denise had told her that the preacher had slapped her, threatened her, and might have assaulted her seriously if Venizelos hadn't shown up and thrashed him. Amie started to flee, but the preacher reached out with cat-like quickness and grabbed her arm, pulling her back, pinning her against the tree. His smile never faded.

His face hadn't felt a razor or even water in months, and his brooding eyes danced in the flickering light from The Texas House's small back windows. Rancid breath stank of old food and coffee. He was a lean wreck with tattered clothes, too thin for the autumn nights in these mountains, no coat or jacket, just a dirty bandanna wound around his neck tightly like a muffler and a misshapen slouch hat full of holes, caked with grime. The Bible in his left hand looked equally misused, swollen and wrinkled from being left outside in sun and rain, the front cover partially ripped. Still gripping Amie's arm with his right hand, he slid the Bible into the front of his trousers, held up with a piece of rope rather than suspenders. He slipped his hand into a mule ear pocket, and withdrew a butcher knife from a sheath, then looked up at the sky, closed his eyes tightly, and said forcefully: "'And upon her forehead was a name written, mystery, Babylon the great, the mother of harlots and abominations of the earth.'" The knife blade moved toward her head as the preacher opened his eyes.

Amie screamed. She fought, but he flung her to the

ground, his strength surprising considering how small he was, and straddled her, pinning her arms with his bony knees, humming a tune she couldn't quite place while lowering the blade. Amie turned her head away from him, but he reached down with his free hand, fingers and thumb pinching her mouth, pulling her back to face him and his knife. She tried to cry out, but couldn't because of his hand, which suddenly clamped over her mouth. Her eyes widened. He hummed a few more bars—"We Shall Gather at the River", she recognized it now—before stopping to concentrate on Amie's face.

" 'If I sin, then thou markest me, and thou wilt not acquit me from mine iniquity.' "

Amie sealed her eyes shut as the blade began a menacing arc, then the weight on her chest flew off, the hand left her mouth, and she sucked in cold air, burning her lungs, and scrambled to her feet. The knife lay at her feet. The preacher lay on the ground, his hat gone, and a figure in black stood over him.

"You yeller-livered bastard!"

She recognized Cameron's voice. He swayed, slurred his words, and pointed at the cowering preacher, who answered: " 'Nor thieves, nor covetous, *nor drunkards,* nor revilers, nor extortioners, shall inherit the kingdom of God.' "

Cameron's response didn't register until some minutes later: " 'And many false prophets shall rise, and shall deceive many.' "

The preacher leaped to his feet. Amie let out an

involuntary gasp as the charging parson ducked a shoulder and buried it into Cameron's stomach before the gunman could react. Both men went down, crashing with groans, rolling over, almost tripping Amie. She shouted again for help, saw the back door open. She spun, kicked out at the preacher.

Cameron swore, and Amie shuddered, realizing her shoe had caught her rescuer in the forehead.

"What the hell?" It was Joe Miller. The fiddle music had stopped, and another man burst through the rear door, screaming Amie's name. Louis Venizelos. Heart racing, she held her breath as the two bartenders ran toward her. Miller went on toward the grunting, pounding figures on the ground. Venizelos stopped, gripping Amie a little too tightly on her arm, asking if she were all right.

Before Amie could answer, Cameron's scream sliced through the night. Miller cursed, kicking at the preacher, and Amie saw the knife in the crazy man's hand. He must have recovered it during the wrestling match. Miller's boot missed its mark; the preacher scrambled to his feet, and disappeared in the darkness. She pulled away from Venizelos, muttering— "I'm fine, Louis."—and hurried to Cameron, who was rocking on his knees, clasping his trembling hands tightly, pulling them close to his heaving chest. For a moment, she thought he was praying, and she recalled him reciting Scripture back at the mad little parson. Then she saw the blood dripping from his fingers, dripping onto his vest.

"Ben. . . ." She knelt by him, but his eyes looked vacant. She wondered why she had called him by his first name.

"Hurts like a son-of-a-bitch," Cameron whispered tightly, his breath stinking of whiskey.

"He get your gun hand, Mister Cameron?" asked Louis Venizelos.

Cameron shook his head. "Left palm." He bit his lower lip and trembled, said something else too slurred for Amie to understand. She reached for him, but Diva's voice chilled her.

"Get inside, Angel," Diva said. Amie looked up to find a crowd gathering around outside, but her eyes locked on Diva, staring down at Cameron with contempt. "You got payin' customers waitin'," she told Amie, although her glare remained locked on the gunman. "Move it, gal!"

"Diva," Venizelos began, "she's shook up. That crazy sky pilot. . . ."

"I don't care. All I know is them Bar J boys won't be here forever, winter's comin' on, and I get fifty cents a poke when this whore's doin' her job and nothin' when she's out here in the middle of the night. Move it, Angel."

She started, but Cameron cried out again, another shout Amie couldn't understand, and, as she spun, she saw him diving to his right, clawing for his gun, hitting the ground, rolling over, shrieking, crying, and she felt embarrassed for him.

"The haunts! The haunts! It's Wes Evans!" He

rolled, screaming in the opposite direction. "For God's sake, Sandoval, don't make me watch!"

The revolver came out of the holster, spun, dropped to the dirt, and Cameron sank to the ground, shivering, pulling himself up like an infant, sobbing. Amie took a tentative step toward him, but Joe Miller had her arm now, leading her back to The Texas House, whispering that she had best mind Diva.

"Drunk piece of dung." Diva snorted. "Throw his traps out with him, Louis. I don't want to see the legendary Scottish Gun in my place again. You hear me?"

"Yes, ma'am."

Chapter Thirteen

Raton, New Mexico Territory

That infant's incessant bawling made Keno Thompson's head hurt. Three nights he had spent here, and the little mutton never shut up. Colic, the barkeep explained. Of course, the barkeep never explained just what in blazes a three-month-old was doing at a whorehouse, but Thompson knew. Mom had to keep her baby girl fed, was doing a pretty good job at it, too.

As hog ranches went, this one fared better than most Thompson had frequented. The Taos lightning didn't burn a hole in a fellow's stomach, and the two whores weren't too ugly. If his money wasn't dwindling, and if Maw wasn't tormenting him something fierce in his sleep, telling him to get a move on and chase down that murdering, scum-sucking Ben Cameron, Thompson would have been tempted to stay here a spell longer.

Tonight would be his last night in Raton. Nobody had seen The Scottish Gun down here, leastways not since the summer of 1887 when he had been dealing poker at the Broken Spoke before lighting out to see some eye doctor in Denver. Hadn't been back since, folks said. That meant Thompson would ride north, come first light, back across the pass into Colorado, veer west to the mining camps and two-bit towns in the mountains: Cordova . . . Stonewall . . . maybe over to Fort Garland . . . Purgatoire . . . or somewhere around Veta Pass.

A puny, bald gent in an ill-fitting sack suit stood at the bar haggling with the barkeep, who also owned the cathouse, over the price of whiskey he was peddling, and a chubby man with a flowing silver mustache and a fancy yellow brocade vest leaned against the bar in the corner, alternately sipping his tumbler and smoking a pipe. Otherwise, except for the chirpies and that screaming baby, Harry's House— the owner didn't believe in some fancy name—was empty. The infant finally shut up; her mother must have gotten her to nurse. Thompson snorted. "Thank God," he said.

That caused the fancy-dressed fellow to guffaw and raise his glass in a toast of appreciation. Harry, the barkeep, and the rail-thin drummer didn't notice, too busy with their bartering. Thompson crushed out his smoke with a boot heel before nodding back at the gent, who picked up a whiskey bottle in front of him and walked over. Thompson hadn't meant to offer an invite to the stranger, but the man was bringing something fancy, not stuff from one of Harry's kegs, so he let him come, although he slid his right hand to his lap, close to the revolver.

The man had a city look about him, and, although he seemed too fat and soft, too pasty and drunk, to be a threat to Thompson's well-being, he just might be some kind of detective, a Pinkerton man or a bounty hunter chasing down Thompson for robbing that cobbler up in Denver, stealing the horse in Wyoming, or any of another hundred crimes he had committed.

"Join you, *amigo?*" the man said with a smile. "I appreciate your singular wit."

He didn't know what that meant, but kicked out a chair. "Welcome."

The stranger grunted as he settled into the chair. He wore a silk ribbon tie, striped breeches and coat, and gold-colored Stetson with just about the biggest crown and widest brim Thompson had ever seen. Greenhorn, that was for sure, and a wealthy one at that, what with those shiny, stovepipe boots with the fancy stitching, and a glittering chain to what Thompson figured was a mighty fine watch. The guy pushed the cork out of the bottle, refilled Thompson's glass with a liquor darker than oak.

"Looks like you've been traveling hard," the man said, leaned back in his chair, pulled a match from a pocket in that pretty vest, and fired up his pipe again.

"Been a fur piece." Thompson tasted the whiskey, and liked it. "What is this?"

The fat stranger turned the bottle so Thompson could see the label, but that did him no good. Maw never saw the need in learning her brood to read and write, although he could cipher half decent, leastways when it came to counting money or cards. Thompson bobbed his head. "Smooth, ain't it?"

"Indeed. Fifteen-year-old single-malt black Caol Ila whiskey, shipped all the way from Scotland's north shore. Hard to find in the States, let alone the territories, my good man. It's my personal stock. Promised to give Harry the bottle when I'm done so he can flim-flam future guests. Enjoy." After laying his pipe on the table, he reached inside his coat, pulled out a wallet—Thompson wondered how much cash this fool carried—and withdrew a business card, which he passed to Thompson eagerly.

"My card, sir. I'm at your service." His hand moved to the other side of his coat and came out with a thin book with a sketch of a man fighting off a half dozen gunmen on the cover. "And this is what I'm all about. Colonel Thaddeus K. Hall."

Thompson glanced at the cover briefly. He didn't know what to do with the colonel's card, so he just set it on top of the cover. The talkative man picked up his pipe and puffed away. "That one is a couple of years old. *Courage of the Scottish Gun; or, Death Comes to Wes Evans.* Sold like hotcakes. I'll autograph it, sir, if you'd like, and perhaps you could help me out." The pipe came out, and he pointed the stem at the barkeep's direction. "That fine man tells me you rode in from Trinidad."

That dark whiskey didn't taste so good now, and the baby had started squalling up a storm again. Harry had a big mouth. He'd remember that.

"Where I come from is my business." He pushed the little novel across the table, where it bounced off the big-talking writer's vest.

"No offense, no offense, sir. It's just that I hear that Ben Cameron killed a man in Trinidad, and I'm looking for him. I thought if you had been there, you might. . . ."

"You friends with Cameron?"

The man's eyes flickered, and he shrugged. "For a while. I haven't seen him lately." He refilled Thompson's glass, then his own. "We had a parting of ways, but, since he killed a man, I think he shall be hot news again. I desire to obtain the details and write another novel about his daring."

"The man he killed, mister, was my brother, Frank Thompson."

Thompson almost wet his britches, pleased at the look on the colonel's face. Even the drummer turned around to see what the commotion was all about. Hall's eyes just about bugged out of his big head. He plucked out the pipe, and his face turned white. Even his well-waxed mustache shivered. *Maybe I should have shot him,* Thompson thought. That might have worked. He could have told Harry and the drummer that this Colonel Hall had insulted him. They might let him go, if he agreed to split the dead fool's loot. Then again, with Raton getting civilized, they might hang him, and Maw would never forgive him for not avenging Frank's death. Besides, a fellow that wrote books probably had a lot of friends, plus being a colonel, likely had a long arm out West.

"Are you seeking Cameron, then?" the colonel asked meekly, having regained his courage. "For family honor?"

"Reckon I am," Thompson said. "And it don't matter that he's done kilt some forty men."

It was the colonel's turn to laugh merrily. "You've been reading too many of my novels, *amigo,*" the fancy talker said. "Cameron has not killed anywhere near forty men except in the pages of my Wide Awake Half Dime Library collection. No doubt he'd be feeding Wyoming's worms if Wes Evans's pistol had not misfired back in 'Eighty-Nine. How about you, sir? How many men have you shot down in fair fights?"

He couldn't believe the man's gall. "You're a pryin' bastard, ain't you?"

"I'm a writer, in need of a novel. Your name's . . . Thompson?"

You didn't ask a man his handle either, not out here. He had let it slip to Harry that he had just come from

Trinidad, and told the colonel about his brother being murdered by Cameron, though, so he said, yeah, he was Keno Thompson.

The pipe returned to the writer's mouth briefly. "Keno Thompson, a fine-sounding name. I'd like to travel with you, sir, if you do not mind, during your search for revenge. I can assist you, too. You better believe I can. Yes, sir, Keno, ride with me, and you'll ride to glory. How does this title suit you . . . *Keno Thompson's Revenge; or, The Death of the Scottish Gun?*"

Thompson blinked, recovered, drained the black Scotch whiskey. "You'd write about *me?*" That might certainly garner Maw's attention, and affection.

The friendliness left the colonel's voice and eyes. "If you kill that son-of-a-bitch."

They just stared at each other a full minute, maybe two, before the whiskey drummer stood beside the table, flipping a token in his right hand, smiling, breaking the silence. "Pardon me," he said. This table was getting a bit too busy for Thompson's liking. "Couldn't help but hear you two talking. Wasn't eavesdropping, just heard a few words, and, well, gentlemen, I'm Charlie Carr, originally from Topeka, Kansas." He sat down, uninvited, staring at the prostitutes, likely trying to pick one to give his token. Neither Thompson nor Hall considered the drummer until he said: "Heard y'all mention Ben Cameron. You know, I just saw him up in Purgatoire less than a week ago."

If he had written it for a legitimate publishing house, and not the Wide Awake Half Dime Library, his editors would have chastised him for this scene: Three strangers gathering at the table in some flea-bitten cavity in the middle of nowhere, two of them looking for the same man and the third pointing to his very whereabouts. Too far-fetched, they'd say, but they didn't know Ben Cameron the way he did. That's what had brought Thaddeus Hall to Harry's, and to other whiskey mills and hell-bending cathouses south of Cheyenne.

Cameron was drifting south, and sooner or later he would wind up at Harry's House seeking the comfort of cheap whiskey, although not likely the cheaper soiled doves. If Cameron never made it to Harry's, Hall knew that eventually someone would who knew where to find him, and the drummer from Topeka had proved him right. Finding Keno Thompson had been a surprising bonus.

The dumb little drummer had shared a drink with Hall and Thompson, then bought them a round of swill before disappearing behind a bear skin hanging from the rafters with the new mother, her infant asleep at last.

Hall tried to size up his new partner, Keno Thompson. Too rough, too stupid to be much of a hero without Hall's sharp guidance, but, of course, Ben Cameron hadn't been more than poor white trash, too young to know the difference between bravery and stupidity, when Hall had met him down in south Texas.

Blood on the Border had catapulted Cameron—and Hall—to international fame. Not bad, Hall figured, considering how he had been nothing but a street hawker for a struggling New York newspaper before the War of the Rebellion. He had joined the Union Army, risen to the rank of corporal—he had promoted himself to colonel for literary reasons—before being mustered out after the surrender. Next, he had drifted West, selling a few five-penny dreadfuls about jungle adventures and one romance set in Scotland, but didn't find his true calling until he wound up in Brownsville, Texas, in early 1876.

Hall had written four more half-dimes about Cameron and the Rangers, all lies, in two years before his editors demanded something with just a hint of authenticity. Thus he had tracked down Cameron, only to find him serving as lawman in some sleepy little burg on the Chisholm Trail. That had potential, but Cameron never did anything more than round up drunks. Readers of the Wide Awake's half-dime novels had heard of Austin, San Antone, Waco, and the Kansas cow towns, but St. Jo? He pulled a few strings, paid off a few city officials, and landed Cameron the job as city marshal in Caldwell, Kansas. Later, he had gotten The Scottish Gun a job with the Pinkerton Detective Agency, always plying his self-made hero with whiskey.

He thought they were friends until he caught up with Cameron in the spring of 1888 in Medicine Bow,

Wyoming. That poor Mississippi hayseed was trying to quit John Barleycorn. He had said whiskey would kill him if he didn't, said he had a good job as stock detective and wanted to keep it. Stock detective wasn't a good job by any means, but it probably paid well, better than Hall had been earning the past year. Cameron had practically blamed Thaddeus K. Hall for getting him fired from the Pinkertons.

He closed his eyes, remembering.

"I never forced a drop down your throat, Benji," he said.

"Ain't blamin' you, Colonel, but you ain't helped matters none. This is hard to say, sir, but . . . well . . . I'd appreciate it if you'd just ride on. Write your books all you want. Maybe when I get a little stronger morally and ain't a drunk . . . maybe then we can talk some more."

"Benji, you really don't think. . . ." He realized Cameron was serious. "Son, where do you think you'd be without me? You'd be playing dominoes at Saint Jo, Texas. By jingo, you wouldn't have gotten that job if I hadn't written about you. You'd be dead with McNelly, or selling farm implements somewhere. You'd be nothing."

"I'd be happy," he replied.

Disgruntled, disillusioned, Hall had taken the Union Pacific to Cheyenne, and quickly gotten roostered—then a thought struck him like a bullet to the head. His jungle and circus novels had not sold well. Truthfully the only books that ever earned him any money had been about Cameron, so, now, he figured, what would sell through the roof? *Death of the Scottish Gun.* He tried to pass off the thought. The law would call what he was thinking accessory to murder, maybe even murder, and Cameron was his friend . . . well, sort of. They had gotten along well enough, but both had been younger, more devil-may-care in the 1870s and early 1880s. When Wes Evans showed up in Cheyenne the following year, Hall, well in his cups, had met him in some low-rent saloon, told him where he could find Cameron, and started plotting out his ultimate masterpiece for the Wide Awake Half Dime Library, *Death of the Scottish Gun; or, The Prowess of Wes Evans*, only Evans's pistol had misfired, and The Scottish Gun had lucked out again. Still, *Courage of the Scottish Gun; or, Death Comes to Wes Evans*, outsold just about everything Hall had ever penned. Meanwhile, Cameron, the legendary Scottish Gun imitated by schoolboys from Liverpool to the Sandwich Islands, had fallen off his wagon, had been hitting the rotgut steadily since gunning down Evans. A fine hero he had turned out to be.

Here, in Keno Thompson, Hall had another chance. They'd drift over to Purgatoire, where Thompson—and Colonel Thaddeus K. Hall—would exact revenge. Of course, if Cameron won again, lucked out and killed Thompson, that didn't matter; he'd just fix up the title a bit.

Keno Thompson's Revenge; or, Return of the Scottish Gun.

Either way, Hall had his next book halfway written.

Chapter Fourteen

Southern Colorado

He stoked the fire in the potbelly stove just to give him something to do. Having that scarred prostitute come to the jail every morning left Joshua Reed in a dither. Glenn Boeke had already cracked a joke over breakfast at the town marshal's expense, and yesterday Potter Stone had asked if Reed planned on giving The Texas House some friendly competition.

First of all, Reed didn't fathom what the Courtland girl saw in Ben Cameron, who had lately been keeping Reed and Randy Johnson up half the night with his screaming, but here she was again, changing the bandage on the killer's left hand and holding his right, giving it a firm squeeze now and then, when he wasn't too far gone, comforting him, even once pretending to be his mother.

Reed dropped the poker in a brass pot, filled his coffee cup, and returned to his desk. Ten minutes later, Courtland came out, shutting the door and asking: "You haven't been giving him any whiskey, have you?"

"No, though I've had a mind to, just to keep him quiet." He jumped out of his chair, snatched the keys off the wall peg, and brushed past her to lock Cameron's cell. When he returned, she hadn't left.

"He's having another nightmare," he said. "I can't believe Stone wanted him to be our marshal. Worthless drunk."

The prostitute fired back at him: "Why isn't that preacher in jail? He assaulted me, almost carved me up with a knife, and he would have if not for Ben Cameron."

So that was why she was here. Owed him her life, or some such nonsense. He snorted and made a snide comment about "assaulting a whore"—but immediately regretted it. She looked hurt, and he felt ashamed, yet he couldn't bring himself to apologize, not to a girl like her. Still, he softened his tone. "My mother always said a man who lets whiskey get the better of him lacks moral strength."

"I think there's more to it than that," she said in a near whisper. "Like a disease."

He tried not to laugh at the notion, likening drunkenness to typhoid or something, and pointed to the trash basket in the corner. She disposed of the dirty bandage before opening the door. A low moan from the jail cell caused her to turn her head, and Reed momentarily thought she might return to her project, but she merely said—"I wonder what's haunting him now?"—and stepped into the chilly morn.

"Well, if you won't sell me that hoss, pard, for a jug, geld him."

Cameron wet his lips, not knowing if the man was joking, but, when the big muleskinner pulled out a Barlow knife and offered it, Cameron quickly shook his head. "Had that horse since he was a colt down in Texas," he stated, but the lust for a drink closed in on him.

"Oh," another voice called from the corral's top post, "you know how stallions are, Benji. How much trouble they cause when they're around a brood mare. A gelding's much gentler, much easier to have around, and face it, amigo, you're not getting any younger. Ol' Goliad's likely to buck you off and leave you afoot."

Clamping his eyelids shut, he shook his head, but, when he opened his eyes, he found the knife in his hand, saw himself running his finger across the blade to test its edge.

"How thirsty are you, Benji?" the man sitting on the top corral post asked, and Cameron looked up.

He rolled off his cot and onto the floor, vomiting, only he had nothing left to throw up. Dry heaving, he felt a few tears drift into his beard as he recalled the nightmare. Nightmare? It had really happened, and he had ducked inside that corral to castrate Goliad for nothing more than a jug of Tennessee sour mash, up at Fort Fetterman in 1889, a few weeks after he had shot down Wes Evans. Fetterman had attracted a hard lot, and he didn't know most of the men there, including the one selling the whiskey. He did know the man calling him Benji, daring him to geld his prized horse, but, until now, he—or more likely John Barleycorn—had blocked out the image of the man's face. He spat out the name: "Colonel Thaddeus K. Hall. Why?"

He sat up, leaned against the iron bars, knew he was in jail, only didn't know the reason. A voice from the neighboring cell said something, and Cameron looked up.

"About time you shut up," said a young man with a scar and knot on the side of his head that must have hurt something bad a few days ago. "You've been keeping us up all night."

Looking around, Cameron didn't see anyone else in the jail. In fact, the door was open to the third and final cell. He became aware of his wretchedness, the stinky smell of a drunkard's sweat, vomit, urine. His mouth felt parched, and he craved water, but he had to crawl to the tin cup in the corner, not knowing if it had anything in it or not. It did, and he drank greedily, emptying the cup, feeling a few drops dribble over his coarse beard.

He found his voice: "How long have I been here?"

"Four days."

Next, he saw his bandaged left hand and tried to remember what had happened. The last thing he could recall vividly was reining Goliad to a stop in front of a place called The Texas House. He closed his eyes, thinking. He saw the dead punk lying in his own blood in a gambling den in Trinidad, remembered riding away, running for his life practically,

151

then nothing. . . . He tried to block out the bad dream, block out castrating Goliad, then he recalled the name of the town. Purgatoire.

"Jamie Courtland," he whispered, shook his head, thought again. "Amie Courtland."

"That the whore who's been looking after you?" the cowhand in the neighboring cell asked.

Cameron didn't know. He wanted a whiskey, but wouldn't find one in jail. He wanted to sleep, but was afraid of the dreams, the visions from his bloody, drunken past. So he just sat there in the corner, pulled his knees up to his chest, and shivered.

The preacher leaned against the fence surrounding the Pendant Mining Company property while Joshua Reed gave him a stern warning. Preach all he wanted—God knew Purgatoire could use it—but he couldn't go around hitting prostitutes or threatening them with knives. It was the law.

To which the vagabond smiled meekly, holding up the Bible, and said: "This is my law."

Reed shook his head in exasperation, pointed in the preacher's face, and said: "I'll run you out of town or lock you up if you don't behave." Some threat. He sounded more like a mother scolding a toddler. Nonetheless, he had wasted enough time on the likes of that tramp, so he walked back to town, kicking at a pine cone, concentrating on it until he finally grew angry and crushed it underneath his boot. That's when he looked up and spotted the buckboard parked in front of the marshal's office, Moses Keller, the stable hand, the spectacle-wearing bartender from the brothel, and Mayor Stone standing on the boardwalk, peering under a canvas tarp, shaking their heads in pure disgust, or maybe sadness. He picked up the pace.

When Reed got there, he realized what lay in the back of Keller's wagon. He remembered when Stone's son-in-law, who had since moved to La Junta, had brought the body of Marshal Horace C. Bentham to the undertaker's office. Reed had been among the miners and townsfolk who gathered about the wagon while the undertaker, Mac Brodie, pulled away the shroud covering the dead man's face. Mac Brodie was also long gone, having departed Purgatoire for Madrid, New Mexico Territory. That's why Keller had brought the dead body to the marshal's office.

"Must 'a' slipped in the river, Marshal Reed, sir," Keller said solemnly. "You reckon I ought to build her a coffin?"

"For a Mexican whore?" Potter Stone guffawed, then remembered the presence of the Greek bartender who served drinks and broke heads at The Texas House. "Sorry, Louis."

She looked so tiny, smaller in death than she had been in life the few times Reed had seen her. His last image of the girl called Vaya Con Dios was of her running down the street in the crisp morning, earlier in the week. He also thought of rancher Randall

Johnson's words to his son: "She's gone, Son. Not coming back, I warrant."

"Hit her head maybe," Stone said. "Slipped in the river, drowned. I've seen that butchered-up chirpie taking a bath in the Picketwire, though God knows how she could stand it sometimes. Maybe this one was thinking about. . . ." Stone became aware of the stares, some humorous, some questioning, and realized his *faux pas,* what everyone was thinking: *You've been spying on that whore while she bathed?* He changed the subject. "How long you think she's been dead?"

No one dared make a guess, although the bartender said she had disappeared three or four days back.

"Reckon she'd keep a spell," Keller said, "cold as it's been getting, what with her in the water, and all. Want me to take her to the pauper's graveyard, Mayor?"

Stone, likely concerned that he might be labeled a Peeping Tom, answered with a nod, and the bartender crossed the street, saying he had to tell Diva. They were writing this off, and who could blame them? A dead whore, and a Mexican at that. Yet Reed felt something tugging at his conscience. He was the law, and, like her occupation or not, like her race or not, he did have a duty to make sure her death had been accidental. He felt almost certain it was, but Randall Johnson's words echoed through his mind again, and he knew that he, not the rancher, would be the one to break the news of Vaya Con

Dios's—no, Consuela's—death to Randy Johnson.

"Bring her inside, Moses," Reed said. "Lay her. . . ."

He ran into another problem. Two cells had occupants, and he wasn't about to put a corpse on his bunk. Even if Randy Johnson had been the only one in jail, he couldn't bring the girl's body in there where he slept, not. . . .

He looked at her face briefly and was thankful when Moses Keller covered it again. "Just lay her on the floor by my desk. I want to examine her. See if there are any clues."

Stone simply shrugged, and Reed hurried into his office.

He grabbed the keys, went into the jail cell, and found Cameron sitting on the floor. Reed couldn't even look Randy Johnson in the face. He concentrated on Cameron and turned the key in the lock. "Get up, Cameron," he said. "You're free to go."

"Why . . . what?"

"You were drunk. Found you passed out. Now, let's go. Stop lollygagging and stand up."

The gunman picked up his hat, pulled himself to his feet using the crossbars in the cell, and swayed, staggered, but finally made it to the office, stopping suddenly when he saw the corpse. The tarp had fallen away, revealing her still face. Cameron started to speak, but Reed slammed the door to the lockup. "Just move it, Cameron. She's none of your business.

"What happened?"

"Likely fell in the river and drowned, or died of

155

exposure. It doesn't matter. Go on, now. *Just git.*"

"Where . . . ?" Cameron licked his lips. "W-wh-where do . . . ?"

He must have worn out his welcome at Diva's place. Reed took great pleasure in pulling a $20 gold piece from his vest pocket and tossing it at Cameron's feet. The coin rolled on the floor, bounced off the gunman's boot, spun, and fell beside a pale hand poking from underneath the canvas. "Why don't you take ol' Goliad out of that livery, rub him down, and give him plenty of water and a bucket of oats?" he said in his best Southern accent. "And then ride out of town."

Cameron knew he had insulted the young marshal at some point, but he couldn't remember when, or why. Damned whiskey. The marshal disappeared back in the jail, pulling the door shut, and Cameron stared at the gold piece near the unmoving, small, wet fingers. He wanted that money, wanted it bad, and had to fight the urge to pick it up and run over to a saloon. Twenty dollars would keep him drunk a long spell. He couldn't leave yet, though. The peace officer had not given him back his guns, the Schofield and the shotgun, plus he had a knife, gun belt, watch . . . or had he sold them off for booze?

Guilt and shame returned, as they always did, making his craving for a drink even stronger, some-thing to make him forget. He had been a good lawman, probably would have been a mighty fine

Pinkerton operative if not for the hooch. He ducked, scooped up the gold piece, ran for the door, but a sudden wail from the jail stopped him.

"Nooooo!" Then sobs. The young cowboy in the jail. He must have known the dead girl. Cameron suddenly saw her again, alive, a little Mexican barely in her teens, running past him at The Texas House. She was Amie Courtland's friend. The vision of Amie replaced the one of the Mexican, and he saw the woman, pretty except for the mutilated cheek, saw her holding his hand, telling him not to worry, pretending to be his mother, saying that the Yankee shelling would soon stop. Then he pictured Amie's face when he told her he had shot her brother.

Cameron found himself suddenly crying. If he didn't stop drinking, he would die, and he was scared of dying.

He made the tears stop, tried to tell himself he was a man if not really The Scottish Gun, not any more, and tentatively, nervously knelt over the corpse, pulled back the canvas a tad more. He owed Amie this much. Owed the marshal he had insulted. Owed himself.

"What in God's name are you doing?" Louis Venizelos screamed upon opening the door to Joshua Reed's office. Ben Cameron looked up, his hand still on Consuela's neck, like some demented freak of nature. Venizelos had seen a lot during his days and nights working brothels and saloons, but never some ghoul like this. Cameron gave him a brief glance, muttered something Venizelos couldn't understand, and went back to studying the poor girl's neck.

Diva barged in behind him, let out a surprising gasp at the sight of her dead prostitute, yet recovered immediately and made for the marshal's coffee pot. Venizelos thought about breaking Cameron's ribs, throttling him good, and kicking him into the street—after all, Cameron wasn't heeled—but he calmed down upon realizing that the gunman meant no harm. He appeared to be studying her body like a doctor or lawman, and everyone knew The Scottish Gun had been a reputable peace officer and detective.

Marshal Reed came in from the lockup, followed by Randy Johnson, who had obviously been crying. Surprised at the visitors, Reed stopped, but the boy ran to Consuela's body and pushed Cameron away, cradling her head in his arms, rocking back and forth, crying. Knocked on his haunches, Cameron stood slowly, but didn't intrude on the young man's grief.

"What happened?" Diva asked.

"Moses Keller found her in the Picketwire," Reed answered. "Your bartender says she disappeared three, four days ago. That sound right to you?"

"Yeah." Diva sipped the coffee.

"I guess she hit her head . . . fell in the river. Something like that, but I haven't made a ruling yet." Reed shot a glance at the overwrought Randy Johnson, swallowed, and shook his head.

Said Venizelos: "Terrible accident."

"Wasn't no accident."

Everyone in the office turned to the sound of the Southern accent. Even Randy Johnson, still sobbing, stopped swaying the dead girl in his arms and craned his neck, staring at Cameron in confusion.

Swallowing, Cameron pointed at Consuela's throat. "Bruises," he said softly. "Strangled to death."

"Christ!" Diva barked, then let out a laugh. "You gonna listen to this drunk?" she asked the marshal.

Reed didn't reply, simply stared at the neck. So did Randy Johnson. Even Venizelos could see the dark marks around the poor girl's throat.

"By someone with fairly big hands," Cameron said. "That's all I can tell."

With a belligerent scoff, Diva placed her hands on her hips and asked Reed if he really believed this drunk. Ignoring the rebuke, Cameron tipped his hat at the marshal, weaved through the crowd, and out the door. No one tried to stop him. A short while later, before anyone had spoken a word, footsteps sounded on the boardwalk, and someone else walked into the office. Venizelos turned to stare into rancher Randall Johnson's hard face. Behind him came a pitiful wail from the Bar J owner's son, followed by a savage curse:

"You damned murderer! You cowardly bastard! You! You killed her! You murdered my Consuela!"

Chapter Fifteen

The water and air had turned too cold to wash laundry in the Picketwire, so Amie Courtland had gotten a fire going behind The Texas House and had placed her linens in the bubbling water in a large, brass tub. She had also become laundress for the other prostitutes— Denise, Rene, Nancy, and Cindy—and would have done Consuela's if she thought the teenager might return to town. She'd collect two bits from each, a dollar for her effort and didn't mind the extra work.

Often Amie daydreamed, how she would have enjoyed being a laundress for some Army post on the frontier, gossiping and laughing with the other washers, scouting out suitable husbands among officers and enlisted men. If her luck had been better, maybe she would have earned a job at Fort Dodge after Stan Gibbs deserted her, but the post was being phased out when they arrived in Dodge City in 1882, and the Army abandoned it that fall.

Smoking a cigarette, Denise Benbrook leaned against a pine tree while engaging Amie in conversation, not really talking about anything in particular, just passing the time. Amie liked Denise, although she didn't completely trust her. They both came from the South, were about the same age, and hated their occupation. Consuela de la Hoya had been more like a kid sister to Amie, whereas Denise was a friend. Not a good friend. You didn't make good friends in this line of work, but a better friend than any of the others. Cindy Haggin was too coarse, too rude, a New Yorker who had been whoring since she was twelve; Ohio-born Nancy Brennan came across as a loner; China Rene spoke little English. And Diva? No one enjoyed the madam's company, especially when in one of her moods.

Smoke and steam snaked through the branches of the rustling tree, and Amie felt at peace this morning, as contented as she could feel here, perhaps because she knew the Bar J boys would be heading down the mountain, making her nights a little less demanding with winter coming on.

Both women heard the footsteps and turned toward the noise in apprehension, for neither had forgotten their dealings with that tramp preacher. Amie spotted him first, smiling in relief at the appearance of Ben Cameron as he swept off his hat and muttered an apology about startling them so, about intruding.

"Ain't no intrusion." Denise flipped her smoke into the washtub, which prompted a reprimand from Amie, but both wound up laughing. That was rude, leaving Cameron scratching his head, wondering what was going on. Amie invited him over, and Denise pulled out a sack of Bull Durham, offering him the makings.

"No, but thank you, ma'am," Cameron said nervously. "Well. . . ." He changed his mind, started to reach for the sack and papers, but stopped, staring at his shaking hands. He shoved them inside his waist-

161

band and shuffled his feet. Amie lost her smile. "If you'd roll one for me, Miss . . . ?"

"Denise."

"Miss Denise, I'd appreciate it. My hands ain't too steady this morn."

"Ain't no 'Miss' to it," Denise said jovially before going about her task. Amie often joked that Denise Benbrook could roll a smoke and light it without spilling any tobacco while engaged in a round of horizontal refreshments with one of the Pendant boys.

Cameron wore no gun belt, Amie noticed, then concentrated on the laundry. "Last load for the winter," she said just to say something while stirring sheets and pillow cases with a cedar branch. Denise rolled the gunman a cigarette, lit it, and handed it to him. Two or three drags seemed to dull the ends of his nerves, and he squatted between the women, feeling the warmth of the fire. He still stank worse than a dead steer, so Amie said: "If I'd known you were coming, I would have prepared you a hot bath. It's better than bathing in the river, don't you think?"

"Ma'am?"

She shook her head. He didn't remember his bath, probably didn't recall much of anything since riding into Purgatoire, but he held out his bandaged hand and thanked her, which surprised her. Marshal Reed must have told him, or maybe his memories weren't totally devoured by whiskey.

"I . . . well. . . ." He flicked the remains of his

smoke into the fire, but remained squatting, rocking on his heels. He closed his eyes.

"You want a drink, Mister Cameron?" Denise asked. Amie felt like belting her, but gave her a scowl, instead. Again Cameron had an unexpected reply: "No . . . I . . . well, no, but thank you, ma'am."

"It's Denise, I done told you. Not *ma'am*."

"Yes'm. My name's Ben."

A twinge of jealousy replaced Amie's anger with Denise.

Cameron stood slowly, looking around, trying to collect his bearings.

"You hungry?" Amie heard herself asking.

"I don't know," Cameron replied. "My stomach. . . ."

"Another smoke then?" This came from Denise.

"Yes'm, I mean . . . Denise."

"Well, once I'm finished with this laundry," Amie said, "we'll go over to the Dead Canary. You can drink coffee if you can't eat, but I think solid food will do you good. You're welcome to join us, Denise."

She knew Denise would decline. It was Monday morning and Louis Venizelos would come knocking on her door around eleven.

"No, thanks. I promised Louis. . . ." She shrugged, passed the lighted cigarette to Cameron, who took it with fingers not trembling quite as much now. She also handed him her tobacco sack and papers.

"Sorry about that. . . . Consuela, wasn't that her name?"

Amie's mouth fell open and her heart skipped. "What are you talking about?" she asked, although, deep down, she already knew.

His dark eyes widened, and he knew he had blundered. Amie let go of the cedar stirring stick and walked to him. Cameron sought out a path of retreat, but found none.

"What do you mean?" Amie practically shouted, and Denise joined in: "What's happened to Vaya Con Dios?"

Cameron stared at the pine straw beneath his boots. "Some colored boy found her in the river this morning. She's dead. I thought your boss or that barkeep had told you already." He looked up, wet his lips, and added: "Strangled to death."

"I didn't kill her," Randall Johnson repeated after Reed had cleared out his office. Moses Keller had taken the girl's body away, although Reed told him to bring back everything he found on her clothing. He had planned on searching the girl himself, but the rancher's presence changed his thinking, and he found it prudent to get the corpse out of here, for Randy's sake if nothing else. Besides, he had seen the markings on the throat, knew she had been murdered. He'd look at whatever Keller found later.

The prostitute would be planted in a pauper's grave near the Pendant, for the Catholic community would never allow her to be buried in consecrated soil; Ben Cameron had vanished; Diva and her bartender had returned to The Texas House. Only the rancher, his distraught son, and Reed remained in the office.

"I didn't kill her," Johnson said again, more to his son than to Reed. "I swear."

His son answered by spitting at his boots, only this time the rancher didn't charge. The quirt dangled at his side. He dropped his head, shaking it, and collapsed in a chair. "You pathetic . . . ," Randy began, but Reed told him to shut up. For the first time, Randall Johnson didn't look so formidable. His face had turned pale, his hands trembled, and his voice no longer carried respect or belligerence.

Leaning against his desk, Reed said: "You can see my problem, Mister Johnson. Cameron was right. That girl was murdered, strangled, or maybe held down in the river and drowned. Either way, it's murder, and it doesn't matter that she was. . . ." He glanced at Randy, decided not to end the sentence. "The only people I know who could not have killed her are me and your son and Cameron, because they were in jail.

"Cameron could have done it," Randy said. "Is that it?" His voice rose in anger as he stared at his father. "Did you bring in that squat assassin to kill her? Is that why he's here?"

"Randy," Reed said, "one more word from you and I'll open the other side of your noggin with my pistol barrel. If Cameron had killed her, he wouldn't have pointed out those bruises on her throat and neck." Reed stopped. *Unless he wanted to ward off suspicion.* No, he decided, that was unlikely, and, considering Cameron's state since his arrival in Purgatoire, he likely couldn't have killed anyone, even a tiny teenage girl. Criminy, from what he had heard, that crazy preacher had almost cut Cameron to pieces.

The preacher. That made Reed think. *The preacher had attacked two of Diva's whores. He. . . .*

Randall Johnson broke his train of thought. "I never saw Cameron till I rode into town. If he killed her, someone else. . . ." He also looked lost in thought, shook his head after a moment, and said: "I'll be leaving, Reed. You know where you can find me."

Shaking his head, Reed stood ramrod straight. "You've got a dozen cowboys with you, Mister Johnson, and every last one of them is a suspect. Until I can figure this out, they can't. . . ."

"Reed, I've got three hundred head of Bar J beef grazing up here, and I'm not going to lose them. Looks like an early winter." The arrogance and command had returned to the rancher's voice and face.

"But. . . ."

"But nothing, Reed. Those boys of mine are good boys. You want an alibi for each of them, well, ask them. They've been working sunup to sundown since they got here, then blowing off steam at that . . . that place, or that other whiskey mill by the mine. I guarantee you that someone saw them with someone else when they were in town, at camp, or rounding up my beef. My boys don't kill women, even. . . . They just don't. Besides, if you believe that drunk, the murderer had big hands. Cowboys are small, Reed."

"Your hands aren't small, Dad."

Reed ignored the son's comment. "What brought you into town this morning?" he asked the rancher.

He heard the bawling cattle and knew the answer. Johnson pulled himself up from the chair, hooking a thumb toward the window facing the street. "That," he answered sternly. "I came to get you out of jail, boy, and take you home. I'm driving my herd to their winter pasture, Reed, and I'm taking my son with me. You want to stop us, you'll have to face down my boys. They don't kill women, but they'll fight you. Come on," he told his son, and put his hand on the doorknob.

"I told you, I ain't coming home. Not with the likes of you."

Silence. The rancher closed his eyes, sighed, shoulders sagging again, and opened the door.

"Mister Johnson . . . ," Reed began, rubbing his hand on the butt of his revolver.

"Give me till tonight, Marshal," the old man said in defeat. Randall Johnson had never called him anything but Reed since he had known him. Now it was *marshal?* "Let my boys take my cattle off this mountain. They didn't kill her, but. . . ." When Johnson looked at his son, Reed thought he detected tears welling in the rancher's eyes. "Let me . . . I might know who killed . . . her."

Reed blinked back surprise. "If you know, if you have. . . ."

"Let me do this my way. Would to God I'm wrong." He stepped outside, barking at Jack Tompkins to drive the herd to a winter pasture along the Picketwire, east of Trinidad. By the time Reed stepped outside, the cattle were tearing down Front Street, taking the trail out of town, driven by the Bar J crew, chuck wagon bringing up the rear. In front of the hitching rail, Tompkins sat on his bay gelding, listening to his boss' orders. Reed couldn't help but stare at the foreman's hands. They, indeed, looked small as he pulled a long-barreled Remington from his holster and handed it butt-forward to Johnson, who stuck his quirt underneath his arm.

"You sure you want me to go?" Tompkins drawled.

"Get my cattle down safe, Jack," Johnson answered. "Randy and I will join you tomorrow." The rancher shoved the .45 in his waistband, and, shrugging, Tompkins spurred his horse, following the herd out of Purgatoire.

"Tonight," Johnson told Reed. "I might be wrong, so let me do this alone." His eyes veered, focusing on his son, and he mouthed: "I'm sorry."

After watching Johnson mount his horse, Reed turned to Randy Johnson. "Stay put," he said, but changed his mind. "Go on, Randy. Go see your girl buried, pay your respects, but don't do anything stupid. I'll get to the bottom of this, I swear."

All this talk about big hands would only confuse

him. Potter Stone was a husky fellow, and so was Glenn Boeke, not to mention the miners at the Pendant, and the word around Purgatoire had it that Diva's fiddle-playing bartender, Louis V-something, had been a professional pugilist. The other bartender was huge as well, and both had had plenty of opportunity to kill the Mexican, but Reed wanted to interrogate another suspect.

He headed straight for the Pendant mine, where he could hear the preacher's sermon above the fading bellows of Bar J cattle.

Louis Venizelos poured himself a drink while watching Denise Benbrook dress. She pulled on a yellow dress, shaking her head until her red hair fell somewhat into place. As soon as she had buttoned her shoes, she began rolling a smoke, and Venizelos drained the rye, stifling a cough.

"When's the stage due, Louis?"

The question caught him off guard, and he had to think. Setting down the empty glass, he shrugged. "Two days, I guess. Wednesday, unless the road's washed out. Leave Thursday morn. Why? You plan on going somewhere?"

Denise struck a match on her thumbnail, and lit the cigarette. She took a long drag, smiling at him, exhaled, and stood. Damn, but she was a good-looking woman, at least to his way of seeing things, and she knew how to treat a man, at least him. She wrapped her arms around his neck, keeping the cigarette at a safe distance, and kissed him warmly on the lips.

"Would you go with me?" she asked suggestively.

If she kept that up . . . well, he had just collected his weekly free turn, although he figured Denise probably wouldn't charge him if he wanted another go with her, no matter how much Diva ranted and raved.

"Anywhere," he said, suddenly wanting another drink.

"Where's that you wanted to take me?"

"Arizona." Was she serious? "I had a boxing match over in Springerville, White Mountains country, honey, and you've never seen such land. No one would know you, or me. We'd start over."

She kissed him again. "Well, hon, we might just leave Purgatoire behind us come Thursday mornin'."

He laughed. "Denise, I couldn't pay even my fare to Trinidad." Not with Diva's wages. Twenty a month he earned, plus the weekly turn with one of the girls, always Denise, but Diva charged him five dollars a month in rent. Meals came extra, exorbitant in a mountain town, and he had never told Denise about his poker debt to Joe Miller. Purgatoire owned him.

"Maybe I'll grubstake you," she said, kissing him again and opening the door. "Now run along, hon. We don't want Diva to think you're gettin' more than allowed." She gave him a wink as he walked out, then whispered in a serious tone: "But trust me, Louis, we'll be on that stage when it leaves."

He looked at her again, a little concerned, and

couldn't help but look at her hands. What a stupid idea! She was so delicate. Denise might be capable of many things, but she had not murdered anyone. Maybe Consuela's murder had her scared. Maybe she wanted to get out of here before something like that happened to her. He couldn't blame her for that reason, but Denise had never been scared of anyone, except maybe that preacher. He'd scare anyone.

"Denise . . . ," he began, but she pressed her fingers against his lips, removed the cigarette with her free hand, and said softly: "Don't tell no one what I said now. All right? Trust me, Louis. Everything'll be fine, just fine."

A hinge down the hall *squeaked,* and Denise blew him a final kiss, and quickly closed her door in his face.

Chapter Sixteen

For the second day, Amie Courtland met Ben Cameron for breakfast at the Dead Canary. She had prepared herself to eat alone, to learn that he was drunk again, but found him sitting on the boardwalk, smoking a cigarette, and petting a stray dog. A few straws had collected in his tangled hair and worn coat, so she guessed he had spent the night in the livery stable. He certainly smelled as though he had.

"You hungry?" she asked.

"I could eat," he answered, flipping the unfinished smoke into the street. He held the door open for her— *When was the last time that had happened?*—as they

171

entered the café, the smell of coffee, ham, and sour-dough biscuits making her mouth water and his stomach rumble. Cameron even removed his hat as they found a seat in the back of the building, and placed it on the table, crown down. Most Westerners never took off their hats except to sleep, but Cameron had not forgotten his Vicksburg manners.

A year ago, the restaurants in town would not serve Amie, or any of Diva's girls, but the Dead Canary never had such qualms, and, even if the owner did resent having a prostitute eat in his establishment, he needed her business. Only the hotel would refuse her service, and few ate the grease served there anyway.

Yesterday, Amie and Cameron had talked about Consuela. He had even offered her a handkerchief when she started crying, and after breakfast they had walked to Amie's laundry, sharing childhood stories about Alabama and Mississippi, only briefly touching on her brother's death. She didn't want to bring that up, and neither did Cameron. He had then escorted her to the makeshift graveyard just north of the mine, where Moses Keller recited "The Lord's Prayer" before shoveling sod over Consuela. Amie had cried again, and Cameron hesitantly had put an arm on her shoulder, pulled her close, let her sob on his chest. She hadn't cared how bad he smelled at that moment. She had just wanted to cry. Consuela didn't even have a coffin, and Keller later told her that the crazy preacher refused to handle the service. Amie was glad of that; she didn't want that man there. So the only persons sending the poor girl off had been Keller, Randy Johnson, Cameron, and herself. Denise wasn't there. Even Diva didn't show up. Or Louis Venizelos, and she thought for sure he would come. After the funeral, Cameron had escorted her to the back door of The Texas House and bid good bye.

Today, Cameron still wore no gun, unless he had a hideaway pistol somewhere. He smoked another cigarette, crushing it out when their plates of bacon, biscuits, and hash browns arrived. He ran his fingers through his coarse beard before picking up fork and knife. His hands didn't seem to be shaking as much today.

"Are your folks alive?" she asked.

Cameron shook his head. "Daddy got killed back in the war, least we think he did. He never come home. He was deacon at the Baptist church, wanted to become a preacher, but went off to fight with Van Dorn. Mama died in 'Seventy-Two when I was seventeen. Heart give out, the doctor said, though she was only forty-three. Anyway, there was nothin' left for me in Mississippi, so I lit out for Texas. Yours?"

She regretted bringing up the subject. "I'm dead to them," she answered flatly.

A horse snorted down the street as Amie and Cameron left the café, something *clicked*, and Cameron spun, jumping into the shadows, leaving Amie standing in the middle of the boardwalk, bewildered. Cameron squinted at a rider coming down

Front Street, asking in a scared whisper: "You know that fella?"

She shot the rider another glance and faced Cameron again, a little disturbed. "He works for the Pendant," she answered, thought of something else, and added: "He's not armed, Ben, except for a rod and reel."

Muttering an apology, he stepped back to her as the man walked his dun horse past them. "Couldn't see his face," Cameron explained, "and I heard. . . ."

"It was Missus Coburn," she said, "turning a key in the lock, opening up the mercantile. How bad is your eyesight?"

"Can't see far, not clearly. No problem readin' or writin', seein' cards in my hands, seein' your face."

Her face. Self-consciously she raised her hand to the collection of scars, but Cameron took her hand in his own and pulled it to her side.

"You got a pretty face, Amie," he said softly. "Them scars can't hide that."

She knew she loved him at that moment. Of course, she had been in love with Ben Cameron since reading *Blood on the Border*. She wanted to help him, wanted to be the reason he stopped drinking, became The Scottish Gun again. "Have you seen a doctor?" she asked. "About your eyesight?"

His head bobbed, and he held out his arm. She took it, blushing just a bit, having forgotten the last time a man had offered his arm to escort her down a board-walk. Stan Gibbs had never done it. Most of the time, when a man grabbed her arm, he was pulling her upstairs.

Once they resumed their walk, he started again. "Talked to a fella in Denver some years back. Said he could fit me up with eyeglasses. Said it was nothin' but gettin' older, spendin' too much time in bad light, starin' at cards."

"What happened to the glasses?"

"Never bought 'em. Any money I had then went to cards or. . . ." He shrugged, or maybe he was fighting off a chill.

"How are you doing?"

"I'm a fright, Amie. I tried givin' up whiskey three or four times, never had no luck, not for long anyway."

"You're doing fine, Ben," she said.

Moses Keller had brought Consuela de la Hoya's personal items found on her body to the marshal's office. Joshua Reed eagerly unfolded the slip of paper the stable hand said had been in her coat pocket. Reed remembered seeing her read the note on the morning she probably had died. He muttered an oath, crumpled the paper, still wet, and tossed it into the wastebasket.

The Picketwire had washed away whatever had been written.

Her other items revealed nothing. Change purse containing $2.37, an engagement ring on her finger. "That Johnson boy, he says he'd like that ring back, Marshal," Keller said.

"He can pick it up." Reed sighed. She hadn't been killed for money, and she wasn't leaving town. No signs of assault. Just strangled.

For nothing.

"What you plan on doing, Marshal?"

"I can't do a thing," he answered. "Dead-end." He knew his limitations. He was no lawman, not a good one at least, and certainly no detective. He wanted to defer the matter to the Las Animas County sheriff, but not even a deputy, let alone the sheriff himself, had been up to Purgatoire in a year.

Reed had questioned the preacher, but the only thing he had learned was the man's name, Ezekiel McGregg. The louse had not seemed concerned that a prostitute had been murdered, refused to preach at her funeral, and had started shouting Scripture in Reed's ears. Briefly he had considered arresting McGregg, charging him with the murder, but he didn't have enough evidence, and the preacher wasn't a large man. His hands were calloused, his fingers long and bony, but not big. Then again, he wasn't altogether certain what Cameron had meant by "big hands", nor would he concede anything to The Scottish Gun. Why should he listen to a drunk? He had told the preacher not to leave town, to which McGregg had replied: "I sha'n't leave till Gomorrah is destroyed."

He still hadn't dismissed the idea of arresting McGregg, but wanted to hear from Randall Johnson first. The rancher had promised to let him know something last night, but Reed hadn't seen him since yesterday. Randy remained in town, moping around the Coal Cave Saloon, a roughshod log cabin near the Pendant that catered to the hardest drinkers. Reed would bet ten bucks that Cameron was getting rip-roaring drunk at the Coal Cave this very minute. He could picture Cameron in that bucket of blood, but not Randy Johnson. Reed didn't know if Randy was drinking away his sorrows, forgetting that deathbed promise to his mother, or simply staying there because it was close to the potter's field.

Maybe Randall Johnson had left town after hood-winking Reed, but he didn't think so. He'd give him till noon, then start looking for him.

A miner came inside, removing a woolen cap, and asking to speak to Reed. Keller took the hint and left, while Reed slid the dead prostitute's items into his desk drawer before grinning at the newcomer. Reed had worked at the Pendant with Seamus O'Flynn, a fun-loving Irishman who spent his time fishing for trout in the Picketwire and other streams when not breathing coal dust.

"You bring me a mess of fish?" Reed asked. O'Flynn shook his head, not even making eye contact, and Reed knew something was terribly wrong. "What's the matter, Seamus?"

When the miner looked up, a tear rolled down his cheek. "He's dead."

Reed could barely hear him. "Who's dead?"

"I took Betsy upstream this morning, Joshua, to wet a line before my shift. Saw him just lying there in an aspen grove, figured he was sleeping is all, only it didn't look right."

"Who?"

"Shot in the back, Joshua. I saw the bullet hole in his coat, just a wee bit of blood, but he was dead. Face down in the leaves." He shook his head and brushed away the tear.

"Who?" Reed's heart began pounding.

"I left him, Joshua. Didn't mess with his body none, figured you'd want to see it yourself. Sweet Mary, mother of Jesus, Joshua, I didn't. . . ."

"Is it Mister Johnson?"

Staring at his brogans, O'Flynn mumbled the answer.

They had reached the back of The Texas House again. Amie pulled away from Cameron's arm, kissed his cheek, and said with a smile: "Why don't you come back here after noon?" She pointed to the washtub. "It'll be warmer then, and, well, no offense, but you could use a real bath, a hot one, and maybe a shave."

"I don't know." He pulled the makings from his vest. The shakes had returned.

She took sack and paper from his trembling hands, sprinkled tobacco into the crease, and rolled the cigarette, licking it, sticking it in his mouth. He struck a match and brought the flame to the tip, thanking her.

"I'll try to be here," he said. "Need to get my guns back from the marshal."

"You do that."

"I ain't much of a man no more, Amie." Another drag. "Probably never was nothin' more'n Mississippi trash. I'm a drunk, I'm. . . ." He shook his head and concentrated on the cigarette.

"You're Ben Cameron." She started to say something, to feed him with compliments, but felt swallowed by her own self-pity. "I'm nothin' but a whore, Ben. That's all I've been for eleven years." She felt like telling him to leave, to ride out of Purgatoire, that the only people who came here were damned, or maybe . . . maybe she and Louis Venizelos, Diva, the marshal, everyone here, Cameron included, were fighting their pasts, their souls, trying to move to either hell or heaven. "I'll never. . . ."

He reached for her hand, squeezed it gently. "All you got to do is say no, Amie."

That took strength, more than she had. She stared into those lost eyes of his, and whispered: "The same holds true for you, Ben."

A silence fell between them. He finished his cigarette, and left, and Amie didn't know if he would return for that bath and shave. *All you have to do is say no.* Tell Diva that she was quitting. Then what? Her hand brushed the scarred flesh on her cheek. Once, she had almost escaped, had all but worked up the courage to quit her profession, until a city councilman in Denver and a madam she thought had been her friend sent her tumbling, squashing her last dreams—her last dreams, at least, until Ben Cameron had arrived in Purgatoire.

The parlor on Market Street was exquisite, not as fancy as Jennie Rogers's House of Mirrors or Mattie Silks's place, but better than a lot of the stone, brick, and frame buildings that lined both sides of the street, and did plenty of business. The main street in Denver's "flesh market" had originally been called Holladay Street, after Ben Holladay, but the heirs of the late stagecoach entrepreneur didn't care to have his name associated with rampant prostitution, so they pleaded with the city council to change the street's name. Holladay Street became Market Street, but the business remained the same.

Amie Courtland had worked her way up from Ernie Jenkins's Dodge City cribs to a better parlor house in the cow town, operated by a madam named Ginger Wier, closer to the deadline. In 1886, Wier sold her interest to Martha Cash, a tall, gregarious brunette who moved the operation, and Amie Courtland, to La Junta, Colorado. Two years later, Martha Cash opened The Cash House in Denver, and again brought Amie with her.

"You have potential, Amie," Martha had told her on the train to Denver. "You can be a queen, with the right coaching, the right wardrobe. I'll look after you, honey, and wait till you see your new home."

Gentlemen callers needed an invitation to get inside the two-and-a-half story Cash House, where they drank champagne, red wine, or brandy, smoked fine cigars, and discussed politics, mining, cattle, and world affairs before going upstairs with one of a dozen well-mannered girls.

Martha outfitted her courtesans with silk stockings, French perfume, and the finest fashions, and she didn't charge Amie, either. "It's yours, honey," she had said. "I spend money on you, and you make money for me and you. I treat my girls right."

Her girls sat politely while the men talked before being asked upstairs. It beat the cribs in Dodge City, and she charged $25 instead of a dollar, plus Martha didn't make her girls pay rent, merely took half their earnings. Amie figured she'd be able to quit and move on, see San Francisco, after all. Martha didn't mind. She always said she wanted the best for her girls, bragging how she wanted them to get married or become a madam like her, albeit not in Denver. She liked turnover in her business. "Keeps everything fresh," she once said.

The councilman's name was Jude Harte, and Amie had entertained him several times. Sometimes he asked her to talk to him before going to bed, saying he loved her accent. Often, he brought her presents, small trinkets mostly, nothing fancy, but the sentiment Amie always enjoyed. That Christmas Eve, however, had been different. He was fairly well in his cups when he arrived, and Martha had admonished him but didn't kick him out, which was the house rule. Instead, she let him drink an entire bottle of champagne and half a bottle of brandy—with good reason, since she marked up the price five hundred percent—and smiled as he led Amie upstairs, scratching the poodle on her lap and telling the councilman and Amie to have a grand time.

Once Amie had closed the door, she sat on the bed, saying warmly: "Merry Christmas, Jude."

"Whore!" he exploded. "Don't be telling me Merry Christmas, you bitch!" She had never seen him like this and never fully understood what triggered the rage, but, before she could apologize, he had shattered the bottle against a bedpost. Brandy and bits of glass sprayed her face, and she screamed, never noticing the ragged edge of the bottle still in Harte's hand. She heard footsteps on the staircase, and ran for the door, but Harte tackled her, cursed her, and pounded her face with the broken bottle. By the time Martha and the bouncer—a towering black man named Harp—had busted inside, Amie lay unconscious while Jude Harte was leaning against the bed, sobbing, moaning: "What have I done?"

Jude Harte was banished from The Cash House. For two weeks, Amie remained bedridden. Martha never visited her until January 9, 1890, when she brought her pet poodle with her, sat in a chair by Amie's bed, and kept everything brief and business-like.

"You'll heal, Amie, but, you know that I run a fancy house, and I don't see anyone paying twenty-five for you. Not any more. I'm sorry, but I have no use for a girl who has lost her charm. Now, I've always told *you that I take care of my girls, and I'm taking care of you. A friend of mine runs a house down in Colorado Springs. His name's Steve Pickett. It's not fancy, but you can't expect that any more. Not with your face a bloody mess."*

Amie just nodded. She had no plans of joining Pickett's house, figured she'd just head west, start over, and asked Martha how long she could stay.

"You're leaving tonight, Amie," Martha replied, and the poodle barked. "I'm losing money and have a girl coming over from Laura Evans's parlor to replace you."

The clothes Amie had worn stayed at The Cash House, even though Martha had promised she could keep them. Martha also charged Amie $300 in doctors' bills, demanding payment before Harp escorted her to the stagecoach station. The madam did pay Amie's fare, so, that evening, Amie left Denver with $37 and a letter of introduction to Mr. Pickett. Six months later, Pickett had fired her, and she was working a crib in Pueblo, charging a dollar fifty cents when she needed to eat. When she had saved up enough money for the stage to Raton, she left Pueblo and found another crib. When that didn't pan out, she moved back to Colorado to a hog ranch near Trinidad fifty cents a poke and plenty of whiskey— where she expected to die before Diva came calling.

"All you have to do is say no," Amie said to herself. After eleven years, could she?

Chapter Seventeen

Almost in a blind panic, Joshua Reed dragged Seamus O'Flynn outside, barreling over Ben Cameron in the process, sending everyone crashing onto the boardwalk. The three men recovered quickly, brushing themselves off, mumbling apologies. Ignoring the bite of splinters in his left palm, Reed motioned for the miner to mount his horse. Nervously he faced the gunman, but immediately realized the infamous Scottish Gun must be just as apprehensive as he was. "You need me for anything?" Reed asked.

"You have my guns?" Cameron studied the warped, rotting planks, and shuffled his feet.

"Yeah. Locked up. I'm busy, but, if you'd come back tonight, I'll give them to you."

He started for the livery, but Cameron cleared his throat, causing Reed to freeze. When he looked back, the gunman stood a little straighter, looked a little more imposing.

"I'd appreciate it, Marshal, if I could have 'em now."

Cameron must have sobered up enough to realize he wasn't heeled and remained paranoid enough to think someone might be gunning for him, up here, at the end of the earth. Sighing, Reed stepped back to the office, asking O'Flynn to ride over to the livery and have Moses Keller hitch up a buckboard. He'd meet him there in a few minutes. As O'Flynn led his horse away, Cameron followed Reed into the office.

"Shotgun's in the gun cabinet," said Reed, fishing out a key before kneeling by the safe. He worked the lock, removed the padlock, opened the safe's door, and pulled out the heavy rig, which Cameron took and began buckling on.

"I owe you anything?" he asked.

"No."

"Nothin'? No fine?"

"Nothing." He locked the safe, slipped the key into a vest pocket, and they left the office. Reed headed for the livery stable only to be stopped once more by Cameron's voice.

"I'm. . . . I reckon I said some things." Cameron focused on his boots, exhaled slowly, and made himself look Reed in the eye. "I don't recollect what all I done, but I didn't mean nothin'. It was the whiskey. That ain't no excuse, and I ain't askin' for your forgiveness. Just wanted to say that I'm sorry, is all, and, if I can do anything for you, well. . . ." He shook his head. "Well, you probably ain't got much use, but . . . anyway, I apologize."

Gunmen weren't supposed to apologize. They took no insult, backed down to no one, rarely even bowed to God. At least, that was what Reed had been brought up to believe, yet now he understood the man facing him was just that, a man, not a legend, not a demigod, just an ordinary gent with strengths, and many, many weaknesses.

Cameron had stepped into the street when Reed

heard himself call his name. The gunman stopped, turned, and stared, wondering.

"Could . . . ?" Reed almost dismissed the thought, was about to tell Cameron to never mind, that it had been a silly notion, but he needed help. Cameron had pointed out the marks on the Mexican whore's throat, and, as much as Reed told himself that he would have seen them, would have noticed something wrong, and realized the girl had been murdered, he'd be lying to himself. Cameron was a lawman, a former Pinkerton agent, and had been the town council's first choice for this job. Reed knew how to arrest an occasional drunk, how to haul off dead animals, how to bill the town council, but he was no lawman, certainly no detective. He also understood that with Randall Johnson dead—murdered!—he needed help. He'd take as much as he could from Cameron before The Scottish Gun lost his willpower and got drunk again.

"Could you come with me?" Reed asked. "There's been another killing."

The coffee smelled surprisingly good, considering he had brewed it himself, so Louis Venizelos decided at the last moment to pour a cup for himself after filling Amie Courtland's cup. She had mentioned the need to refill the lanterns and lamps, but he had been putting that chore off. Maybe later in the week.

He took both cups to the table—"The Scottish Gun's booth", patrons had been calling it—and stretched out his long legs after sitting across from

Amie. Unfortunately the coffee smelled better than it tasted, but Amie didn't seem to mind and Venizelos's mouth and stomach had become used to it. He pulled a handkerchief from his vest pocket, pried the eyeglasses off his nose, and began cleaning the lenses.

"How long have you been wearing glasses?" Amie asked, as if noticing his spectacles for the first time.

"Since I quit the ring. Got my head pounded so much, I'm myopic."

He put the glasses back on, smiling, and saw her shaking her head, uncomprehending. "Near-sighted," he explained. "Means I can see up close but not far away."

Her eyes remained trained on his spectacles, but she didn't appear to be seeing anything. After a moment, she blinked, looked out the window toward Front Street, and asked: "Is that your only pair?"

"I have an old pair up in my room." Lifting the cup, he began shaking his head, knowing where Amie was going. "These are stronger. Got them in Denver two years ago because my vision had gotten worse. Probably could use stronger lenses now." He followed his sigh with a chuckle. "Part of getting old, I guess."

She stared at him, now seeing him, purpose written in her face. "Louis, do you think I could buy that old pair from you? I . . . well. . . ."

"He's no good, Amie," Venizelos told her, and her chin dropped against her throat. "He'd just sell them for a drink."

"I . . . think . . . maybe. . . ."

Venizelos finished his coffee. He had always been

honest with Amie, and, although he didn't want to hurt her feelings, he had to speak his mind. "He's a killer, a drunk. As God as my witness, I don't see what you see in Cameron, Amie. I could picture Cindy with him, maybe even Nancy, but not you."

Her eyes revealed hurt when she looked up at him again, and Venizelos tried not to stare at the scars on her right cheek. "He's sober today, Louis," she said, "and I think he can stay that way if he just has the right person." The head fell again.

"You're his guardian angel?"

"No." She sobbed softly. "He knew my big brother, and . . . never mind."

He caught her arm as she stood, pulled her closer, waiting until she looked him in the eye. "If you wait here, I'll go fetch that old pair of glasses, Amie." He liked seeing her smile again. "They might not be strong enough, Amie, or they might be too strong. Either way, he should see an eye doctor the next time he's in Denver or Santa Fe. I don't know. Colorado Springs might have one."

"How much do I owe you?" she asked.

Venizelos rose, handing the empty coffee cups to her. "Make us a fresh pot, will you, and I'll call it even." That would keep her busy for a while, give him time enough to run upstairs, find that old pair of spectacles, and maybe knock on Denise's door, see if she still planned on leaving Purgatoire, still planned on taking him with her. The stage would be here tomorrow.

• • •

Someone just stepped on your grave.

That's what his mother had always said whenever he shivered for no apparent reason. Cameron didn't know what made him think of that old saying, but he knew why he had shivered. He squatted over the dead body, staring at it, the rustling of the trees and the gurgling of the river sounding out of place amid such a violent scene. A golden aspen leaf fluttered through the air before settling on the linen duster near the bullet hole that had smashed Randall Johnson's spine.

He wet his lips, took a deep breath, exhaled slowly, and plucked the leaf from the corpse, then made himself look a little more closely, fingering the bullet hole in the fabric. "He was shot up close," Cameron said nervously. "Powder burns. Really close, inches away. Almost set his duster a-fire." He closed his eyes and envisioned the killer standing over the body, lowering the revolver, pulling the trigger. Cameron's hands grabbed the rancher's arm and turned the body over. The miner gasped, and the marshal told him to go back to work but not to tell a soul what he had found out here. The Irishman didn't need further prompting to vamoose.

Blood stained the rancher's shirt and the leaves underneath where he had lain. The miner had reported that Johnson had not bled much, but he had only seen the bullet wound in the back, and the leaves and straw had soaked up much of the blood underneath his stomach. A Remington revolver was tucked

189

in the rancher's waistband. His eyes remained open, staring at Cameron as he worked. That unnerved him even more, so he reached out and gently closed the man's eyes. He found the bullet hole just below the sternum and pressed his little finger into it, a trick he had learned from McNelly. Johnson had been shot with a .45. Next he reached into the pockets of his vest and trousers, pulling out a wallet, cigar case, well-chewed pencil, some matches, and one of those note pads he had seen countless ranchers up in Wyoming reading and writing in from time to time. He thumbed through the pages in the note pad, but found only records of cattle, horses, and expenses. He set everything beside Reed, who had worked up the nerve to come closer. The marshal picked up the wallet and glanced at the contents.

"Wasn't robbery," Reed said. "There must be two hundred dollars here, or close to it."

Cameron agreed. "He was shot in the chest first," he explained, "and fell here, on his face. The killer walked over and shot him in the back just to make sure. Wasted shot. Doubt if he lived more'n two minutes after the first bullet hit him."

"How far away was the killer on that first shot?"

"No powder burns. Farther'n six feet. I'd guess ten or twelve."

Reed contemplated the area before pointing to a thick pine. "Maybe the killer was hiding behind that tree. That looks about a dozen feet from here. He was hiding, shot him, and then. . . ."

"Angle's wrong for the bullet trajectory," Cameron said. "I'd say the killer was just waitin' here by the river. Johnson walked up, and bam." He pointed to the Remington in the waistband. "He knew who it was, didn't try to pull that hogleg."

"How long ago?"

Cameron shrugged. "Last night." He sounded like he knew what he was saying, yet he never had considered himself a detective. Whiskey had erased just about anything he had learned from the Pinkertons and Rangers. That young lawman was scraping the bottom if he had to turn to him for help.

"Could we track him?"

"Wouldn't do you no good, Marshal. Tracks would lead back to town if we could find any, then you'd lose 'em once you hit the main street." His hands began to shake, and he balled up fists until his knuckles paled. "What did he tell you?"

Shaking his head, Reed tossed the wallet beside the other items. "Said he might know who had killed the Mexican whore, but wasn't certain. Asked me to give him until the evening."

And you did. The young lawman had certainly botched things. Even in his cups, Cameron would have known better than to agree to something like that, or, if he had, he would have followed the rancher.

"Randall Johnson got whatever he wanted in this town," Reed said, as if reading Cameron's thoughts. "Anything else?"

191

He shook his head. "No, nothin' that I can see. I'd get him back to town, send word to the county sheriff."

"The *sheriff?*"

"This ain't in the town limits, is it?"

"No."

"Then it's out of your jurisdiction. That dead whore probably ain't your concern, neither."

Reed shook his head. "The sheriff won't come here. If he does anything, it would be to deputize me, tell me to handle it. Maybe the Johnson cowboys would put pressure. . . ."

Cameron read the fear in Reed's face, fear of the dead rancher's men. Those cowboys had seemed a harmless lot, as much as Cameron could recall, but he had seen cowboys turn angry, turn mean. Reed's fear likely was not that unjustified.

"Let's get him back to town." Cameron walked to the buckboard, threw the tarp over his shoulder, and returned to the murder site. After unrolling the tarp, he grabbed the dead man's shoulders while Reed lifted the corpse by the boots, and they unceremoniously dropped the body onto the sheet of canvas.

Cameron began covering the body while Reed collected his personal effects.

Suddenly Reed stood straight and blurted out: "His quirt! Where's Johnson's quirt?"

He definitely wanted a hot bath, needed to wash everything off him after poking around Randall

Johnson's dead body, almost craved the soap and water more than he longed for a drink. Cameron didn't tell Amie about his morning. No sense in troubling her.

He made her turn her head while he undressed and climbed into the tub. It felt good, and he tried to remember the last time he had bathed. Amie brought him shaving gear, and he smiled as he trimmed the beard with scissors, then lathered the remnants. The smile vanished, however, when he picked up the razor and felt his hands trembling again. Slowly Amie took the razor, whispering: "I'll do it."

"I went to those hot springs in Arkansas once," he told her after the shave, just to talk, to forget about his nerves, to kill the image of Randall Johnson's blood-soaked corpse. "In the dead of winter. This is kinda like that. Cold air, hot water."

"If you stay in here much longer, the water will be just as cold as the air." She handed him a towel.

She turned her back as he stepped out of the tub, finished drying off, and dressed quickly, feeling the bite of autumn. A pungency remained embedded in his clothes, which now felt uncomfortable on his clean body, and he thought he might walk over to the mercantile and outfit himself in some new duds, something that didn't remind him of whiskey, vomit, urine, or sweat. He'd do that immediately, before the stink of his clothes permeated his body. New long johns, everything . . . and he'd buy some more Bull Durham and papers. He was about out of both, and he wanted a smoke, so he began rolling a cigarette.

"I never knew you had the habit." Amie had turned around.

He lit the cigarette and took a long drag. "Never smoked much, but it keeps my hands busy, gives me somethin' to do."

"Come on," she said, and he followed her into the kitchen, where she filled two cups with coffee. After they had sipped for a few minutes, she brought a leather pouch from her handbag and slid it across the table.

"Try these."

To his surprise, he pulled out a pair of wire spectacles. He studied them a moment, then tried them on. The wires pinched the back of his ears and the bridge of his nose, but when he looked up, his mouth dropped open. Amazing, how clear became Amie's face, and he could read the label on the can of Arbuckle's ariosa sitting on the counter top behind her, although he couldn't make out the smaller print. His head began to throb slightly around his temples. Still, the improvement was immeasurable.

"Louis Venizelos gave these to me to give to you," Amie said. "He's the bartender here. The nicer one. Plays the fiddle."

He could only nod.

"He says you should still see an eye doctor when you can."

Another nod.

A hinge *squeaked* upstairs, and a door slammed. "You'd better get out of here, Ben," Amie said, "before Diva comes down. If she finds you here, there'll be hell to pay. Go on." She added with a smile: "Can I see you tomorrow for breakfast?"

What he wanted was to see her tonight, wanted to sweep her into his arms and kiss her. That surprised him. He couldn't remember the last time he had had such an urge, but it felt strong, good, right. She remained sitting as he stood and headed for the door. He put his hand on her shoulder, squeezed it, and enjoyed the touch of her hand when she reached up and squeezed him back. He could hear the stairs creaking but couldn't move, or wouldn't move, until she looked up at him. Leaning forward, he kissed her softly on the lips.

"Thank you," he whispered, and headed out the door.

Chapter Eighteen

The lightweight wool underwear set him back $1.75, the blue flannel bib shirt was another dollar, $3 for corduroy pants, fifty cents for suspenders, $1.50 for vest, ten cents for socks, two bits for bandanna, and $15 for a broadcloth coat. After pricing the boots, Ben Cameron decided his weren't that bad, but he picked up a pair of gauntlets for eight bits, and found a silver belly Stetson that fit for another four bucks. At the last moment, he added two more pairs of socks and some cheaper shirts, three for a $1, before laying his plunder on the counter beside the sack of Bull Durham and Mail Pouch papers.

"Anything else?" the gleeful, silver-haired woman in the apron asked hopefully. She had not likely done this much business in months.

He had almost forgotten about matches, and also opted for a twenty-ounce plug of Kylo tobacco, just in case the cigarettes didn't do enough. She began wrapping his purchases, and he leaned against the counter, staring through the doorway. With his new glasses, he could read the sign above the Dead Canary. The special, written in big block letters on the chalkboard, read: ELK STEAK AND FRIED POTATOES. Grinning in satisfaction, he scanned the rest of the store, mesmerized at the colors so clear, bolts of cotton prints, axe handles in the keg, calico dresses, dusters, and Mackinaws. He straightened when he came to the dresses on display in the window.

"Ma'am?"

The woman tied a piece of twine around the brown paper containing his shirts. "Yes, sir?"

He pointed. "How much is that dress?"

She had to adjust her own spectacles. "Oh, my goodness," she said, "that's the only one I have, and it's forty-four dollars. Do you know the lady's size?"

"No, ma'am."

"Is she in town? I mean, could she come in to try it on? I can do some alterations . . . wouldn't be much

. . . I'd just hate for you to spend that kind of money on that dress and it not fit.

He hesitated. She wouldn't let Amie come into her store, not a prostitute. Of course, most towns didn't allow houses of ill repute to operate on the main street. Still, he wasn't about to risk bringing Amie here, not to be insulted, embarrassed. He walked closer, listening to the woman's sales pitch: It was a reception costume. Grosgrain silk, a fine garnet, with six bands of contrasting gimp in navy blue and a satin ribbon bow, also blue. It had been sitting in that window for almost two years. A wonder moths hadn't gotten to it. On second thought, she'd throw in the alterations for free.

His head bobbed slightly as he told her to wrap it up.

She bolted from behind the counter before he could change his mind, smiling, shaking her head, telling him: "You must be taking the stagecoach out of town, heading to Denver or Santa Fe. Nobody's had reason to wear a dress like this in Purgatoire since I got it. You think it'll come close to fitting? How tall is she?"

He shrugged. "Five five, maybe."

"Not heavy set, I hope."

"Not hardly. She's right skinny."

"Then this will probably come close but, like I said, just send her in. Is it Charlie Prescott's daughter?"

"No, ma'am."

She cocked her head and pursed her lips, about to fire off another guess, but stopped, shrugged, and carefully folded the dress, finished the wrapping job, and began totaling the purchases in her ledger book.

"Seventy-eight dollars and forty-seven cents, sir," she announced.

He was glad he didn't go shopping every day. He tossed his old hat and ratty Mackinaw in the trash bin, pulled on the new Stetson, tipped it to the grinning lady, and tucked the packages underneath his arm. He turned left on the boardwalk, wondering where he would spend the night. Not in the livery, not again. Diva didn't want him in The Texas House, but she might not even recognize him once he put on his new duds. Maybe he'd get a room at the hotel, but he didn't think so. The hotel had a saloon, and he wanted to keep temptation as far away as possible. He paused to think. That was the first time whiskey had entered his mind and he hadn't started shaking. He felt satisfied, and stepped off the boardwalk to cross the alley between the vacant billiards hall and The Texas House. When he heard the scream, he dropped the packages in the dirt and ran.

Louis Venizelos had just stepped outside of The Texas House, heading to the privy, when he heard the *pop,* felt the searing pain in his neck. He reached out to clamp a big hand on his collar, sensing the blood, mumbling—"What the hell?"—while tumbling backward. He had been looking for Denise, hadn't seen her since that morning, and thought she might be in the privy. He felt awkward, hadn't figured out how he would call out her name as he approached the two-seater, but it was 4:30 and Diva would turn ugly when she learned that one of her girls wasn't ready for work. He also kept choking down the worry, remembering the fate of Consuela, who also hadn't shown up for work a few days ago.

He glimpsed the little man standing by the old washtub, saw him rearing back, and spotted the weapon. Venizelos raised his right arm in a defensive measure to protect his face and eyes. The heavy leather bit into his forearm and his left knee buckled—sending a bolt of pain up and down his leg—and he dropped, crashing on his face as the whip—no, too short for a whip, but a quirt—ripped through his woolen vest.

" 'Forty stripes he may give him, and not exceed . . . lest, if he should exceed, and beat him above these with many stripes, then thy brother should seem vile unto thee.' "

That damned little sky pilot.

Venizelos rolled over, tried to stand, but his knee had given out, just as it had in three or four of his boxing matches, ending his career. He'd be able to pound that little jackass, throttle him good, maybe even send him to his Maker, if he could only stand up. The quirt slashed his cheek, and Venizelos screamed, not from fear or even pain, simply rage.

The preacher raised the quirt again, took a step forward, whispering another bit of Scripture, while

Venizelos crawled backward like a coward. He had never wanted to kill anyone . . . until now.

A gunshot left his ears ringing—it sounded like a cannon had fired just over his head—and Venizelos swore again. The preacher checked his advance, his gaze turning left. Venizelos tried to control his breathing, raised his hand to wipe away the blood. Words sounded behind him, but he couldn't make them out, not with his ears pealing so. The preacher dropped the quirt, and said something else, but again Venizelos couldn't hear.

He groaned as the back door opened, and out stepped Cindy, followed moments later by Nancy and Amie. At least Joe Miller remained inside; the bartender would have tormented him for the next six months if he had seen Venizelos on his backside, bleeding, a gimp, almost crying, beaten up by that God-loving little cock-of-the-walk who couldn't weigh much more than an aspen sapling.

Ben Cameron stepped into Venizelos's line of vision, holding a smoking Schofield. The preacher lifted his hands over his head, and the ringing stopped for Venizelos to hear the tramp say: " 'And now whereas my father did lade you with a heavy yoke, I will add to your yoke . . . my father hath chastised you with whips, but I will chastise you with scorpions.' "

To which Cameron replied: " 'A whip for the horse, a bridle for the ass, and a rod for the *fool's* back.' "

That shut up the preacher.

The gunman holstered the .45, and offered Venizelos his hand. "You all right?" he asked.

Cameron looked different, clean-shaven, although still in dirty clothes. New hat for sure, though, and . . . Venizelos forced a smile. "Yeah, I'll live. How do you like your spectacles?"

A brief grin stretched across Cameron's face, and he pulled Venizelos to his feet.

Venizelos limped over to the back door, fighting back the urge to strangle that miserable zealot. Cindy and Nancy walked down the steps to help him, while Amie's eyes locked on the preacher. More footsteps drew Venizelos's attention.

The marshal rounded the corner, almost slipped on the wet grass, and slid to a stop. "What's going on?"

Cindy answered: "This damned fool was beatin' hell out of Louis here. With that." She pointed to the quirt lying at the preacher's feet.

The young lawman's eyes widened, and he just stared at the intricately braided piece of leatherwork as if in a trance. Finally he swore, pushed back his coattail, and fumbled for his revolver. "You're under arrest," he managed after thumbing back the hammer. "You killed Randall Johnson and that Mexican girl."

Joe Miller and China Rene had drifted outside by now, and, choking back the pain, Venizelos watched as Reed picked up the quirt with his free hand and motioned the preacher to start walking. For some reason, the lawman asked Cameron if he'd tag along, and the gunman simply shrugged and followed.

"Let's get inside," Venizelos said through clenched teeth, "before Diva raises hell." His knee wouldn't bend, not without excruciating agony, and he had to lean on Cindy and Nancy to climb the steps. Miller's grin irked him, but no one said anything until they were in the saloon and Miller was pouring Venizelos a drink.

"You need a couple of stitches," Miller said after sliding the whiskey in front of Venizelos and examining the cut on his cheek. "Can you work tonight?"

The whiskey felt good, took his mind off the pain. "I got a pair of crutches up in my room," he said. "This old knee's given out on me before. I'll be fine in a day or two." He hoped so, anyway. As far as stitches were concerned, well, Amie Courtland had done a pretty good job on Ben Cameron's hand, using a fine thread slick with beeswax. Some old sawbones down in Trinidad might frown on the method and materials, but there hadn't been a pill-pusher in Purgatoire since Doc Driebe pulled down his shingle back in May. Besides, Amie wouldn't charge as much as the gent over at the Pendant who stitched up cuts and set broken bones when not swinging a pickaxe. Miller refilled Venizelos's tumbler, and a customer, one of the boys who ran the Pendant company store, entered the front door. China Rene went to greet him, and Miller returned to duty behind the bar.

Venizelos had just finished his second drink when Diva came through the kitchen entrance, stopped to stare at his face, and cackled. "I thought you give up the ring, Louis," she said after shedding her coat. That prompted a chuckle from Miller, busy pouring a beer for the Pendant clerk. "Well," she demanded when no one followed up on her joke, "is somebody gonna tell me who tried to make Louis look like my Alabama Angel?"

No one laughed at that. Venizelos caught a glimpse of Amie and frowned as her head fell in shame.

"I ain't got all day!" Diva bellowed.

"The preacher killed Consuela," someone said. Then voices rang together. "An' he was 'bout to kill Louis, too."

"The marshal says Randall Johnson's also been kilt."

"Says the preacher done that, too."

"I had just opened the front door when I heard this scream."

"Cindy ran outside first."

"The preacher was about to whip Louis ag'in when Ben Cameron came up an' fired a warnin' shot."

"His knee's frettin' him some, Diva, and he might need stitches in that cheek."

One voice suddenly sounded clear, halting the meaningless banter. "Has anybody seen Denise?" Amie Courtland asked.

Ben Cameron didn't seem interested in Joshua Reed's interrogation of Ezekiel McGregg, but it didn't matter. Reed would hold the prisoner in jail until the sheriff got off his butt and came up to Purgatoire himself or sent a deputy to bring the prisoner down to Trinidad. He would finish his letter and send it down with the stagecoach Thursday morning. It was a relief, having the two murders solved, but he had hoped the preacher would give him a motive. Maybe he didn't need one. Everyone in town thought the parson mad.

Reed had asked Cameron to help march McGregg to jail with hope that Cameron would suggest something about the questioning, but all the gunman wanted to do was take off his filthy clothes and put on his new outfit. Reed had loaned him the empty cell, hammering McGregg over and over, getting only Scripture for answers to his questions, or nothing when the preacher turned mute.

They left the preacher locked in the third cell with his Good Book after twenty minutes of questioning. Reed dunked a mug in the water barrel and drank greedily, forgetting his manners. After apologizing, he offered Cameron a drink, but the gunman shook his head and began rolling a cigarette.

"You do think he killed Randall Johnson, don't you?" Reed asked.

Cameron shrugged.

"It makes sense," Reed explained, more to himself than Cameron. "He assaulted the red-headed whore, then went after the one that . . . the one who looked after you. And that's Randall Johnson's quirt. Here's my thinking . . . he killed the whore. I don't know what he was doing, maybe he thought he was baptizing her. Johnson suspected him, went to him, to bring him in, and then he shot him dead and took the quirt."

Cameron took a drag on the cigarette, exhaled, blew a smoke ring, and watched it disappear. "You find a gun on him? Forty-Five caliber?"

"No." Reed sank into his chair. He had found a butcher knife, the one the preacher had used to slice Cameron's palm. "But he could have thrown it away." His eyebrows arched. "How could you tell it was a Forty-Five?"

"Size of the bullet hole. I can just get my pinky in a Forty-Five hole, not quite all the way in if it's a Forty-Four."

"It doesn't matter," Reed argued, "because he's got the old man's quirt."

Another drag. Reed waited for Cameron to explain that the preacher's hands were too small to have strangled the Mexican, but he wasn't going to buy that. Ezekiel McGregg had done more than a fair job on the Greek bartender at The Texas House just minutes earlier, and Cameron's left hand remained bandaged from the knife wound caused by the preacher. He had to be the murderer, small hands or not. At least the sheriff wouldn't raise many questions. Men had been tried and hanged with less evidence. Criminy, as much weight as Randall Johnson carried, Ezekiel McGregg would likely be lynched in Trinidad by the Bar J boys before the circuit judge held the next term of court.

"You tell Randy Johnson about his daddy?" Cameron asked.

"Yeah."

"How did he take it?"

Reed straightened. Surely Cameron wasn't suggesting that Randy killed his father, that the preacher merely came by the dead body and picked up the quirt to help him deliver his sermons about whips and stripes. Randy Johnson had plenty of reasons to despise his father, but murder him? Randy had been in a sorry state when he broke the news, but the boy didn't look capable of even carrying a pistol.

"Randy was drunk," Reed answered sharply, and immediately regretted his choice of words.

Cameron's eyes misted over. He crushed out the cigarette and began fumbling in the pocket of his new vest, pulling out a plug of chewing tobacco. He bit off a mouthful and began working the quid. His hands had started shaking again.

Hoofs sounded outside. Stagecoach? No, too early. It wouldn't be here until tomorrow. Cameron rose stiffly, picked up the remaining packages, and walked to the door while Reed tried to soften what he had said, explaining that the boy merely looked shocked, probably hadn't gotten over his girlfriend's death, and that he would likely take the body back by stagecoach to Trinidad, then on to the ranch for a proper funeral.

Cameron stopped after opening the door. "Marshal . . . ," he began.

Reed jumped to his feet, rounded the desk and

stove, and stood behind the gunman, peering over his shoulder. He muttered an oath.

Jack Tompkins and a half dozen Bar J boys had ridden back to town.

Chapter Nineteen

This colonel, Keno Thompson had decided, was all right. Thaddeus K. Hall could drink with the best of them and, better yet, didn't mind sharing, even now as the stagecoach creaked on its hard, winding climb up the mountain toward Purgatoire. Hall had just pulled an engraved pewter flask from his coat pocket, unscrewed the cap, and offered a drink to the fancy lady in the pink calico dress sitting across from them.

To his surprise, the woman accepted Hall's generosity, didn't even wipe off the top—by jingo, she didn't even cough after swallowing the stuff, pure Trinidad forty-rod instead of the colonel's smooth-tasting Scotch—and she returned the flask with a warm smile, saying something about the nectar of the gods, which Thompson didn't understand. The colonel laughed before passing the flask Thompson's way, and Thompson drank greedily.

They were the only paying customers on the ride out of Trinidad. Thompson had been worried about returning to the town, figured those smart-aleck law-dogs might take exception to his being back, but no one had recognized him at the station—they had only stayed in town about four hours, anyway—and the colonel footed the bill for Thompson's breakfast, whiskey, and ticket. Yes, sir, he wished he had run across this gent a long time ago. It certainly beat having to rob cobblers in Denver and back-shoot rustlers in Wyoming to make a living.

"What brings you to Purgatoire?" Hall asked the woman.

Trying to woo the gal—Thompson couldn't blame him. She wasn't the prettiest petticoat he had ever laid eyes on, but he admired that curly black hair and she had the look of a woman who could entertain a fellow. She had just enough meat on her bones, a wicked little mouth, and he couldn't help but stare at those heaving breasts, almost busting out of that too-tight dress.

"Business," she answered. "And you?"

"A mix of business and pleasure," Hall replied, took a swig, and passed the flask back to the girl. Hell's bells, she drank again, handing it this time to Thompson. "I hope to see an old friend," Hall continued. "So does my associate, Mister Thomas."

Thomas? Oh, yeah. Thompson had almost forgotten. It was his alias for the deal. The way Hall had explained things, Thompson would just hang out in the hotel room, drinking whiskey, maybe running a few whores if he could find the time and money, while Hall set things up with Ben Cameron. Then he'd kill Cameron, and the colonel would make him famous. It sounded pretty good, although Thompson wouldn't be disappointed if Cameron had left Purgatoire. Maybe the colonel would continue to pay their way across the West looking for that walking whiskey vat.

Back in Raton, Hall had even sent a wire to Thompson's mother. Well, actually, he had wired Thompson's Uncle Preston Zeske in Van Buren, asking him to tell Keno's mother what had happened to Frank and explaining that Keno was tracking down Cameron to avenge his brother's death. Uncle Preston was to wire Hall in Trinidad. The reply had been waiting for the colonel at the telegraph office after they stabled their mounts. "Your mother's proud of you, son," Hall had said. "Says you're showing a lot of courage."

Maw would be even prouder after Uncle Preston read her Colonel Hall's book about him, *Keno Thompson's Revenge; or, The Death of the Scottish Gun*. He liked the sound of that, could just see himself being treated to free drinks and being asked to make his mark on a copy of the book. Right now, though, Thompson was more interested in the hard-drinking lady who had just given him another toothy smile. She had rosy lips and smelled of lilac. Her teeth weren't all that good, but he did like that mouth. Yes, sir, he surely did. He'd bet the horse he had left back in the Trinidad livery that this woman was a sporting gal.

"My name's Susan Falconer," she said. Thompson also enjoyed her Texas drawl.

"And I am Colonel Thaddeus K. Hall, profiler of

heroes and heroines of the West for the Wide Awake Library and several newspapers. This is my associate, John Thomas. I hope you do not find me overly forward or presumptuous, but we'd be honored to be your escorts while in Purgatoire. We're at your service, Miss Falconer. It's a rough town, I've heard, and Mister Thomas is quite handy with a six-gun."

Susan Falconer had the gumption to reach for Hall's flask. After a long pull of whiskey, she wiped her lips and returned the container. "Colonel, I thank you for your offer, but I've been in rougher towns than Purgatoire, and I won't be on the streets once we arrive. But, if you don't find me overly forward or presumptuous, perhaps I can service you."

She reached into her purse and withdrew two coins, placing one in the colonel's hand and giving the other to Thompson. He pushed back his bowler and grinned when he realized it was a bawdy house token.

"Just ask for me at The Texas House," she said cheerily. "You can't miss it."

It had been a hard night, what with the Bar J boys riding back to town and blowing off steam at The Texas House upon learning of the murder of their boss. Most of the older cowboys, like the foreman, Tompkins, and Quincy, the cook, spent their time draining the liquor supply, but some opted to escort the girls upstairs where the boys, generally pleasant but eager, turned unpleasant and angry.

Amie wanted to stay in bed an hour or two longer, but Diva started howling, demanding that her girls file downstairs. Groaning, she tossed off the covers and managed to sit up. Her head throbbed, her mouth tasted like burned piñon ash, and a wave of dizziness almost sent her reeling. The Bar J boys had not left until almost dawn. She gingerly touched the bruise underneath her left eye. Closing her eyes, she replayed the scene once more.

"You miserable little trollop," the freckle-faced cowboy had shot out, and slapped Amie suddenly, sending her crashing against the headboard after she asked for her dollar. "If not for you or that Messican bitch lustin' after Randy, Mister Johnson'd still be alive."

He had hit her again before leaving.

A rough night, indeed.

All you got to do is say no, Amie.

She wasn't as strong as Ben Cameron thought, although she wished she did have the courage to tell Diva she was finished. The words of a prostitute back in Dodge whose name she had long forgotten rang through her mind, too: *They can buy your body, hon, but not your soul, damn them.*

Diva's vocal demands rocked the timbers, and Amie forced herself to her feet, took a hit of gin for courage—what would Cameron think of that?—and threw on a robe, joining China Rene, Cindy, Nancy, Joe Miller, and Louis Venizelos downstairs. Still no Denise, and Amie feared the worst. Diva, in her garish kimono and puffing on a cigar, stood in front of the bar, talking to a raven-haired woman in a pink calico dress, all smiles as she sipped a beer. Amie had never seen her, nor could she recall finding Diva so happy this early in the day. Well, one-fifteen in the afternoon came early for Diva.

"Ladies and gents," Diva said, flicking ash onto the bar, "this is an old friend in the business. . . ."

"I ain't that old, Kate," the new woman said, and Diva let out a belly laugh.

"This is Susan Falconer. She'll be replacing my Vaya Con Dios. Come up from Trinidad to get the chance to work for me one more time."

"And to buy you out."

Diva's smile faded quickly. "In time." The grin reappeared. "Anyway, make her feel at home, will you?" She made the introductions, then let Susan Falconer tell everyone a bit about herself, as if anyone really cared. She hailed from west Texas, had been in the entertainment business twenty-one years—she didn't look that old—and had come up from Trinidad as soon as she read Diva's letter. Her plan was to work through the winter, and, if she liked the prospects, she'd buy out Diva and take over The Texas House. She truly believed the railroad would run a spur to Purgatoire after the financial panic faded away.

"If Purgatoire becomes civilized," Nancy Brennan said, "those fickle city officials won't let us operate here. Not on Front Street."

"Then we'll move," Susan Falconer said, "and I'll turn this place into a legitimate saloon."

Cindy asked another question: "If you got the money to buy out Diva, why work all winter on your back?"

"I have to sell my place in Trinidad first, girlie," she answered, "and I ain't like some madams." She winked at Diva. "I ain't lost my looks, and I enjoy a man's company."

Diva's frown hardened. Amie only wanted to go back upstairs, get some sleep, and maybe find Ben Cameron for a late dinner or early supper. She didn't know if the Bar J boys would come back tonight. Maybe not. Joe Miller had said they were talking about hanging that crazy little deliverer.

"You replace Denise?" China Rene asked Diva. "If she no return?"

Amie glanced at Louis Venizelos, whose face could not mask his hurt.

"No rush with winter comin' on," Diva announced, and ended the interview. "C'mon, Susan, lemme show you to your room."

Joshua Reed had watched two strangers and a woman get off the stagecoach. He was curious about the men who headed for the hotel and the woman who strolled over to The Texas House. He wanted to find out what they were doing in town, but he could not leave his office, not with the Bar J waddies in town. They had spent most of the night at the brothel before riding out to the Coal Cave to consort with Randy Johnson and get even drunker, angrier . . . working up the nerve to hang Ezekiel McGregg.

His palms turned clammy as Jack Tompkins rode up, reining to a stop in front of the hitching rail but not dismounting. Tompkins looked tired, his eyes bloodshot, but he carried no six-gun. Reed remembered that the foreman had loaned Randall Johnson his Remington, and that revolver was locked up in Reed's safe. There was a Winchester in the scabbard, however, but Tompkins didn't appear to be interested in gun play. He rested his hands on the saddle horn and leaned forward.

" 'Afternoon."

Reed nodded in reply.

"No need in beatin' 'round the bush, Reed. Me an' the boys been wonderin' what you got in store for that preacher man that killed Boss Johnson."

"I'll turn him over to the county sheriff." Reed tried to sound confident, but his voice betrayed him. "He'll stand trial for murder, two murders actually."

"Why not just turn 'im over to me an' the boys?"

"You know why."

The grin on Tompkins's face unnerved Reed. "Cheaper for the county. Hell, we'll even foot the bill for the scum's buryin'."

"Why don't you just take Mister Johnson and Randy home, Jack? The law will handle this."

Tompkins shook his head. "We already got Boss Johnson loaded up in the chuck wagon in the coffin that darky at the livery put 'im in. Got Randy, all liquored up, loaded up, too. So we're all ready to go, after we finish up our business here."

"You've got no business here."

With a cackle, the foreman pulled on the reins and turned his horse. "You ain't no Scottish Gun, Reed," he said, trying to sound jovial to mask his anger as he rode away. "Do yourself a favor an' find some place else to sleep tonight."

"What happened to your eye?" Cameron asked, frowning when Amie shrugged. He didn't push her, though, simply lifted the package from his lap and placed it on the table before their supper arrived. She stared at it, wet her lips, and, finally, shyly glanced at him. Someone had given her a shiner, and he wanted to know who, wanted to track down that piece of dung and teach him some manners, but Amie would never tell, and, when her eyes began to sparkle, he forgot all about revenge.

"Open it," he said eagerly.

He smiled as the paper crinkled and her tiny fingers worked the knots the old lady had tied back at the mercantile. *When was the last time I bought a woman a gift?* he wondered, but couldn't remember the answer. It didn't matter. He was content living in the present, not the past, watching as she finally pulled the paper away and gasped.

"Ben . . . it's . . . it's beautiful!"

"Ain't sure it'll fit," he said. She held it up, wanting

to find a mirror. He wouldn't trade this moment for anything. This would be the way he always pictured Amie Courtland. The waitress set their plates and glasses in front of them and left. Everyone in the Dead Canary stared. Cameron didn't mind that one bit.

"I. . . ." Amie started crying.

He reached inside his pocket and realized he had bought no handkerchiefs and had thrown his old ones away with the rest of his miserable clothing. Of course, he could untie his bandanna, but what kind of gentleman did that? Suddenly he felt like a fool and looked around uncomfortably, trying to figure out what he could give her. Maybe the waitress would bring him a napkin. Maybe. . . .

He froze.

"Ben Cameron, as I live and breathe!" shouted the fat man with the big hat and mustache. "It's been far, far too long, *amigo.*"

Colonel Thaddeus K. Hall sat down at the table, uninvited, and Amie must have read something in Cameron's face because she quickly began stuffing the dress into the brown paper. Ignoring her, Hall just kept on talking, smiling, and puffing on his pipe.

Can I ever be shun of him? Cameron shuddered.

"What brings you to Purgatoire, Benji?" Hall asked.

"I might ask you the same." The contents in his stomach started roiling.

Laughing, Hall tapped his pipe against the table. He never even considered Amie, and Cameron hated him even more for that. "Pursuit of a story, Benji," the colonel said. "What else? You look dapper in those eyeglasses, by the way. Mother of God, I don't believe I've seen you look this good in ages. How long has it been, *amigo?"*

He honestly couldn't remember. *Cheyenne . . . Fort Fetterman . . . Denver?* He had likely been drunk. No, they had both been drunk wherever it was—no *likely* to it.

If Hall heard Cameron's sigh, he didn't let on. For a time, Cameron had blamed Hall for his own drunkenness, but now considered that hatred misplaced. Maybe Hall fueled the flames, but Cameron had been no stranger to John Barleycorn when he had met the journalist down in Brownsville seventeen years ago. He had shared a few beers and several shots of rye and tequila with Jamie Courtland, Sergeant Armstrong, and others. Truth be told, he had been known to sneak away from his mother in Vicksburg and sip the swill the Rebels called corn liquor during the Yankee siege. Yet whiskey had never bested him, controlled him, consumed him, until Hall entered his life, and Cameron clearly recalled that, when he had tried to quit drinking before, he had never started backsliding until the colonel showed up.

Now, Hall was back.

Cameron stood, his meal untouched.

"Don't run off, Benji," Hall began, but stopped, unable to match Cameron's stare. The colonel cleared his throat before rising, said something about catching up later, when Cameron wasn't so rushed, and wandered out of the café.

How in hell did he find me . . . again?

He didn't realize Amie stood by his side, dress underneath her arm, until she nudged him. "You can stay here and finish your supper," he told her wearily, but she shook her head. He tossed a coin onto the table, and led her outside. The colonel had vanished, inside the hotel most likely. Cameron wanted to leave Purgatoire now, ride out, take Amie with him. He could sell his horse, buy a ticket on the stagecoach, and roll out at first light. No, he couldn't sell the horse. Not Goliad. He should go check on the gelding, had been neglecting him far too long.

The few people on the boardwalks had stopped, staring down Front Street, a few fingers pointing, most of them whispering. Cameron adjusted his new eyeglasses and frowned. He had seen this sight too often all across the West. A body, covered by a gray woolen blanket, had been secured over a saddle, and a horse was being led by a man on foot. A sudden sob from Amie startled him, and he whirled to find that she had dropped the dress and backed against the café's wall, hand over her open mouth, lips trembling. Cameron turned for a better look at the somber procession that had upset Amie. The man, a townsman Cameron had heard called Boeke, looked solemn as he pulled horse and body toward the marshal's office. The corpse's face remained covered, but Cameron now knew who it was.

Chapter Twenty

Red locks spilled from underneath the blanket before Glenn Boeke uncovered the body in the marshal's office. The door opened partway as Joshua Reed worked up the courage to kneel over the dead prostitute, staring up at him with green eyes coated with death's film, streaks of dried blood stretching down pallid cheeks from both corners of her open mouth. Her front teeth had been knocked out, and her cotton blouse, ripped, was also matted with brown stains.

Ben Cameron told somebody to wait outside, slid through the narrow opening—keeping it that way to protect anyone from seeing the corpse—and closed the door. Cameron shuddered as he focused on the gruesome body, which somehow made Reed feel a bit of relief, knowing that a hardened lawman such as The Scottish Gun could be affected just as much as he was.

"She put up a fight," Boeke said to no one in particular, "more than Johnson or that other whore."

The out-of-work newspaperman went on. He had gone out riding south of town that morning in hopes of bagging a turkey for supper, and had hobbled his mount at the abandoned gristmill over on the Picketwire, about a quarter mile from the Masonic Lodge. He just happened to look down and he spotted dried blood on some leaves by the dilapidated building. Suspicious, he pushed open the door and stepped inside. It was dark, and he didn't notice the dead woman until he tripped over her body.

Boeke's eyes suddenly widened, and, when he spoke, his voice trembled in panic. "Should I have left her there, Joshua? I didn't even think about that. I can tell you where I found her, if you want me to, show you everything."

Shaking his head, Reed assured Boeke that everything was fine, then rose, hoping his knees wouldn't betray him, and asked Cameron if he would mind examining the body.

The gunman squatted. "Knifed," he said. "A lot. Looks like a dirk. Dead a day or more, I guess." He gently closed her eyes.

"What was her name?" Reed asked.

"Denise . . . give me a sack of tobacco once." Cameron shook his head sadly, and lifted the dead woman's right arm, stretching out her cold fingers.

Reed tried to think. Could Ezekiel McGregg have murdered this one, too, before he had been arrested? Perhaps. A new theory ran through his mind: The preacher hated prostitutes, had murdered the Mexican and this one, and had killed Randall Johnson because he found out. It made sense to him.

"He's right." Cameron nodded at Boeke. "She did put up a fight. Scratched whoever killed her. Scratched him pretty good. Blood underneath three fingernails."

"Some damned crazy man's killing those whores," said Boeke, his eyes suddenly alight over the shock of finding a brutally murdered body, and realizing that he had a fantastic newspaper story if only he had a newspaper to publish.

Reed didn't care about that. He hurried across the office, jerked open the heavy door, and walked to Ezekiel McGregg's cell. "Take off that coat," he commanded, "and roll up your shirtsleeves."

"This hotel's all right, Colonel."

Stretched out on the bed in his socks and puffing on a cheap cigar, Keno Thompson grinned as Thaddeus K. Hall closed the door behind him.

What would you know about good hotels? Hall thought savagely, but held his tongue. *You've never slept anywhere but wagon yards, bunkhouses, and hog ranches.* The Picketwire Hotel was a dismal excuse, a seedy affair with bad food, dirty linens, and an unfriendly staff. Hall had stayed at the Exchange, Driskill, St. James, Dodge House, and the Vesey, fine accommodations across the West, even the Astor in New York. Now he was forced to live like a rat.

"It's gettin' a mite chilly, Colonel. Mind shuttin' that winder?"

And live with rats, as well. Fuming, Hall crossed the room, slammed the window down, collapsed in an uncomfortable chair, and fumbled for his flask.

"When do I get to kill Ben Cameron?" the drunken oaf asked.

Hall took pleasure in watching the smug little face turn sour when he said: "He's sober."

Plucking the cigar from his mouth, Thompson rolled over to face Hall. "I thought you said he's been roostered for years now. That's what I heard, too."

He shook his head. "He's sober." The drink felt good as it burned its way to his stomach, calming him after seeing Cameron's dark eyes burning into his soul. Ben Cameron had come to hate Thaddeus K. Hall almost as much as Hall hated The Scottish Gun he had created.

"Don't worry, Thompson." Hall took another pull on his flask. "I've seen Cameron try to dry out before. He'll be drunk as a skunk in a day or two."

"Maybe I should just kill him sober," Thompson said. "I ain't a-feared of that piece of trash."

That amused Hall, who shook his head with a chuckle. "You wouldn't stand a chance. I've known Benji more than fifteen years. Call it luck, providence, or whatever, that man has instincts like none I've ever seen. When he's sober, you can't touch him. So just sit back and relax. You'll kill him when he's drunk."

Thompson set the cigar on the end of the table, not even searching for an ashtray, and produced that token from his vest pocket. "Maybe I should pay that Susan what's-her-name a visit."

"No."

"Why not?" The fool looked like a petulant child. "You said I could have me some whores while we was waitin'."

"That's before I knew Benji was on the wagon. I

don't want him to see you until you're killing him."

Thompson pushed the coin back into his pocket. "Why is it you want to see him dead so much, Colonel? That part I ain't figured out."

You'd never figure it out if I spelled it out for you. Hall closed his eyes. A simpleton like Keno Thompson would never understand Hall's hatred. He had made Ben Cameron a name every schoolboy from Sacramento to Savannah knew, had gotten him jobs, had bought him clothes and watches, had shown him Chicago, St. Louis, New York, and Washington, D.C. In return, Cameron had dropped Hall like a hot stone, dismissed him, disliked him, blamed him for his problems with whiskey, his failing eyesight, everything that had gone wrong in his life. Without Cameron, Hall had seen his own career sink. *Look at me now, drinking bad whiskey, bunking with a lunatic, and hanging my hat in this hell-hole.* Soon, however, he would have a second chance to taste success, and revenge. Cameron would be dead, and Hall would be wooed by publishers, governors, and ladies.

"It's no concern of yours," he told Thompson. "You just think about your mother, how she wants Cameron dead, how much that will please her so. Sit tight. I'll go fetch us a bottle and supper."

Ben Cameron felt like he could kill a man for a drink, yet he steeled himself, pulled Amie Courtland closer, and let her sob on his chest. He held her tightly, and she likely thought he was consoling her, comforting her, but he needed her as much as she needed him. Tighter. The longing for whiskey passed, and he lessened his hold. Amie pulled away, dabbing her eyes with her sleeves, saying she had to tell Louis about Denise. Tucking the dress underneath her arm again, she crossed the street. Cameron followed her.

How could today have gone so wrong, turned out so badly? One minute, Amie glittered like a beacon, beautiful, happy, and then the colonel had arrived, souring Cameron's stomach, making the walls close in on him. Moments later, they had seen the body of Denise, one of Amie's friends. He had to get out of Purgatoire and take Amie with him.

He glanced at the unhitched stagecoach over by the livery stable. The jehu was pointing to the left front wheel, talking to the black stable hand. They'd leave Purgatoire after dawn, and Cameron wanted to be on that stagecoach, needed Amie to be beside him, wearing her new dress. To hell with Goliad. He'd sell him. He'd do anything to put Purgatoire behind him. He tried to close his eyes, but kept seeing Denise's face . . . and the face of the young Mexican . . . and the face of that other whore, the one strung up in some sickening crucifixion back in Fort Worth.

Cameron had been working for the Pinkertons then, and some wealthy cattle baron from Tarrant County had hired the agency to look into the prostitute's grisly murder. No one asked the cattleman's interest in the dead girl—lover? family? friend?—because he was paying the bills, and the Pinkertons respected their clients' privacy and need for diplomacy. As far as Cameron knew, that case remained unsolved. He had been too drunk to do any sound investigating, the client had given up on the matter, and Cameron—and Colonel Hall, he now remembered—took a train back to Chicago.

He couldn't really suspect Hall of being a killer of prostitutes, could he? Crazy. He shook his head, telling himself he was becoming just like Joshua Reed, coming up with theories for everyone.

"What?"

They stood in front of The Texas House. Cameron looked at Amie, forced a smile, and shook his head. "Nothin'. Was just thinkin' aloud, I reckon."

When she put her right hand on the top of the batwing door, Cameron touched her shoulder gently, whispered her name, and froze when she turned. Words failed him. She considered him a moment, and started to go inside. It was already past four o'clock, and Diva would raise hell, but now he blurted it out: "Let's leave, Amie. Get out of Purgatoire."

Before someone murders you. He shuddered again, had to look away from her, to get that thought out of his head, but, instead, he saw the long bar, saw the two bartenders pouring beers, and the need for a drink started to crush him. He made himself look back at Amie. "We can take the stage tomorrow mornin'."

"Where would we go?"

He smiled, genuinely. "Wherever."

225

She leaned against him, hugging him. "Do you mean it?"

He barely heard her. "Yes." He was running away again, but this time he had a good reason. Purgatoire didn't need him. Joshua Reed had his suspect locked up, and Cameron owed the marshal nothing. He had pointed out Consuela's bruises, had helped out with the other murders. That was payment in full. He'd run away with Amie, leave Purgatoire, the murders, and Colonel Hall behind.

"I'll tell Diva."

"Not yet," he said, although he didn't know why. "Don't tell anyone. You just come down for breakfast, or to wash your clothes, and leave. Don't pack. Don't do nothin'. Just leave." He smiled again. "Just wear that pretty dress."

"But, Ben . . . I have books, letters, some. . . ."

"Nothin', Amie. I mean it. Don't tell anyone, don't bring anything. We'll send for it, maybe, later." He kissed her forehead for reassurance. "Trust me."

As if he could trust himself.

"All right." She kissed him warmly, but all too briefly, and the batwing doors flapped noisily as she left. He checked his timepiece, the one Amie had returned to him. It felt suddenly colder, and he looked up at the gray clouds. The wind became more pronounced, and he headed to the livery to see about buying a couple of tickets to Trinidad. Then he'd sell Goliad. No, he couldn't sell that old gelding, but he had a pretty good idea who might look after the horse a while. He would send for Goliad and Amie's traps sometime . . . after they got settled.

"There were no scratches on the preacher's arms," Reed told Cameron as he poured the gunman a cup of coffee. Shaking his head, Reed went on: "No scratches anywhere that I could see."

Cameron didn't look surprised as he accepted the tin cup. "Still, that redhead was a whore," Reed continued, "and she could have scratched one of her customers, not just the killer. I hear those Bar J boys got out of hand last night. And I still have enough to hang him for Mister Johnson's murder."

It was irksome, Cameron's shrug, the way it dismissed Reed's theories without comment. Cameron sipped his coffee, crossed his legs, and asked: "Did the preacher ever say how he got the quirt?"

"Says he found it. Says it was just laying there, a gift from God. Says Johnson had no need for it any more."

Another damned shrug.

"Well, what do you think?" Reed had had enough. Jack Tompkins and the Bar J boys would be coming in tonight, to lynch Ezekiel McGregg, and he couldn't hold them off. His nerves felt raw, so he snapped at Cameron. "Don't just sit there and shrug. I have three murders on my hand in a week."

The legs uncrossed, and Cameron set his cup on the floor beside him. Pushing back his hat, he reached inside his coat pocket and pulled out the makings.

Reed tossed two more logs into the stove to pass the time, knowing by now that Cameron wouldn't say anything until he had taken at least one drag on the cigarette.

"I'm not much of a detective, son," Cameron finally began. "Don't believe those books by. . . ." He shook his head, leaving the sentence unfinished. "The Mexican was strangled to death. Johnson was shot at close range. Denise was stabbed."

"McGregg had a butcher knife," Reed fired out.

"With a dirk." Cameron had shot him down again.

Reed held his hands over the stove. It was getting cold, really cold, and an early snow would not surprise him. "You're not suggesting three different people killed them, are you?"

"I ain't suggestin' nothin', just layin' down facts. It could be three murderers, or it could be a smart one."

"Just say something, mister! Anything. Make a guess. I'm at my wit's end."

He finished the cigarette before complying. "All right. My guess is you have one killer. He strangled the little Mexican. Figured she wouldn't put up much of a fight. You said Johnson suspected who might have killed her, so he went to confront the killer. He got shot for his troubles. Johnson was a powerful man, so the killer didn't give him no chance. Then he kills Denise, stabs her, but she puts up a fight, gouges his arm, cheek or something."

"Why not shoot her? Or strangle her like the other one?"

Cameron started to shrug, but stopped himself, and grinned, which Reed couldn't help but return. "That mill's close to town. Likely the killer didn't want no one to hear the shot, figured a girl wouldn't put up much of a fight. She'd be just like Consuela, but maybe too strong to strangle. So he stabbed her, but she was tougher than he figgered. Got him with her nails." He flicked the remains of the cigarette into a spittoon, and picked up his cup. "Anyway, that's just a thought. I'm probably way off. And I ain't got no idea 'bout a reason for the killin's, 'ceptin' Johnson's."

Reed liked the theory, though. Now, all he had to do was find someone with scratch marks on his body, but he could also use a motive. If Ezekiel McGregg were innocent, who had killed them, and why?

"Thanks," Reed said.

"It ain't nothin'," Cameron said. "Anyway, I come to see you about . . . well, I was wonderin' if I might pay you to look after Goliad, my horse, till I can send for him."

Reed straightened. "You're leaving town?"

When Cameron nodded, Reed couldn't help but stare at the man's arms. He wore a heavy shirt and coat, but who didn't in this weather? Still, three people had died after Cameron had arrived in town, and he had spent a lot of time at The Texas House. Cameron had killed before—thirty or forty times, if you believed the penny dreadfuls—and the jehu for the stage line had told him that afternoon that The

Scottish Gun had killed a fellow down in Trinidad before coming to Purgatoire, had killed him with a knife. Cameron said the redhead had been killed with a dirk, and a dirk was a Scottish weapon, wasn't it?

"Want me to roll up my sleeves?" Cameron suddenly asked.

Reed swallowed, recovered, and shook his head with an apology. "He's a good horse," Reed said, changing the subject. "Sure, I'll look after him. When are you leaving?"

"On the stagecoach, day after tomorrow."

That caught Reed by surprise. "The stage leaves tomorrow," he said.

"Something's busted on one of the wheels," Cameron said. "That's what the messenger told me. Won't leave till Friday."

Reed softly swore.

"I ain't happy 'bout it neither," Cameron said as he stood to refill his coffee cup.

Hearing a horse whinny above the wind, Reed walked to the window, pulled back the curtain, and cursed again. "Wait here," he told Cameron, lifted a Winchester from the gun cabinet, and stepped outside into the bitterly cold night.

Chapter Twenty-One

They came with violently flickering torches that cast eerie shadows, walking their horses, rifles cradled in laps or butted against thighs. Tightening his grip on the carbine, Reed stepped to his right, away from the door, closer to the wooden column and water barrel, the only shelter he would have if the Bar J boys started shooting. Jack Tompkins, Quincy, and, to Reed's astonishment, Randy Johnson took the point, reining up a few paces from the marshal's office. Even in the dim light, Reed could tell that Johnson could barely sit in his saddle, he was so drunk, but the rest of the cowhands appeared resolute.

"We've come for the preacher, Reed!" Tompkins had to shout to be heard over the wind.

Reed's head shook. "You're making a mistake, Jack. I don't think McGregg killed your boss."

"You still got 'im locked up in the calaboose."

"For his own protection," Reed lied. "Listen, the red-headed whore scratched her killer, and there's not a mark on McGregg."

Quincy spoke this time: "All that proves, boy, is that *maybe* that little parson didn't kill her. But he sure killed Boss Johnson, stole his quirt."

"Killed him with what?" Reed suddenly realized how wrong he had been. He should have read Cameron's shrugs and non-answers. Ezekiel McGregg hadn't killed anyone, never should have been arrested. What a pathetic job he was doing as town marshal. "He doesn't have a gun. He told me he found Mister Johnson dead, picked up the quirt, and that's all. The only thing he's guilty of is poor judgment, petty theft."

Tompkins swung from the saddle, and Quincy followed the foreman's lead. Another cowboy produced a lariat with the coils of a hangman's noose, but remained in his saddle.

"Randy!" Reed cried out in desperation. "You can stop this." He wasn't sure about that, couldn't quite figure out why Randy had ridden with them. The boy had loathed his father, had blamed him for his girlfriend's murder, but now the rancher's son only gripped the saddle horn tighter. Tompkins and Quincy had likely talked the boy into coming along, building up the revenge obligation, and Randy Johnson was too drunk—forgetting that pledge to his mother—too distraught to know better.

"I tol' you to spend the night somewhere else, Reed," he heard Tompkins saying. "Now put down that gun. Don't be no fool."

Tompkins stepped up beside him. He carried only a torch, no weapon that Reed could see, but most of the cowboys now had their guns trained on him. Reed didn't drop the carbine, just held it against his chest, unable to move or speak. With a nod from the foreman, Quincy stepped up behind Tompkins. The two men exchanged whispers, and Quincy opened the door to Reed's office.

The explosion was deafening.

Quincy was catapulted backward into the street, horses reared, men shouted, but still Reed could not move. Things happened slowly, as if in a dream. Tompkins dropped the torch, started to spin around, reaching behind his back for a pocket Remington, then let out a rabid cry and dropped at Reed's feet. Another explosion and a blinding flash of savage light. The cowboy holding the hangman's rope reeled, dropping the lariat, sliding off his mount, bouncing off the saddlebags of a spooked horse, and landing on the dirt, covering his head with one arm for protection against pounding hoofs.

"How many of you sons-of-bitches want to die tonight?"

Movement and noise sped up considerably, and he breathed in the heavy scent of gunpowder. Only then did Reed see Cameron, standing over the supine form of Jack Tompkins. Cameron held a shotgun in his left hand, the double barrels stuck in the foreman's mouth, and the Schofield in his right, pointed at the cowboys, the dancing flames reflecting off Cameron's eyeglasses and giving him a ghostly appearance. Tompkins's nose had been turned into an ugly mess, hardly recognizable, his mustache soaked in blood. Quincy lay writhing in pain, while the other wounded cowboy had managed to crawl in front of the horses, away from the hoofs, and had clamped a hand over a crimson shoulder, mumbling something about his mother before passing out, or maybe he was dead; Reed couldn't tell.

Flames licked from dropped torches, and the cowboys regained control of their horses. The only sound came from the wind, and Quincy's unnerving screams: "Gawd A'mighty, Gawd A'mighty, my legs, my legs! Gawd A'mighty, boys, I'm kilt for certain."

Reed felt his heart pounding and suddenly reacted. He swung the Winchester up to his shoulder, jacked a round into the chamber, and covered the lynch mob. Footsteps sounded, and he could make out the forms of townsmen hurrying to investigate.

"Well?" Cameron demanded. "Come on, you yeller bastards! I'm gonna blow off this cowboy's head, then shoot as many as you stupid peckerwoods as I can. You wanted this dance, now who'll start the ball?"

The townsmen stopped, keeping a safe distance. No one moved; no one spoke again, except Quincy. The wind wailed.

Reed glanced at Tompkins, his bloody face pale, eyes wide in fright, gagging on the shotgun rammed in his mouth. He couldn't make out Cameron's face, except the reflection from his glasses, because of the shadows, but he didn't need to, or want to. He had seen the gunman shaking so much over the past few days, but now the heavy Schofield did not waver. At first, he thought the shotgun was Cameron's Parker, but he realized it was his own weapon, one he used for goose hunting. Cameron must have lifted it from the gun cabinet. Reed found his voice, told the cowboys to drop their weapons.

Now they moved, slowly, pitching their rifles to the ground, unbuckling gun belts. A few dismounted to help the wounded, and Cameron lifted the shotgun out of Tompkins's mouth, and the foreman rolled underneath the hitching rail, leaving a trail of blood, and scrambled to his feet.

"Go on," Reed told the townsmen. "Go on, now. It's all over."

He watched the Bar J boys load their wounded and retreat, leaving the hardware and torches on the ground. They disappeared in the darkness, and only then did Reed realize how much he was shaking. He started to say something to Cameron, but the gunman had gone back inside the office. Reed left the guns and torches in the street, stepped through the open door to find his goose gun on the floor and Cameron in a chair by the stove, just staring, Schofield still in his right hand.

Reed pulled the door shut, bolted it, and walked to the cabinet, lowering the hammer on the Winchester before placing the rifle in its cradle. He let out an audible sigh. His knees buckled, and he quickly retreated to his desk, collapsing in his chair.

Seconds passed before Cameron spoke.

"Now you know why I drink," he said.

His head cleared, and Cameron eased down the hammer before holstering the Schofield. A drawer scratched, followed by the sound of a bottle against wood, the pop of a cork, and the gurgling of liquid. He blinked, looked up, and found Reed filling two coffee cups from a half empty bottle of rye. Reed brought over the cups, placing one in Cameron's trembling hands, then killing his drink quickly, stifling a cough, muttering a curse, and falling back in his chair.

He could smell the whiskey, almost taste it, tried not to look at it, only he couldn't help himself. His mouth watered as he stared at the three fingers in the tin cup. *Just one drink. just this one. To steady my nerves.* He needed this one, needed it something fierce, needed it so much even Reed knew it. If anyone deserved a drink tonight, it was Ben Cameron. He had stopped a lynching, had wounded three men, two of them perhaps mortally. Jack Tompkins had been a good sort. Cameron recalled joking with him at The Texas House, reliving Cameron's days as city marshal in Caldwell, yet that had not stopped Cameron from smashing the waddie's nose with the shotgun's stock, then jamming both barrels into the frightened man's mouth, busting out his front teeth.

Cameron didn't even know why he had given Reed a hand. He couldn't even remember going to the cabinet and picking up the long-barreled shotgun, checking the breech. All he remembered was the door flying open, and the face of a silver-haired gent with a fat belly, seeing a mask of terror replace a determined grin a second before Cameron cut loose with one barrel and rushed outside.

The faint report of a gunshot made him blink. It also snapped Reed from his trance. Cameron remained in his seat, staring at the cup filled with rye, as Reed walked past him. A blast of cold wind attacked him, then nothing. The door shut, and he was alone.

Cameron looked again at the whiskey, lifted the cup, and threw it savagely across the office. It *clanged* against the gun cabinet, splashing its contents everywhere before falling to the floor. He immediately regretted his actions, scrambled to his feet, raced across the room, and scooped up the cup, looking at it, cursing its emptiness, and throwing it across the room again. He fell on his backside, crawled to Reed's desk, jerked open the bottom drawer, and pulled out the bottle.

Empty! Why did Reed put an empty bottle back in the desk drawer? Cursing the marshal, he smashed the bottle against the open drawer, cutting the fingers on his right hand. He was out of breath now, staring at the bandage on his left hand, the one hiding the stitches, and he thought again of Amie.

He had to see her, had to be with her. She gave him strength. She could stop him from getting drunk again. So he pulled himself to his feet and staggered outside, leaving the door open.

An excited Joe Miller was telling Potter Stone, Diva, Susan Falconer, and Celestial Cindy Haggin what had just happened over at the marshal's office when the batwing doors banged open. Louis Venizelos had only been half listening to Miller's report, unsure how he really felt about Cameron and the marshal stopping the Bar J outfit from lynching that fiend, how he wished he had killed that sky pilot a few days back, after the preacher had slapped Denise. If he had done that, Denise might still be alive, and maybe they'd be leaving town on the stagecoach to start over. He looked up at the doors, and swallowed.

Ben Cameron made a beeline for the bar.

"Diva," Venizelos whispered, and jutted his chin in Cameron's direction.

"Aw, hell, Louis," she said with a smile after spotting the gunman. "I reckon he's got reason to celebrate. Pour him a drink, Louis, a Scotch, on the house." With a laugh, she headed for her office.

Venizelos couldn't bring himself to pour The Scottish Gun a whiskey, but Joe Miller had no qualms, and slid a glass to him. Cameron caught it, stared at it briefly, then shook his head.

"Some night, huh?" Cindy said.

"I want to see Amie." Cameron spoke to Venizelos, who shook his head sadly and poured himself a drink.

"She's busy, cowboy," Susan Falconer drawled, "but I'd be happy to make your acquaintance."

"Busy?"

Even the hardened Cindy dropped her head and wandered off to an empty table with China Rene.

"Busy," Falconer repeated, "but I ain't."

Cameron's fist swallowed the glass, and Miller laughed as he walked to the end of the bar with Potter Stone to fetch cigars.

"My name's Susan," the woman told Cameron, who stood there, struck speechless, suddenly sweating despite the chill. "Just got to town. Rode up on the stagecoach from Trinidad, and, yes, sir, I heard all about you, Mister Cameron. Folks are still talkin' 'bout what you done there. You should have spent your money at my place. Anyway, I got a letter from Kate . . . that's Diva, you know . . . packed my bags, and came up on the next stage, and I'm glad, because I've certainly wanted to meet The Scottish Gun since I was plyin' my trade down Fort Stockton way."

Cameron took his glass and fell in the nearest chair.

Frowning, Susan Falconer shook her head, downed her own drink, and looked up at the sound of a door closing. "Well, suh," she said, "I reckon Amie ain't so busy a-tall seein' how her latest customer's finished now."

Venizelos finished his drink as Cameron spun in his chair, his shoulders sagging as the man straightened his hat and bounded down the stairs angrily. The new-comer stopped halfway down, recognizing Cameron. Venizelos didn't know what to think, couldn't understand what was happening. Cameron said something, although he couldn't hear clearly, and the man on the staircase smiled suddenly as Cameron lifted the drink and killed it.

"Another round, my good man," Thaddeus K. Hall ordered the bartender, "for me and my old *amigo*." He had been so scared at the sight of Ben Cameron, he had almost soiled his britches, but The Scottish Gun returned to his old form and drank a shot of whiskey. Hall hurried down the stairs, slapped Cameron's back, and pulled up a chair behind him. "Good to see you, Benji, me boy," he said cheerily as two more whiskies arrived, delivered by the whore he had met on the stagecoach.

"Colonel," Susan Falconer demanded in jest, "I hope you did not use that token I gave you on Alabama Angel!"

Hall threw down his drink and let out a hoarse laugh, fishing out the coin she had given him on the stagecoach. "Of course not, Susan, and I'll be spending this on you in short order, but not tonight!" He pinched her buttocks as she walked away, delighted at her squeal, and returned the token. "Drink up, Benji," he told Cameron, and stopped himself. *Don't push him. He has had one whiskey. Everything will be fine, but don't rile him up so that he kills you.*

"You were up there . . . ?" Cameron began.

"Well, that's where you go in places like this." He changed the subject. "You deserve a drink, Benji. I hear you thwarted a lynch party this evening. Bully for you. You're The Scottish Gun, a hero, and it does me good to see you standing on your feet again." He ordered two more whiskies, although Cameron's remained untouched.

Fear returned, palpable, and his hands suddenly turned clammy. He thought those spectacles would make Cameron look less like a killer, but the lenses could not mask those cold eyes. Cameron's right hand had disappeared underneath the table, and Hall thought he might have pushed him too far. He wondered if he could reach for the pepperbox pistol in his coat pocket before Cameron killed him. Cameron was standing now, the legs of the chair scraping against the floor, making Hall's skin crawl.

When he had barged in on them at the café, Hall had pretended not to notice the carved-up whore at Cameron's table, but, when he saw her at The Texas House, he had decided on another way he could hurt Cameron, so had whisked her upstairs while Susan Falconer, who he had come to see, was busy entertaining the town mayor, or so he had been told.

Now, he was about to die, unless he told Cameron, of all things, the truth.

"Benji. . . ." He picked up Cameron's untouched whiskey and downed it. "Your lady's honor is intact." He laughed, shaking his head, and met the gunman's ghostly stare. "Hell, *amigo,* she told me *no!*"

Chapter Twenty-Two

Hearing the pounding of boots on the staircase, Amie Courtland corked the bottle of gin and slid it underneath her bed, standing up quickly, trying to think of what she'd tell Diva, or the man she had just insulted by telling him he could keep his dollar and leave. She pictured Denver again, the councilman hitting her, slashing her with the broken bottle, and considered it a miracle the big man had not attacked her minutes ago. She feared he was coming up the stairs. Worse, it might be Diva.

The door jerked open, and she gasped, unbelieving, as Ben Cameron swept her into his arms and kicked the door shut.

"You told 'im no!" Blabbering like a baby, kissing her face.

She had remembered the big man from supper at the Dead Canary, knew he was Colonel Thaddeus K. Hall, biographer of The Scottish Gun, and felt the tension between author and gunman. Yet she would have told anybody no, even Mayor Stone, on this night. She had found her courage, and had to credit Cameron for her strength. She kissed him back, trying not to laugh, but tasted and smelled whiskey on him, and suddenly pulled away.

"Ben. . . ."

"I know." He pulled her to him, hugging her tightly, almost crushing her. "I had a drink . . . one

. . . my last one, Amie. I promise you that."

She prayed he couldn't detect the gin on her lips and tongue.

"We're gettin' out of here," he said, and they fell onto her bed. "Takin' that stagecoach on Friday."

"I heard gunfire," she said.

"It's over. Tell you 'bout it later."

She pulled him close, running fingers through his hair, feeling his heart pounding, as well as her own. She felt so alive, so happy. This was real, not like Stan Gibbs. They needed each other, loved each other.

They crept downstairs early that morning, surprised to find Louis Venizelos filling lanterns with coal oil at the far end of the bar, and were shocked even more at the sight of Diva puffing on one of her foul-smelling cigars, a goblet in front of her. Cameron squeezed Amie's hand, nodded a greeting to both the bartender and the madam, and made his way toward the front door.

"It's locked!" Diva called out. "You'll have to use the back one. You ain't washin' your sheets this morn, Angel?"

Amie simply shook her head, and Diva didn't say anything else until they stood beside Venizelos, at which point she reminded both of them that the price for a full night remained $25. "And seein' how I somehow don't think my Alabama Angel collected, I'll take it, Mister Cameron. Right now."

243

The hard-frowning Venizelos dropped his right hand beneath the bar, likely searching for that night-stick, or maybe a revolver. Cameron reached into his vest pocket, counted out the greenbacks, and laid them in front of the lanterns and bucket on the bar.

"You missed all the excitement last night," Diva said, cheery again. "Randy Johnson blew his head off down by the livery after that little set-to at the marshal's office."

Amie let out a soft moan and shuddered, while Cameron glanced at the bartender for verification. Venizelos confirmed the news while reaching for the greenbacks and telling Diva: "We're out of coal oil. I'll have to get more when Miz Coburn opens up."

"Finish it this afternoon. Go on and get some sleep, Louis. Get Amie's lantern, and my other girlies' lanterns or lamps and bring 'em down and fill 'em up later." Her eyes remained locked on Cameron and Amie. "Wanna hear my theory?" She didn't wait for an answer. "That boy's pa kilt my Vaya Con Dios, and the boy kilt his pa for revenge. And he kilt Dirty Denise when she tried to blackmail him. What do you think of that, Mister Detective?"

Cameron had heard enough theories. He shrugged and led Amie out the back door.

They ate breakfast at the Dead Canary. Cameron's funds were dwindling, and he'd be glad to get out of Purgatoire, although he wasn't sure what they would do for money once they reached Trinidad, or afterward. He might have to sell Goliad, after all.

The Bar J boys had taken both dead Johnsons and their wounded down the mountain, they learned, and Marshal Reed and Mayor Stone seemed to concur with Diva's theory, although no one had checked Randy Johnson's body for scratch marks. Cameron tried to shake off his thoughts, telling himself he was finished with everything about Purgatoire. They ducked into the vacant billiards hall, where he picked up his Parker shotgun.

"This . . . ," Amie said incredulously. "This is where you've been sleeping?"

He shrugged, joking that it was less expensive than the hotel, or The Texas House for that matter, and more comfortable than the livery and jail. In truth, he had stayed there because he wanted to be closer to Amie, to protect her from whomever it was killing prostitutes. He handed her the shotgun. "You sneak this back upstairs," he said. "Keep it. It's loaded with buckshot, kicks like ol' Goliad."

She hesitated. "You don't think . . . ?"

"I don't know," he said. "Just take it . . . for one more night."

When they walked out of the abandoned building, someone shouted his name. He stepped away from Amie, pushing back his coat, but relaxed almost immediately upon recognizing the stagecoach driver.

"We got 'er fixed, Mister Cam'ron," said the man, out of breath. "That ol' colored boy's a pretty fair wheelwright, so we'll be lightin' out 'bout four-thirty this afternoon. Wanted to let you know, since you bought the only tickets."

He could scarcely believe his luck. Not another night, just a matter of hours. The old jehu glanced at the shotgun in Amie's arms suspiciously, then spit out a mouthful of tobacco juice.

"Isn't it a late start, down that mountain?" asked Cameron, not believing this turn of fortune.

"Can be risky." The jehu nodded, moved the plug of tobacco to his other cheek, and pointed skyward. "But she's lookin' threatenin', and I don't want to spend another night in this piss pot." Cameron had to agree with him there. "'Sides, we got mail to deliver, and them guvment contractors nitpick like sons-of-bitches. Anyway, four-thirty. I gotta go see if them gents I hauled up here wanna ride back down today." He tipped his hat, and crossed the street toward the hotel.

Excitedly Cameron led Amie to the back door, kissed her gently on the lips, and told her to meet him at three-thirty. She could tell anyone, if questioned, that she was taking an early supper before business started at four. They'd be gone before anyone realized it. Amie offered him the shotgun, and he started to take it, but shook his head. "Keep it," he said, and stopped himself from adding: *Just in case.* He kissed her again. "Wear that new dress," he said with a smile.

He didn't know why he was there. Cameron pushed open the door to the old mill, where Denise Benbrook had been murdered, and struck a match. Diva's theory sounded as good as anything Marshal Reed had ever offered, maybe even better, and she even had a motive: Denise had been blackmailing the killer. Cameron had never even thought of that. He felt sober, clean, confident, better than he had in years. He put last night's shoot-out with the Bar J boys behind him and thought of the future, a life with Amie. He had once been a pretty good lawman, might have made a good detective if not for the binges, but something gnawed in his stomach. As much as he told himself he could leave Purgatoire without a regret, he wanted everything to add up, and he didn't want some lunatic stalking Amie in their new life, although that sounded as far-fetched as some of Marshal Reed's theories.

He left the mill unsatisfied, walked back to town, and mounted his horse at the livery. Being in the saddle again felt good, and he gave Goliad plenty of rein as they rode past the mine to the spot where Randall Johnson had been murdered. Holding the reins, he knelt, closed his eyes, tried to picture what had happened. Randall Johnson had come here to meet the killer, the man who had murdered the young Mexican, but he had left his revolver in his waistband. Why? Cameron did not know the rancher, but the man had not struck him as a fool. He had borrowed a gun from his foreman, but he had not pulled the weapon. Why would he meet Consuela's murderer here? What had brought him here? What was his part in this whole affair?

He dropped the reins to let Goliad drink and graze while he wandered about the site, crossing the river, studying the ground, trying to find something. He waded the Picketwire again, leaned against a pine, and sighed. Cameron checked his pocket watch. It was well past noon, so he gave up, and rode back to town.

"Nice ride?" the stable hand asked.

"All right," he answered.

"You got a good hoss. He needed some exercise."

Cameron tossed the man a quarter tip, thanked him, and started to leave. "Did you find Randy Johnson's body?" he asked.

"Yes, sir." The man stared uncomfortably at his brogans. "Heard the shot, right after you and Marshal Reed had turned back them cowboys. Come out here . . . found him by the corral. Shot hisself in the head." He shook his head sadly. "He'd been drinkin', just a-mopin' 'round since his gal got . . . since she died."

That made sense. The one thing he felt certain of was that Randy Johnson had committed suicide. Nothing else added up, though.

"You find any marks on his body? Other than the bullet hole?"

"No." He shook his head. "Didn't really look, though. Marshal Reed come by right after it happened, but then some Bar J boys rode back up, took Mister Randy's body away. They done left town this mornin'. You don't think . . . ?"

"I don't know what I'm thinking." He thanked the stable hand again, and walked toward the marshal's office.

Keno Thompson had been waiting long enough. He told Colonel Hall he needed open spaces, that he wasn't used to living like some cooped-up chicken, hiding out in a hotel room, but the colonel just told him to shut up and wait. Hell, the colonel had made at least one trip to that fancy cathouse across the street, had been to the saloon downstairs, even that eating house, while Thompson had been playing solitaire poker since he had never learned how to play regular solitaire, drinking whiskey, smoking cigars, and wishing some chambermaid would come here and clean out that pot.

Well, the colonel was gone again, had said something about seeing if Cameron was drunk, but he had been gone too long, and Thompson couldn't stand staring at the walls any more. This waiting around bored him even more than the times up in Wyoming when he hid out to dry-gulch some rustler. He fingered the token the fancy lady in the pink dress had given him, found the colonel's token by the wash basin, and decided it was high time he treated himself. He buckled on his gun belt, checked the loads in his Colt, pulled on his bowler, and opened the door just enough to peer down the hall. He didn't see anybody, so he stepped outside, hurried down the stairs, and raced across the street. The front of The Texas

House was all locked up, but he darted down the alley, turned the corner, headed up the steps, and tried the back door. It swung open, and he laughed. He could picture the colonel's face when he showed back up at that hotel. That was fine with Thompson. It was about time the colonel figured out who bossed this outfit.

He went through the kitchen and stepped into the parlor, only this parlor looked like a mighty fine saloon. Except that it smelled like coal oil. He saw a big fellow with eyeglasses, handing some scarred woman a lantern, and watched her take it upstairs. Then the big man spotted Thompson, and started to say something.

"It's all right, Louis."

Keno Thompson grinned, recognizing the voice.

Susan Falconer stepped into his view, took him by his arm, and led him to a table, asking the big man with the spectacles to stop with his lanterns and bring them a couple of stiff whiskies.

Amie set her lantern on her chest of drawers before undressing. She pitched the wool dress on her unmade bed, and picked up the fancy outfit Cameron had bought her. She held it against her body and stared at the mirror, smiling, catching herself in some solo waltz. Amie pulled on the dress, nervously working the buttons, and looked at her reflection again. The sight took her breath away. She hadn't worn anything this fancy since her nights in Martha

Cash's parlor houses. *I'll need new shoes,* she caught herself thinking and laughed aloud, stopping at a loud noise.

Downstairs someone was banging on the front door, cussing up a storm, and Louis Venizelos was yelling back, telling the visitor that The Texas House was closed, then shouting: "All right, all right, hold your horses."

A door *squeaked* open down the hall, and, moments later, someone tapped on the doorjamb. She glanced at Cameron's shotgun in the corner, dismissed the notion. The Texas House was closed. No visitors, except maybe the guy Venizelos was about to let in downstairs. She opened the door.

The only reason Louis Venizelos let Colonel Thaddeus K. Hall inside was because Susan Falconer told him to. She said Diva wouldn't mind, and that Hall had a lot of weight, might even write about The Texas House.

The colonel ripped off his big hat and walked with determination to Susan Falconer and the ugly little jackass in the dark bowler. "I told you to stay put!" Hall snapped, but Thompson just smiled and shook his head.

"Sit down, sit down," Susan Falconer was saying, and the colonel finally settled into his chair. "Bring the colonel a Scotch," she told Venizelos.

He was filling a tumbler with the last of the Scotch when he heard a shout upstairs.

"So you let the preacher go?" Cameron asked.

Joshua Reed nodded. "He left town, too. Took off right after I opened the cell door. Guess the lynch mob scared him out of town, and good riddance. Moses said he saw him walking down the road to Trinidad. Anyway, you were right. I had nothing on McGregg. I just fouled everything up. Some lawman I turned out to be."

Cameron's tone was placating. "I've fouled up more'n you, Joshua. More'n you'll ever know. Just put it behind you and keep goin' forward."

He couldn't remember Cameron ever calling him by his first name, and he beamed. He had loathed The Scottish Gun when he had ridden into Purgatoire, but Cameron had loathed himself back then. Reed liked this man, however, sober, calm, soothing, although those eyes still unnerved him. Excitedly Reed explained the theory, his newest, although he had to give Mayor Stone, and the madam, Kate "Diva" Weiss, most of the credit.

"Randall Johnson murdered the Mexican. He lured her to the Picketwire with a note, maybe promising her money, maybe letting her believe she'd be meeting Randy there instead. Then he killed her, to keep her from ruining his son. You told me yourself that Mister Johnson kept coming to The Texas House. And we both know Randy blamed his father for her death, so he murdered him. That would explain why he never tried to protect himself. He didn't think his son would kill him, didn't think his son had the nerve to pull the trigger. The redhead found out about it . . . maybe she saw it . . . and tried to blackmail him. Randy killed her, then couldn't live with himself, and wound up shooting himself."

He waited for Cameron to shrug, but the gunman's head bobbed slightly. "It's as good a theory as I've heard."

"Yeah." Reed wished he had checked Randy's body for scratches, though. "Anyway, as soon as the stagecoach leaves town with the mail, it'll be out of my hands and up to the sheriff. But I do thank you for your help, Mister Cameron."

"The name's Ben."

Reed shuffled some papers on his desk. He would miss Cameron, but would enjoy looking after that horse of his. Thoughts of the Tennessee Walker left his mind, and he started shaking his head again. "The one thing I can't figure out is why Mister Johnson met his son that far out of town, or let's say he was there to meet someone else. How did Randy know to find him there? I guess he followed him."

"Like you said," Cameron said, "once your letter. . . ." Cameron crushed out his cigarette with the toe of his boot. "Son-of-a-bitch!" he snapped, and bolted out the door.

A startled Reed leaped from his seat, grabbed a Winchester, and followed.

Chapter Twenty-Three

"Can I help you pack?" Diva asked.

Amie couldn't lie to her boss, no matter what Cameron had said, and there was no point in it now. The fancy dress, the books Amie had stacked on the bed, the look on her face . . . Diva knew. Cameron had told her not to bring anything, but she couldn't leave behind the letters, the dime novels about the man she hoped to marry. Besides, Diva had been good to her, well, most of the time. Some of the time.

"You . . . understand why . . . ?"

"You gonna marry him, honey?" Diva asked.

He hasn't asked me. She shrugged, a habit she had picked up from Cameron. "I don't know. I just . . . I'm sorry, Kate."

Diva let out a sad smile, and Amie felt for her. She looked like a wreck, kimono open, hair disheveled, hands behind her back, leaning against the open door. "It's the dream of every whore, Angel," said Diva, her voice distant. "To get married. Get out of the business. I bet you wouldn't believe it if I tol' you I had me some beaus . . . back in my early days. Was even engaged once. Turned yeller, he did. Damn' coward. Probably just as well, though."

Suddenly nervous, Amie wanted Diva to leave. "I don't need any help packing, Diva. I won't be taking much. Don't have much. Thank you. You'll tell Louis and the girls . . . good bye?"

Diva shrugged. She reached up with her left hand to brush the locks from her eyes. Amie turned, picked up Cameron's autobiography. It registered then, the marks on Diva's arm, and she spun around, raising the book, screaming as the dirk ripped through the cover and pages, the weight of the enraged madam overpowering her, both of them off balance, falling onto the floor. The point of the dirk bit into her, just below the ribs, and she felt the blood, a sharp pain. Diva jerked the weapon free, but it slipped, went bouncing across the floor.

"You think you can leave me, you little whore?" Diva shrieked. "You . . . that Mexican . . . Denise. Nobody leaves me! Not to get *married!*"

Diva shifted, looking for the weapon, but it had landed outside the room, by the staircase. She turned indecisive, and Amie took advantage, twisting, squirming, knocking Diva to one side, her head crashing against the mattress. Amie pulled her legs free, bent both knees, kicked the madam in the face. Blood spurted from Diva's nose, and she screamed even louder, falling backward, rolling, crashing against the chest of drawers. The lantern fell, cracked against the headboard, coal oil spilling, soaking the mattress.

Amie was on her feet, forgetting the shotgun, just wanting to get out of that room, downstairs, to Louis Venizelos, Ben Cameron, anyone who might help her. She made it out the door, but a hand jerked her ankle, and she pitched forward, the floor peeling off a layer of skin on her elbows as she slid toward the staircase. She saw the dirk, grabbed it, rolled over, threw it.

Diva held the shotgun, quickly lowered it in a defensive move, muttering something unintelligible, twisting, firing one barrel accidentally as the knife's handle struck the trigger guard. The concussion tore the shotgun from Diva's grasp. Amie gripped the balustrade, pulled herself to her feet, tried to move, but Diva smashed into her. They crashed onto the floor, and Diva's giant hands swallowed her throat, crushing the breath out of her. She smelled smoke from her room, somehow understood that the muzzle flash from the shotgun had ignited the coal-oil-soaked linens. What she couldn't understand was the sudden detonation of gunfire downstairs. Amie struggled, but Diva wouldn't budge, her face a hideous mask of anger, and Amie's strength failed.

Everyone looked upstairs, trying to figure out what in blazes was going on. Keno Thompson figured it was some kind of cat fight and couldn't help but grin, then he saw that the big, fat madam had a shotgun. The gun exploded, the woman fell, but jumped back on her feet, tackling the scar-faced whore. Susan Falconer yelled something, and the batwing doors flung open.

Thompson knew it was Cameron and figured the gunman came to kill him, although as to why he had bolted up the stairs, Thompson didn't have a clue. It didn't matter. The great Scottish Gun didn't even notice Thompson, simply ran for those brawling doves. Thompson whipped the Colt from his holster and fired. Fired again.

"No!" Colonel Hall yelled, and fancy Susan Falconer started screaming, too, only she was running out the door. So was the big bartender, not the one with the eyeglasses, but the other one.

Standing, Thompson cursed himself, firing a third shot. That one hit the railing on the staircase and showered Cameron's face with splinters. The gunman's gun was drawn, though, but he fell, halfway to the second story, crashing through the railing, landing on a table, which overturned. No movement now, so Thompson smiled grimly. Maw would be proud. He started over to put a bullet in Cameron's head, but Cameron lunged forward, snapped a shot that took off Thompson's bowler. Thompson jumped back, fired again, turned over the table, and took cover behind it.

Someone else stormed through the batwing doors, swinging a Winchester in Thompson's direction. To his amazement, Colonel Hall had drawn his little pepperbox, and fired at the newcomer, hitting him and flinging him back through the doors. Hall sent another shot at Cameron before ducking behind the table beside Thompson.

"Damn it!" Hall swore. He turned savagely to Thompson. "Why did you shoot?"

"Why did you?"

That stopped the colonel. "Didn't have time to think. I. . . ."

Cameron had fired again, splintering the wood above Hall's head, and the colonel cried out like a baby and began crawling on hands and knees, heading for the rear door. Thompson took another shot at Cameron, firing blindly, and ducked again, watching as Hall leaped to his feet and darted for the back door, chased by two bullets from Cameron's gun. Neither shot struck the colonel—one tore a chunk out of a wall painting and the other blew a hole in that can of coal oil. The colonel leaped through the back door.

Good riddance, you damn' coward. Only the colonel then did something peculiar. He struck a match, tossed the Lucifer on the floor, and the coal oil, spilling from the can, burst into flames. It spread fast, and Thompson realized the colonel had sealed off the back door. There was only one way out now. He turned to face Cameron, sent another bullet through the overturned table, then glanced up to see smoke pouring from one of the whoring rooms. The big madam had straddled the littler whore, as three other doves darted down the stairs, running out the front entrance. That left only Thompson and Cameron downstairs. No, the four-eyed barkeep was here, too. Thompson considered him briefly, but he just stood there, frozen stiff, staring at the flames, the violence, not even blinking.

He heard something, lifted his head. Cameron

pulled the trigger, but the hammer snapped loudly, and Thompson had him dead now. Only his Colt clicked empty, too, and both men disappeared behind their tables.

Thompson thumbed open the gate, began ramming out the empties. He pushed out .44-40 rounds from his shell belt, letting them roll by his thigh, and shoved one in the cylinder, another, another, feeling the heat from the growing flames both upstairs and down. He heard something else, too, couldn't figure it out, then he knew. Footsteps.

He was still trying to finish loading his Colt when he saw Cameron standing over the table, Schofield in his outstretched hand, and Thompson realized his mistake. He had been putting six beans in the wheel while Cameron had loaded only one round. Desperately Thompson snapped the loading gate shut, pulled the hammer to full cock. He was swinging the Colt around when the muzzle of Cameron's .45 flared.

Ben Cameron tossed the empty Schofield on the body of the man who had been trying to kill him. He had never seen him before, but didn't give him another thought, for now. He turned, hurried upstairs, lunging, flying, burying his shoulder into Diva, knocking her off Amie. He rolled over, coughing from the smoke, surprised to find that Diva had also recovered, charging. She lashed out at him, but he grabbed her wrists and, seeing the scabs on her upper right arm, knew he was right. He sum-

259

moned all his strength and shoved her backward, sending her disappearing into Amie's smoke-filled room. He heard the breaking of glass, the smashing of furniture. He chanced a look downstairs. Louis Venizelos stood at the bar, unmoving, while flames raced across the tinder-dry floor and walls. The heat from Amie's room almost took his breath away, so Cameron went to Amie and pulled her close. Her eyes fluttered, and he almost cried in relief. She was still alive. He stood, cradling her against him, then started down the stairs.

He tripped—no, Diva had tripped him, had crawled out of the room—and he dropped Amie, who tumbled downward, bouncing, sliding to a stop about where he had crashed through the railing when Colonel Hall and the stranger had opened fire on him.

"Nooooooo!"

Cameron rolled over, saw the screaming Diva, smoke billowing behind her, perhaps her kimono smoldering, too, and he recognized his Parker shotgun in her hands. He started for his Schofield only to remember he had tossed it aside, and sprang forward, covering Amie's body with his own. The explosion left his ears ringing, and he felt . . . nothing, no shotgun pellets riddling his body. He pulled himself up, looked at Diva.

She staggered against the wall, bringing the shotgun against her body, as blood pumped just below her left breast. The Parker slipped from her grasp, dropped at her feet, and she crashed over the railing, landing with a sickening *thud* on the floor below.

Amie groaned, and Cameron helped her to her feet. "Go," he said, as he spotted Louis Venizelos, a revolver in his hand. The bartender had snapped out of his shock, had killed Diva, saving Cameron's and Amie's lives, but now he stood frozen again. Cameron helped Amie downstairs. A burning timber crashed against the bar. "Get out of here," he told Amie, but she didn't budge, too tired, as he ran behind the bar, pried the Webley from Venizelos's hand, left the revolver on the bar, and pushed him, guided him, sent him through the flapping front doors. Amie just stood there, leaning against the wall, shaking her head.

"Come on," he said, and grabbed her, shoving her in front of him, stepping into the cold air, seeing the crowd lining the street. Then came the gunshot, Amie crashed against him, and they both fell.

Everything had turned out wrong for Thaddeus K. Hall. He had shot the town marshal, could see him lying in the street. There might be witnesses. He'd be sent to the prison at Canon City, or hanged, and Cameron would live. He had panicked, shooting Reed and setting the place on fire for some reason that made sense to him at the time, maybe hoping to burn Cameron and that fool, Keno Thompson. If Thompson had stayed in the hotel room, if he hadn't gone crazy and started shooting at Cameron. . . . He still had no idea what had started the brawl upstairs, or how everything had soured. He only knew he would be charged with murder and arson, but he could take Cameron with him.

That's why he drew the Ethan Allen .31-caliber pepperbox when he spotted Cameron standing behind the batwing doors. That's why he pulled the trigger. The little hideaway gun misfired, though, discharging all four remaining rounds simultaneously and ripping the gun from his hand.

He cursed, backing away from the stunned crowd of spectators and fire fighters, realizing his mistake, and started to say something, to explain everything. Ben Cameron had started the fire. Ben Cameron had killed the marshal. Ben Cameron. . . .

The town marshal, his shirt front covered in blood, had rolled over. Cameron was pulling himself to his feet, ignoring Hall, lifting the whore, carrying her across the street as flames and smoke leaped skyward from The Texas House. Hall swallowed, looked back at the marshal. He was alive. Maybe he wouldn't hang. Only the marshal was drawing his revolver.

"No!" Hall held out both arms. "I'm unarmed . . . !"

The pistol bucked in the marshal's arm, and a sledgehammer crushed Hall's chest. The world turned black, but only momentarily. His eyes fluttered. He lay on his back, staring at the gray sky. He couldn't move his arms or legs and felt so thirsty. He wet his lips with his tongue, tasted something, felt something stinging his face.

"Hey, it's snowing," Colonel Thaddeus K. Hall said, and died.

He was crying. Ben Cameron's tears had embarrassed her, angered her, the first time she saw him cry, but these were different. He had carried her across the street from the burning Texas House, and now held her tightly in his arms. She was vaguely aware of the heat from the inferno, the noise of the fire fighters and bucket brigade, and of the crowd gathered around her and Cameron.

Amie felt numb and cold—but no pain. That surprised her. She became aware of the dampness of her new dress, and knew she had peed on herself; that embarrassed her. She felt warm blood spreading across her chest and heard a horrible sucking noise from her chest, which, strangely, did not bother her. What bothered her was that this dress, the fancy get-up Ben Cameron had bought, was ruined.

She focused on his face, wanted to apologize for the dress. He reminded her of her brother when he was eight or nine years old. *A wagon running over their blue-tick hound, and Jamie picking up the mangled dog and carrying him a mile back home. He dropped the dog*—Hank was its name; she had almost forgotten—*on the porch and dashed inside, yelling for help. The sight of Jamie, hysterical, covered in blood, scared Amie and her mother half to death. They were both checking Jamie for some awful cut when their father stormed into the house, demanding: "Who the*

*hell killed Hank and what's the sum-bitch doin'
bleedin' on our doorstep?"*

She tried to lift her hand and brush away Ben
Cameron's tears, but her arm wouldn't move. Nor
could she swallow. When she tried to tell him that
everything would be all right, a coughing fit erupted
and burned her lungs. He pulled her close, and she
vomited, some breakfast but mostly blood, and
groaned as the pain finally came.

She gasped for breath, couldn't find air, and tears
welled in her own eyes. Her chest burned savagely
while the rest of her body was freezing. After
Cameron wiped her mouth with his bandanna, she
tried to mouth the words *I love you,* but again all she
could do was cough. Her strength faded. Numbness
spread from her legs to her chest. It was as if she
could feel the life draining from her body. *Was this
how Jamie felt before he died?* she wondered.

Amie closed her eyes, and fought off a wave of pain
and nausea. She stared at Cameron again, locking on
his face, wanting him to be the last thing she saw on
this earth. She didn't want him to cry. Spasms shook
her, and she screwed her eyes shut, felt blood bubbling on her lips, forced her eyes open again.

Only now she couldn't find him. Just blackness.
Then she saw a light, brilliant, shining in the distance,
growing brighter, heading toward her. She forgot
about Ben Cameron, her brother, the pain racking her
body. Instead she just focused on the light. *If I can
reach it,* she thought, *everything will be fine.*

Chapter Twenty-Four

A dusting of snow covered Amie Courtland's grave as Cameron knelt, holding an unopened bottle of King Bee whiskey in a gloved right hand. Her name was carved into a small wooden cross, out of place among the marble headstones in the cemetery proper, but he vowed to order a fine tombstone in Trinidad, one that would outlast this dying town.

The priest raised a holy stink about burying a whore in hallowed ground, but Cameron refused to allow Amie's final resting place to be in the pauper's grave-yard out behind the coal mine, lying with those he held responsible for her death. Cameron had lost his Schofield in the fire that consumed The Texas House, but he didn't need a gun to convince the man of God to see things his way. So the diggers had lowered her in the grave yesterday morning. No preacher read the Bible. No one gave a eulogy. Only the two Mexican miners from the Pendant, the stable hand, and Ben Cameron attended the funeral.

Moses Keller, who had buried Consuela de la Hoya and Denise Benbrook, handed Cameron the bottle of whiskey as he and the miners left, leaving the gunman to grieve alone. He stayed there all night, even as it snowed again. Keller must have brought old Goliad there at some point, because Cameron found the gelding saddled and tethered to the fence surrounding the cemetery. The sun broke through the clouds that Saturday morning, but no one stirred in town.

A distant bullwhip cracked, followed by faint curses that grew louder. Eventually he saw clearly through the new eyeglasses that pinched the bridge of his nose the first oxen as freighters toiled up the mountain road. He made out whiskey barrels on the wagons as the team stopped in front of the smoldering ruins of The Texas House. The freighters silently gaped at the charred debris.

He could recall the theories, the guesses, being discussed after the fire. Cameron had figured most of it out, but he had been too late . . . for Amie Courtland, and he'd always blame himself for that. Susan Falconer said she had gotten the letter from Diva, asking her to come on up, to replace the dead Consuela de la Hoya, only Consuela had been alive when the stagecoach had left Purgatoire, carrying the mail. Diva had mailed that letter *before* she had murdered Consuela. Likely, she had sent the young girl a note, inviting her to the river, and strangled her to death—to collect money from Randall Johnson.

Johnson had probably wanted nothing to do with a murder, simply wanted Diva to get rid of the prostitute, but Diva killed her anyway, maybe out of jealousy, maybe something else. Who knew for sure, what with Diva dead? When Johnson had confronted her at the river, an agreed-upon meeting place most likely, Diva had shot him without warning. The rancher hadn't expected her to kill him, but she had probably planned on that, too. That's why she had invited Susan Falconer to Purgatoire. Falconer told Mayor Stone and others that Diva had offered to sell her The Texas House at two bits on the dollar. She hadn't thought much of it, just figured that Diva had seen enough, didn't think Purgatoire would live much longer, so she wanted out. They'd keep the sale price a secret. That fit, too. Wherever Diva resettled, she would claim the money Randall Johnson paid her for getting rid of Consuela came from the sale of her brothel.

Denise Benbrook had either seen or heard enough, though, and had blackmailed Diva, trying to buy enough money to get out of town, to start over with Louis Venizelos. It was Diva who had suggested blackmail when no one else had. So Diva had killed her at the mill.

He had never solved a case during his brief career with the Pinkertons, but he had figured out this one. Too late, though.

Venizelos had left on the stagecoach, which didn't depart until Friday, after all of the excitement and early snowstorm. So had Susan Falconer, Joe Miller, and the three other surviving prostitutes. Falconer, seeing her investment in Purgatoire disappear in flame and smoke, had offered Miller, Cindy, Nancy, and China Rene a job at her house of ill repute, which she would not sell after all, down in Trinidad. She had promised Louis Venizelos a job, too, but he had turned it down. Cameron had given him his ticket, told him to leave, and the bartender had quietly accepted.

There was nothing left for him in Purgatoire, either.

Cameron felt for Louis Venizelos, as had Amie. They had been friends, and he knew how Venizelos hurt. The barman had loved Denise, only to see her die, to hold himself responsible. The same guilt haunted Cameron. He also felt sorry for Joshua Reed, who had killed Colonel Hall. There would be talk, questions, about that, seeing how Hall had thrown down his gun, but Reed would handle that . . . if he survived the bullet wound.

Cameron had also identified the man accompanying Hall, the one he had killed inside The Texas House. Glenn Boeke had pulled a telegraph paper from Hall's vest, and read it aloud. It had been wired to Hall in Trinidad, sent by one Preston Zeske in Van Buren, Arkansas.

REGRET TO INFORM YOU AND ALASTAIR OF THE DEATH OF MRS. THOMPSON ON 3 DECEMBER 92. STOP. TELL ALASTAIR AM SORRY TO BEAR THIS NEWS AND LEARN OF HIS BROTHER'S DEATH.

Alastair would be Keno Thompson, the man-killer whose brother Cameron had killed in Trinidad. Colonel Hall had hired him, or likely bribed him, to kill Cameron. Hall had set things in motion, but Hall was dead, buried in the potter's field beside the burned remains of Diva, Keno Thompson, and two of the three people Diva had murdered. The Johnson bodies were probably planted by now at the home ranch. It was over.

Boeke, the former newspaperman, had volunteered to take the badly wounded Reed to the doctor in Trinidad shortly after the gun play. Boeke wasn't being a good Samaritan, though. With no telegraph wire in Purgatoire, Cameron felt sure the one-time editor had gone to Trinidad to send his sordid newspaper lies across the nation. Cameron's reputation would grow again. There would be more dime novels, maybe another stage play, making a few hacks and ne'er-do-wells money, and Cameron nothing. Perhaps some good would come from it, though, maybe a legitimate job as a lawman.

But at what cost . . . ?

His horse snorted again, and Cameron slowly rose. Snow crunched under his feet as he walked to the gate and gathered the gelding's reins. He slid the bottle into his coat, and removed his gloves. The lock of Amie's hair caught his eyes. While Moses Keller had built Amie's coffin, Cameron had braided and, after removing the bandage and stitches from his hand, had slid the keepsake on his ring finger. Now, he stroked it gently and swallowed.

Amie Courtland had been a whore, but she was better than anyone in Purgatoire. She helped him regain his self-respect and, ultimately, had given him his life. Ben Cameron loved her . . . more than anything. He wished he had told her, especially when he had held her dying body. She knew that. She had to.

He would not despoil her memory now by becoming the wretched man he was when he first rode into town. He reached into his coat pocket, withdrew the whiskey, took a deep breath, and dropped the bottle onto the ground. It would be a hard fight the rest of his life, but Cameron owed Amie at least that much.

He swung into the saddle, glanced at the grave once more, and turned around. The freighters barely even noticed him as he walked Goliad down Front Street, heading toward Trinidad, the hoofs making a sucking noise as the roan struggled through snow-covered mud.

A dog barked. His horse snorted. The town slept.

Center Point Publishing
600 Brooks Road ● PO Box 1
Thorndike ME 04986-0001 USA

(207) 568-3717

US & Canada:
1 800 929-9108
www.centerpointlargeprint.com